WHEN FALLEN ANGELS FLY

BOOK FIVE OF THE ARIZONA SERIES

ROMEO PREMINGER

CONTENTS

BOOKS IN THE SERIES

THE ARIZONA SERIES

1

NINETEEN-NINETY-EIGHT was the year I got custody of my niece, my daddy became a U.S. senator, I made it as an author, and I died. That's probably spoiling the story a bit. I just never liked pulling the rug out from under anybody so I thought you should know this here is the end of my story. It was my last year living in the world, and at thirty years old, I sure didn't see it coming. Now I promise you're going to see some twists and turns along the way. I would've liked things to have turned out different, but even so, I can say now, I lived an extraordinary life. Why, people still be talking about me, and I'm not even bragging.

I was living in Thibodaux, Louisiana with my six-year-old son Chase, and my twelve-year-old niece, Dinah. Nineteen-ninety-seven had been what you'd call a transitional year for me. Preston Montclair, the man I thought would be my partner for a lifetime, moved out on his own at the start of that year. My heart was broken, but we said we were always going to be part of each other's lives. We just couldn't figure out how to do that as lovers, so we were giving it a try as friends.

Meanwhile, I had a book going through production at a major publishing house, and an agent and a marketing team pushing me to build my career as a writer. I was working with editors, proofreaders, and my marketing manager, Rafe Mansoor, while writing my next book, traveling to conferences, and taking care of two kids.

I had some help with the latter. Chase had a live-in nanny named Sophie Loeffler, and she was a pretty young girl from Strasburg, France who took good care of him when I was traveling or needed peace and quiet to write. Preston and I had an informal agreement that he would take Chase and Dinah for weekends once a month, and my daddy was always happy to have his grandson over when he was in town. Daddy's estate, Whittington Manor, was only forty-five minutes away in Darrow. I called Chase my angel. I could've probably left him on his own for days, and he'd have stayed out of trouble. Dinah was a different story.

My stepsister, Dolly, had her when she was thirteen years old and living in foster care. We'd grown up together in the dirt poor Fanning family till I was fifteen and us four kids got sent off to separate places. My daddy, Gaston Bondurant, stepped in to claim me and told me about my history. Anyway, Dolly was raped by her foster father, and when Dinah came along, he claimed Dolly messed around with a boy. He took Dinah in and sent Dolly to a Christian home for wayward girls. She ran away from that home and got herself involved with prostitution, drugs, and a series of bad news boyfriends.

I'd tried to help Dolly get her life together and even paid off her evil foster father so I could bring Dinah home to live with her. Dolly had begged me to do it, but she never could stick around to be a mama to her girl. It was really Dolly's daddy, Gus, and my stepbrother, Duke, who raised Dinah from the age of six to eleven. Then Gus died at the end of 1996, and Duke got a job on an oil rig. Dolly and her boyfriend of the hour cleaned out every valuable from Gus's house down to the copper pipes, and they disappeared in the night. I moved Dinah in with me, got her enrolled in Chase's Catholic school, and went to family court to petition for guardianship.

We didn't share a drop of blood, but I'd always felt a bond with that girl. I certainly wasn't about to let Dinah become a ward of the state and live with strangers. I knew about traumatic childhoods and being abandoned by people who were supposed to love you. I saw some of myself in her, and it wasn't just the broken parts. She had a real good head on her shoulders, and she loved reading and writing. I knew it wasn't going to be easy, but I swore to myself back then I was going to do right by that girl.

We went through some tough times when she started living with me. First, she broke just about every rule they had at St. Thomas' Academy, from showing up late to smoking in the bathroom to cursing out her teachers. Next, we tried the public school in town, but that didn't work out any better. Dinah nearly got me into a lawsuit when she knocked the front teeth out of another girl's mouth, and that was just after one week.

I considered homeschooling her, but that was going to be near impossible. I needed time to write and travel, and once my book came out, I had a long schedule of book signings and media appearances ahead of me. Dinah was a real terror when she was home alone with poor Sophie. She got mouthy and wouldn't do anything Sophie asked her to do. So, I found a private school called the Waldron Academy that had small classes and could give Dinah extra attention. It was twenty miles away and twice the cost of Chase's school, but if they could get her on track, it was going to be worth every penny.

That just about brings us to the place where the story starts. January, 4th 1998. Le Moyne Parish Courthouse. It was the final hearing for my petition for permanent custody of Dinah. I'd been looking forward to it but worrying about it at the same time. I dressed up in a suit and made sure Dinah was looking her best in a blouse, sweater, and skirt. Sophie and Chase came along, and Duke, Preston, and Preston's parents were sitting on the bench behind us. My daddy's personal lawyer, Lawrence Barbet, had found me the best family attorney in the state, Annette Dougherty. Annette was sitting next to me in her pinstripe power suit and big blond updo. She was a big deal, but she had a quiet, reassuring manner. While I waited for the proceedings, I needed as much reassurance as I could get.

Getting custody of a child who's not related to you isn't easy, regardless of the circumstances and particularly for a gay man. Annette had built the strongest case I could hope for. She'd shown the court how I'd taken care of Dinah financially over the years and given her a place to live all the times Dolly had been absent. She had reports from Child Protective Services documenting Dolly's abandonment. Both CPS and Dinah's law guardian were at the courthouse to tell the judge they hadn't been able to make contact with Dolly, and they supported my petition.

Meanwhile, we'd had Duke, Preston, and my good friend, Katie, testify that I was a responsible, loving father, and I'd had social workers over at the house a half dozen times for interviews and observations. All that had gotten me was a series of temporary orders of custody, and now, ten months later, a judge had scheduled this final hearing for a permanent order to go through. Dolly's court-appointed lawyer had told Annette she'd never been able to make contact with Dolly either. As far as any of us knew, Dolly had run off with some man named Bobby and forgotten all about her daughter. Still, if she showed up that morning, that's all it would take to send the legal process back to square one and possibly send Dinah back to living with her mama.

The hearing was supposed to start at 9:15 a.m., and a minute shy of that, Judge Walters entered the room. He didn't look too happy about the vacant seat where Dolly was supposed to be with her legal counsel, but he accepted her lawyer's request to give her client a little more time. I was on pins and needles, and my heart bled for Dinah. She'd brought along my paperback copy of *Watership Down* and was paging through it impassively. They say a watched pot never boils, and I can tell you, watching that big clock above the door to the judge's chambers didn't make time pass any faster either.

Finally, at quarter to ten, the judge called the attorneys up. They had a quick conversation, and then the judge announced

Dinah was remanded to my custody, and I was recognized as her permanent guardian.

I drew a lungful of air and stretched my arm around Dinah to give her a squeeze. I thanked Annette and shook hands with Dinah's law guardian. As soon as I turned to the row behind me, Duke gave me a great big hug, and then I was hugging everyone from Preston to his parents to his brother Earl, who was also Duke's best friend. I was overwhelmed by all the support.

The Montclairs had said they were having everyone over for lunch regardless of the outcome, and now it was going to be a celebration. Well, a funny kind of celebration. I kept glancing at Dinah to get a read on her, but she wasn't letting on much with her blank face and little nods to people who came over to say they were glad she had a permanent home now.

About fifteen years ago, I'd been in a courthouse in Baton Rouge where a family court judge announced to a nearly empty room that I was going to live with my daddy Gaston Bondurant. So, I knew Dinah had to have some feelings about that day. As much as I hated my stepdaddy, Gus Fanning, at the time, it was like I'd been socked in the gut by him again. He hadn't tried to fight for me, just like Dolly hadn't fought for Dinah. At least Dinah was surrounded by people who loved her. Maybe it was different for her. I didn't know.

We all caravanned over to the Montclair's house on St. John's Island, which was a working-class bayou town where both Preston and I had grown up. As soon as I stepped through the door to their little blue brick ranch with Dinah and Chase, I smelled the food and saw it laid out on tables in the cramped living room. Preston's mama had made a huge buffet of roast pork, chicken, and red rice with sausage and beans, along with macaroni salad and deviled eggs.

Dinah ran off with some of Preston's nieces and nephews, and Preston took Chase to a back room to play with the younger kids. With all of Preston's aunts and uncles and cousins wanting to say congratulations and ask how I was doing, I barely got beyond the first few feet of the living room. Preston's family had known me since we'd been in sixth grade, but they hadn't always been so friendly. They were Cajun, and I'd grown up with the Irish Fannings. They'd come around real quick when they found out my daddy was the CEO of B&B Sugar, but that's not to say, they weren't good people. I didn't like their evangelical beliefs and politics, but I had to admit, when it came down to it, they had nothing but love for the people they cared about, no matter who they were. Preston's Uncle Willy even told me he'd voted for my daddy in the senate election. Now, none of them besides his aunt Eugenia and his brother Earl would've said out loud that Preston and I had been boyfriends and lived together for six years, but I'd come around to seeing people can be real complicated. The Montclairs would fight to the death for anyone they considered family, and that included me, Chase, and Dinah.

Earl and Duke pulled me away, telling me that we could drink and smoke in the screen porch in the back of the house. I followed them, and Earl got me a can of Budweiser from a cooler. They lit up Salems and offered me one, but I politely declined. I'd been doing well kicking the habit for about a month.

Duke bumped his shoulder against mine in a brotherly way. "Gus be proud of you. You givin' Dinah a good home."

I rubbed his back. I was proud of him. Working on an oil rig wasn't easy. He was offshore forty-four weeks of the year, though it was the kind of work that allowed him to save money for his future. I'd helped him get a little rental apartment in Houma, which was closer to Port Fourchon where he shipped out.

"I gotta go back to work on Thursday," he said. "But I back for two weeks in Feb'uary if you need help wit' Dinah."

Duke always meant well, though he couldn't give much help. Dinah was going to school almost an hour and a half away from where he lived. He was only one year younger than me, but he hadn't had the advantages I'd had. I was glad he'd gotten on his two feet after Gus died.

"I ain't surprised," Earl said. "A Bondurant always gonna win in court. You got a hand that turn everything to gold."

Earl could get a little confrontational, but I don't think that was his intention. Gaston Bondurant was like royalty in John's Island. B&B Sugar employed a good third of the residents, and now he was their representative in Congress.

"I'm sure the name helped," I told Earl. "But I'm just looking out for Dinah's future."

He took a big draw on his cigarette and let out a long exhale. "Preston been lookin' out for her future too. You think 'bout that?"

Well, he was getting confrontational after all. Earl was a proud heterosexual, but he'd also been the front cheerleader for Preston and my relationship. The last time I'd seen him, a good ten months ago, he cursed me out for breaking up with his brother, though he didn't know the full story.

"Preston is always going to be a part of Dinah's life," I told him.

"Arizona gonna do right by Dinah," Duke broke in. "That what he say, and we gotta respect it."

Earl stared me down, and I held my own, trying to be compassionate at the same time. Since Preston and I split, I'd stopped going to Montclair family affairs, and I figured Earl had feelings about that. I wanted and needed Preston to have a relationship with the kids, but we both needed to move on with our lives. I was about to say something about that, but then Preston strolled out to the porch.

"This where they drinkin' beers?" he said.

"It where the good folk drinkin' beers," Earl said. "Padoo folk gotta drink outside."

Preston play-lunged for his brother. We all had a chuckle. Earl scrounged out a beer from the cooler and handed it to Preston. After a short silence, he turned to Duke.

"I ain't shown you that new rifle scope my père got me for Christmas. C'mon. It over in the garage."

Duke looked at me. "Arizona might wanna see it too."

Earl squinted at him. "He ain't wanna see it. What you think? Arizona Bondurant took up huntin' in his spare time? He don't wanna ruin his manicure."

"You all go on ahead," I said.

The two went out the back door with their beers and cigs. I was pretty sure Earl was being cute and wanting to give Preston and me some privacy to get reacquainted. Hope sprang eternal with that boy.

"How you doin'?" Preston asked.

"I'm doing good. Thank you, Press. For coming to court this morning. Taking the day off from your shop. You rounded up your entire family to be there for Dinah."

Preston ran a gas station and automotive repair shop in town. It was his pride and joy, and he rarely took off on a weekday.

"Us Montclairs travel as a herd." He sipped his beer and scowled. "I ain't have to ask nobody to be there for Dinah. She family. Everybody have the day marked off on their calendar for weeks."

"I'm just saying, I appreciate it is all."

Preston nodded. I could read that boy like a book. He was irritable, and I didn't take it personally. It had to have been an emotional day for him as well.

"How *you* doing?" I asked.

"I don't know if I should say." His gaze shifted here and there. "Press, I'll tell you something. For all the lawyers and social workers I had to deal with this past year, there was a part of me still hoping Dolly would show up today. I can give Dinah a stable home, and be a good uncle to her. That's a piece of cake. But helping her come to terms with her mama…it's going to be hard. So, it would be okay if you felt the same way too."

"Dolly ain't even sent a letter to Dinah?"

I looked off to the side and shook my head.

"I don't understand it. How can somebody just give up her own child?"

I didn't know what to say. Preston knew Dolly's history. He'd been there for a lot of it. Still, I think he'd been even more hopeful than me that Dolly would come around to wanting to be part of Dinah's life.

"I guess there ain't no point in staying mad 'bout it," he said. "Dinah got a good home with you. You know I'll help out where I can." He took a draw on his beer. "I hear Dinah say she like her new school."

"It's only been a month, and that includes a week off for Christmas. She just hasn't figured out how to tunnel out of the building yet."

Preston grinned. I still got warm inside when I made him smile.

"She a perfect angel when she stay with me."

"Now what am I supposed to say to that? I'm the one who has to get after her about her schoolwork and chores. You get to take her go-kart racing and let her stay up all night watching movies on the weekends."

"It ain't all fun and games. I make sure she do all her home-works and tuck her bed in the morning. You just need to bone up on your parenting skills."

I smirked at the wise guy. "Well at least I'm doing well with Chase. He's *my* little angel. I don't know what I'd do if both of them were hellraisers."

Preston tossed back another slug and was quiet for a while. I don't know what I'd said to get him thinking, but something was brewing in his head.

"Chase ain't no angel all the time. He got some airs 'bout him. He say he only eat his eggs and toast the way Sophie make 'em, and he won't go on sleepovers wit' his little cousins. He say he can't sleep in a sleeping bag on the floor."

I smiled at first. Chase had inherited his granddaddy's taste for the finer things in life. He was top of his class and real mature for his age, so I didn't see the harm in it. But I picked up that Preston felt differently. "I'll talk to him about his manners."

Preston looked quietly amused. "It the *manners* that are the problem. He actin' like a miniature Gaston Bondurant. He even try to sass me last weekend when I say he gotta get his clothes in the hamper."

Now Press had never been a fan of my daddy, and he had his reasons. I was shocked, though. "I never saw that side of Chase. But I'll sort him out."

"How often you seen any side of him lately?"

I glanced at Preston twice.

"I jus' sayin', the way he talk, he spend all his time with Sophie." He cut me off before I could defend myself. "I know you busy and have every right to hire help. It jus', well, Dinah ain't the only one who have a lot of adjusting to do this year. Used to be Chase jump right into playing with his cousins, and today, he got my mama to set him up in her room to watch TV by himself. He don't seem to want none of my attention, so I thinkin' he lookin' for yours."

"Press, I'm doing my best juggling both kids. You know that Waldron School is all the way in Vacherie, and they don't have buses. I've gotta leave out no later than seven fifteen every morning to get Dinah to school and turn around and head back by quarter to two to pick her up."

"Sophie could take her sometimes, couldn't she?"

I snorted. "She could. If I wanted to start World War Three. You know how Dinah cops an attitude with her. Believe me, it works out better this way. And Chase, he's getting plenty of attention. Why, I'm taking him up to Washington, DC this Thursday to see his granddaddy get sworn in. He tell you about that?"

"Sophie coming along?"

I was getting a little heated. "Yes, she's coming along. She's never been to DC. Barely has a chance to get out of the house."

"You a softie is what you are. I s'pose Dinah gets to see the Capitol, too."

"Preston Montclair, you picked a hell of time to tease me about my parenting. If teasing is what you're doing."

He held up his hand. "I back off. But it wouldn't be a problem for Dinah to stay with me. When you gonna be away? Thursday through Monday?"

I glanced at him crookedly. "You're gonna get her back and forth to school from Franklin?"

"You was planning for her to do the commute from Washington?"

"No, smartass. I'm pointing out you'd have to take three days off from work."

He gave a little shrug. "Nothing saying I can't take her to work wit' me. When her cousins get out of school, she can go to Francine's. Dinah like spending time with them."

"I don't know when you got so laissez-faire about your job, but this is all decided. Dinah's looking forward to the trip. I talked to her teachers. They're considering it an educational experience. She just has to write a report to read in class when she gets back."

"Hm. Sound like the two of you will be spending a lot of time on that report."

I glared at him. I did help Dinah with her homework, but it's not like there wasn't a reason for it. With everything going on, she'd been struggling to stay motivated in school. I didn't want her to feel worse by getting bad grades.

"Press, when're you going to find yourself a boyfriend so you can pick on him instead of picking on me?"

He smiled in satisfaction. "You got a long time to wait on that. After you, I think a boyfriend is the last thing I need." He must've noticed me looking moody. "Arizona, I ain't saying you ain't a real good father. You is. Way you stepped in wit' Dinah, she lucky to have you. I jus' needed to say what I gotta say since, y'know, they still like my own, Chase and Dinah."

Our eyes met. You could say there were some feelings expressed on both sides in that moment. I didn't know what to do about it. I'd spent a whole year trying to get over us splitting up.

"Press, if I give Dinah extra attention, it's only because she needs it," I said. "I've been in her position, and I can talk to her about things from the heart." Preston didn't say anything so I went on. "Right now, I've got the time, but that's going to change real soon. Starting at the end of the month, I'm going to be traveling to promote my book. To tell the truth, I'm worried about how I'm going to keep up with everything."

Preston looked up at me. "You always got my support."

I wanted to give him a hug, but we didn't do that anymore. It wouldn't have felt right anyway since I'd been trying to move on specifically with my marketing manager Rafe Mansoor. I'll get to that in a minute. Preston and I just tossed back our beers in silence for a while, and then his cousins René and Beau came out to the porch to smoke and drink. We made some small talk and joked around and passed a good time that afternoon.

2

I GOT HOME with the kids around seven that night. Dinah had been in a good mood driving home. She got along real well with Preston's nephew, Louie, and his nieces, Gracie and Stella, and they'd been playing games in the basement all day long. She told me she wanted to get Pokémon trading cards, which was something her cousins were into. Remembering my talk with Preston, I tried bringing Chase into the conversation, but he was preoccupied with his Gameboy in the back seat.

Sophie was ready to take the kids off my hands. They'd had plenty to eat, but it was a school night. Chase had a couple of pages to do in his math workbook. Dinah had a chapter to read in her textbook for her science class. Sophie got them set up at the dining table, and she told me Rafe had called a couple of times on the house phone.

I went up to my bedroom to get out of my suit and call him on his mobile. I had a mobile too, and I explained to him I'd turned it off at the courthouse and forgotten to turn it back on. Truth be told, I wasn't crazy about that mobile phone. Half the time, the sound went in and out, so I only used it for emergencies.

"Well? How did it go with your niece?"

I gave him the highlights. Rafe and I had been seeing each

other long distance for over a year, but we never talked too deep about Dinah and Chase. He met them once, just briefly, when he came down to NOLA for New Year's Eve. I'd gotten us a hotel room for the night because I wasn't ready for the kids to see him sleeping over. He wanted to see my house, so we drove over New Year's Day and spent an hour or two with everybody before I had to give him a lift back to the airport.

"I'm glad you're finally done with the court drama," he said. "And I've got some more good news." He paused dramatically. "The review came out in *Booklist*. It's starred and full of praise."

I hadn't thought about my book all day, but I switched into author mode in a hurry. "Starred? For real?" Only a handful of fiction titles got starred reviews from *Booklist* each month.

"Yes, for real. I'll read it to you." He cleared his throat. "'Bondurant's raw, honest storytelling is to be enjoyed, though perhaps it's not his greatest triumph. What he has accomplished so well is a tale that is at once tragic and life-affirming.'"

A grin spread over my face, and I covered it with my hand. "Well...damn."

"This is only the beginning. The review from *Kirkus* comes out next week, and next month, we've got *The New York Times*, *The San Francisco Chronicle*, and the *Boston Globe*."

"A starred review from *Booklist*."

"I'll fax it to you. Or better yet, I'll bring it to you. I can come down this weekend."

I wiped the dampness from my brow. "Not this weekend. I'm bringing the kids up to DC for my daddy's swearing in."

"Of course." He hesitated. "I could pop down with the review on Saturday or Sunday. It's a quick flight from New York. I wouldn't even have to stay over."

He sounded so excited about the idea, I felt terrible having to let him down. "I'm sorry, Rafe, but it's going to be a jam-packed weekend. My daddy's got breakfast, lunch, and dinner planned all four days and somehow we're fitting in the Smithsonian, the Lincoln Memorial, and the National Zoo."

"I see. It was only a suggestion."

"I know, and I appreciate it. I'm coming up to you at the end of the month for the conference." He'd booked me for the annual Literary Writers Conference in New York.

"I can't wait. We'll finally have time to ourselves." He chuckled lightly. "Well, I admit, I have some ideas for introducing you to some media people in the evening, but we'll definitely have time for a romantic dinner or two. You have to tell me what you're in the mood for. Aquagrille? Le Bernardin? We can always order in to my apartment if you prefer."

My stomach sank again. I hadn't told him I'd booked a suite at the Peninsula Hotel for me, Dinah, Chase and Sophie. I wanted to introduce the kids to New York since I was thinking of moving up there as a long-term plan. I managed to break the news to Rafe, though I left out I was also going to be catching up with my best friend Jonathan while I was in town.

"I guess I'll have to settle for a coffee break in between the conference sessions," he said.

"It's not like that—"

"It's fine. You can do these things when it comes to our personal relationship, but as your marketing manager, you're going to need to follow my lead. I'm getting interest from TV and magazines with a national reach. If you want your book to go somewhere, you can't pass up those opportunities."

That hit me the wrong way at first. Of course, I wanted my book to go somewhere. I wanted it flying off bookstore shelves and climbing the bestseller lists, and I knew my publishing contract obligated me to media appearances. Beyond that, I felt bad about letting him down twice in one phone call. We'd never "defined" our relationship as he liked to say, but we screwed every time we saw each other, took a trip to Greece together last summer, and I'd slept over at his place a half dozen times in the past year. I'd been thinking that made us boyfriends by most accounts.

"Rafe, I want to see you. It's just a busy month." I snuck my hand inside my unbelted trousers. "I'm missing you real bad. Just hearing your voice has got me feeling things, if you know what I mean."

"I can grab a flight to New Orleans and be there by midnight."

I sighed. I had to get Dinah to school in the morning. It just wasn't a good time, but our reception was working well, so I tried smoothing things over differently. I eased back on my bed, pulled down my pants and briefs, and told him I needed his help.

3

_____

THAT THURSDAY, I flew up to DC with Sophie and the kids.
My daddy had bought himself a massive brownstone in the heart
of tree-lined Georgetown, and he'd insisted on putting us all up
there. That nineteenth century three-storey house was pretty damn
impressive. I think Daddy said Tip O'Neill used to own it, but I
wasn't always listening when he dropped names. It was ivy-covered,
whitewashed brick on the outside, and inside were gorgeous hard-
wood floors and tall, paneled walls. It had five bedrooms, so there
was plenty of room, and he had a live-in housekeeper and a part-
time cook. We only had to bring in our luggage, and the four of us
were well taken care of.

Dinah got a little moody, making a big deal over her room on
the third floor. It was cold and creepy, she said. The house was
furnished in an old fashioned, colonial style, which I guess wasn't
her cup of tea, but she had a nice big bed and a view of the gardens
in the back. I showed her how to adjust her radiator to warm it up
and reminded her it was just for a few nights. I'd suggested that
Sophie take the other bedroom on that floor so the two of them
could share a bathroom. That could've been why Dinah had a bug
stuck up her you know what. She was always resisting any attempt

to have a relationship with Sophie, no matter how nicely Sophie treated her.

Our visit was scheduled almost to the hour, so it was hectic. No sooner had we gotten settled in than Daddy called me on my mobile and said to bring everyone over to the Willard International Hotel. There was some kind of gala dinner going on for the Democratic delegation, and he said our names would be on the guest list.

That was a swanky affair, but the main event that weekend was the Senate swearing in ceremony on Friday. I coordinated things with Sophie to get the kids dressed up proper. Chase was no problem. He looked like a little gentleman in his houndstooth suit and his blond hair parted and set in place. Dinah, naturally, was a lot more work. She waited until that morning to announce she hated every dress she'd brought, and she didn't like any of the alternative outfits Sophie suggested. She finally agreed to wear a blouse and sweater and denim jeans. That was underdressed for the event, but we were running late so I let it go. She was giving me gray hairs at twenty-nine years old.

That morning, we passed through the security line at the Capitol, and we were packed into the Senate chambers with hundreds of guests, politicians, staffers, and reporters. I nearly couldn't believe my eyes being up close to so many people I'd seen on TV or read about in the newspapers. The ceremony was aired live by CSPAN, and I was really proud of my daddy when he was called up to the dais and sworn in by Vice President Al Gore. Gaston Bondurant and I had our differences over the years, but I had to admit, he was one hell of a go-getter. He ran a Fortune 500 company, and at forty-eight years old, he'd decided to go into politics against the tide of so-called Christian conservatives sweeping the South. Nine years later, he was a US senator. That man never slowed down.

After the ceremony, they had a long itinerary of photography for the newly elected senators and their families. It was a lot of standing around for the kids while we waited our turn to get in front of the photographers with Daddy in the well of the chamber with its starred carpet and towering red drapes. The big shot was making his rounds chatting with his colleagues. He looked like he'd belonged in Congress for years with his American flag pin on his suit lapel and his easy manner. Finally, someone announced his name over the microphone, and I headed to the spot with Chase and Dinah.

When Daddy came along, he stooped down to Chase and lifted him into a big hug. He waved me over, and I stepped toward him a little tentatively. I wasn't sure what the protocol was, and I was kind of starstruck seeing Al Gore standing there for our photo.

Daddy patted my back and pulled me closer while Chase stood in front of him. He turned to the vice president and told him, "This here is three generations of Bondurants. My son's a graduate of Columbia University. He has his first novel coming out from Random House in March. And you're going to see big things from my grandson here."

I shook the vice president's hand and introduced myself. Then I glanced at Dinah who was standing off, not knowing what to do, and I whispered in Daddy's ear, "Dinah's here too."

He said nothing. Then, in an instant, an aide came over to get the four of us positioned. Cameras clicked and flashed, and Daddy shook Al Gore's hand and ushered us along. I was speechless.

Sophie must have seen the situation. She had made her way to Dinah's side with a sympathetic hand on her back. When we joined them, Daddy put on his charms thanking Sophie for coming. I don't think he looked at Dinah once while he was fussing with his grandson and telling Sophie about the French architect who had designed the Capitol. Then he told us he had other things he had to move onto.

"I've got what they call an orientation session this afternoon, so I'll have to meet you all for dinner." He fixed on me. "You've got the address? You just call yourself a town car. The reservation's at eight."

I'd written down the address for the restaurant. I knew it was a busy weekend for him. Still, I wasn't happy about him leaving Dinah out of the photo. He knew I'd been awarded custody of her just recently. He hadn't even made the time to come to the court hearing.

I chose not to say anything. It wasn't the right time to have that conversation. I glanced at Dinah while Daddy gave Chase a hug goodbye. The poor girl looked like she wanted to disappear.

THAT WEEKEND, WE attended a congressional breakfast, took a tour of the Capitol and the monuments around the Washington Mall, and went to a fancy ball where I shook hands with President Bill Clinton himself. It was surreal. Otherwise I might have given the president my opinion about him signing the Defense of Marriage Act, which prohibited same-sex couples from getting married.

As it was, I'd been trying to take everything in that weekend while giving Dinah my attention so she didn't feel left out. I kept reminding her to take photos with the top-of-the line Nikon camera I'd bought for her school project, and I pointed out things she could write about. We got in some good pictures around the mall while Sophie and Chase walked ahead, and we talked about how she could organize her report with respect to the Capitol's history. Funny, we'd flown up to DC to see my daddy, but I'd barely talked to him with all his running around.

Then Sunday afternoon, he surprised us by showing up while we were visiting the National Zoo. He'd left out early that day for a pre-congressional session at the Capitol, and I thought he said that was going to keep him busy through dinner. Lo and behold, he tracked us down at the panda exhibit, and of course, the first thing he did was lift up Chase and spin him around. Then he set Chase down, gave me a look, and said Chase should go on with Sophie and Dinah to take in the exhibits, and we'd all meet up later at the gift shop by the main gates.

Daddy linked our arms and led me off the main way to a quiet trail through the wooded grounds. We passed a couple pushing a stroller, but nobody else was on that side route. It was a chilly day with dark clouds threatening rain, which must've kept the crowds away.

"Don't tell me you're being derelict in your constitutional duty already," I teased him.

"No such thing. We're in a recess till three."

I glanced at my watch. It was two forty-five.

He gave me a playful yank. "I always have time for my Number One. Leave the clock-watching to me."

I hadn't been his "Number One" since Chase was born six years ago. I figured he'd popped over because he couldn't resist buying out the gift shop for his grandson, but I was glad we finally had some time to catch up.

"If I could get you to spend a week or two instead of a couple of days, it wouldn't have to be so rushed." He stepped over to a recess off the trail and lit up a Camel. I understood then why he'd taken me aside. He needed an accomplice to his bad habit. Well, I couldn't resist myself when he offered me one.

"It's the middle of January. The kids have school," I reminded him.

"I'm talking about you. Sophie can look after Chase for a few weeks, can't she?" He fixed on me chummily. "I think you'd really love this town once you spent some time here. You've got museums, theater, great restaurants. A whole neighborhood for fellows like you over in Dupont Circle. You could get yourself a beautiful house for the price of a one-bedroom apartment in New York. And they've got great schools for Chase. I'll have one of my aides send you some information."

I had no interest in moving to DC, but I didn't want to argue on his big weekend. With my daddy, you just had to ride things out sometimes.

"I think it would be perfect for you and Chase," he went on. "You've got a great quality of life up here and all kinds of cultures and communities. It's like New York without the crime and with a lot more elbow room. And you can get up to New York anytime you want to visit your friends."

"How about this? You get Congress to repeal the Defense of Marriage Act, and I'll move into the townhouse across the street from you."

He waved me off. "That's easy. I already spoke to Senator Feinstein about it. She's working with a group of senators to get a new civil rights bill through Congress. But listen here, as a matter of fact, DC is one of the best places in the country for gay people to raise children. They've got a non-discrimination law and domestic partnerships."

As they did in New York City. I took things gently. "I appreciate you researching things. It's just not the time for me to be looking to move anywhere. You should see the lineup my publisher has for me starting in two weeks. I'll be on the road, trying to sell my book."

"Well, that's going to be a big success. I told you I've got a good feeling about it."

I watched him as he drew on his cigarette. In fact, he'd never told me that. Daddy was put together as usual in a cashmere overcoat and shiny wingtips, but I noticed his hair thinning on top and the creases around his eyes. In a room full of people, he was vivacious and hardly looked his age, but in these kinds of private moments, I could see things weighing on him.

"How's Virginia doing?" My grandmother Virginia had suffered a stroke a little over a year ago. We'd never been close. To tell the truth, we detested each other so much, we barely spoke. But I'd been thinking about her absence, seeing all the other senators with their wives.

"She's doing all right." He took a long draw on his cigarette. "She's not well enough to travel, but we've got a good live-in nurse working with her." He stomped out his cigarette in a nearby trash can. "I'll be getting back to Louisiana when I can." He came back to me with his face brightening. "What do you say to coming up here with Chase for spring break? The two of you can see DC's famous cherry blossoms."

"Daddy, if I didn't know better, I'd say you were worried about living up here alone."

"No such thing. A busy man doesn't have time to worry. You want to talk about a lineup, you should see my schedule for the next six months. They've got me on the Agricultural Committee, Health and Human Services, and now the party wants me working on Nominations." He smoothly lit up another cigarette.

"That's why you're worried?"

"Who said I'm worried?"

"Seems like you're worried about something."

He glanced at me. "The only thing I worry about is you and Chase. With me being in the public eye, I think you'd be safer living in DC."

I smiled to myself. "Daddy, you've been in the public eye for years. And if someone's wanting to hurt a senator's family, don't you think the first place they'd look is DC?"

"I just don't like the idea of you living on your own. I've been talking to my colleagues, and what some of them do is hire private security. If I can't get you to move up here with Chase, I think that's something we should look into."

"You want a bodyguard for your grandson?"

"And you."

I was kidding, but evidently he wasn't. "We don't need body-guards, Daddy. I don't want Chase growing up that way, and I certainly don't want somebody tagging along with me wherever I go." I looked him in the eyes. "We'll be fine. We really will. You've got a beautiful house up here, and we'll be up to visit again as soon as we can."

"How about Chase's school break in April?"

I couldn't hold my tongue about him leaving Dinah out of the conversation again. "The kids have different breaks now that Dinah's going to a new school. Daddy, you realize this past Tues-day, I got permanent custody of Dinah."

"Yes. I remember you mentioning that."

I could tell he had opinions I wasn't going to like hearing, but I looked at him expectantly. We couldn't keep dancing around the subject all the time.

"Son, I told you before, it's a noble thing you're doing for that girl. But how's that going to work out for you on a permanent basis?"

"What do you mean?"

"I mean, you've got Chase. Your son by blood. He needs to be your primary focus."

I was a twenty-nine-year-old man, but I still felt like a kid slapped in the face when Daddy said things like that. It took me a moment to regroup. "Chase *is* my primary focus. And so is Dinah. Daddy, people have three, four, ten kids, and it doesn't mean one suffers because of the other. Why, it wasn't so long ago you were saying Preston and me should have another child because you heard somewhere it would help with Chase's development."

"I was talking about him having another sibling by blood. Bringing another Bondurant into the family." Before I could react to that statement, he went on. "What you're doing is bringing a troubled girl into the boy's home. Now, I like Dinah. Always have. But she comes from a family that's had nothing but problems for generations. You planning to spend all your time correcting that? I'm telling you, one way or the other, Chase is going to suffer."

Part of me was outraged by his snobbery. I'd grown up with Dolly and Duke, and it was true, their family had problems, but mostly that had to do with being poor and trying to get by as best as they could. My head twisted up because Preston had also raised concerns about Chase. I guess you could say I was thrown. I wanted to believe there was enough of me to spread around to both kids. Like I'd told Preston, Dinah needed more of me right now, but that was just due to her circumstances and her age.

"Daddy, I made a commitment to raise Dinah, and you're going to have to accept that. Even if you couldn't see your way to being at the courthouse to support me for my adoption hearing."

"That has nothing to do with what I'm saying. You know I've always been there to support you, and that's regardless of whether or not I agree with your choices. I had to be in town January second to get the house settled and meet with the party delegation. It's not my business what's going on with you and your stepsister's daughter, but when it comes to my grandson's welfare, that *is* my business."

He hadn't found the time to attend my own hearing at family court when I was released from juvenile probation and remanded to his custody at fifteen years old. But he sure had strong opinions about his six-year-old grandson's welfare. A lot of issues were swirling in me.

"Chase is hardly suffering. He loves Dinah like his sister, and thanks to you, he gets anything he wants at the drop of a hat."

I was about to mention that all of Daddy's spoiling was giving Chase an attitude. Then his mobile rang. He brought it out of the inside pocket of his overcoat, glanced at the screen, and held up his finger. I watched him drift away a few yards and take the call.

His bearing was tense and secretive. He was speaking low into the phone, but I could make out most of the conversation.

"*Cher, I had to pick you up, but I told you I'm in sessions all day...I miss you, too...Now why would you say that? I put you up in the best hotel in town because I wanted to see you...I told you I have a schedule...I'll be over to see you as soon as I can shake myself free...It may be nine o'clock or it may be later...C'mon, you know I'll make it up to you...*"

I wandered away from him. It always got me queasy being a witness to his affairs. I don't know why I'd been feeling sorry for him. Gaston Bondurant always managed to find companionship, even on a weekend he was supposed to be spending with his family.

4

I SPENT THE next couple of weeks getting the kids back into their routine with school. Now, if I'm being honest, my time was tied up with Dinah more than Chase, but like I said, she needed more of me. First thing I did when we got back from DC was schedule an appointment for her with a psychologist. She'd been really moody since the court hearing, and I couldn't get her to open up about how she was feeling. She needed to talk about her mama with somebody neutral. Well, Miss Dinah didn't like that idea, but I told her it was non-negotiable.

The truth was, I think Dinah had it a lot worse than me growing up, which is why she got in fights so much and gave Sophie a hard time. Her mama had never been in her life for more than a month or two, and she didn't know anything about her father. That was probably a good thing, actually. Dolly had told Dinah her daddy ran off before she was born, but he was actually Dolly's foster father, a Bible-thumping pedophile. Dinah was getting to an age where she'd have more questions about her daddy, and I had no idea what to tell her. I was looking forward to talking to a professional about that myself.

I found a real nice lady who specialized in children and had an office right in town. I gave her some background information over the phone, and she said for starters she'd meet with the two of us together. Then, on the day of our appointment, I nearly had to drag Dinah out of my car. When we finally sat down in the psychologist's cozy office, Dinah wouldn't say a word. She just clammed up, really bratty. The psychologist told me it could take some time to get a twelve-year-old to talk about her feelings, and we made an appointment for the following week to try again.

Meanwhile, Dinah needed help at school. They had a whole different approach to the sixth grade curriculum at that Waldron Academy. I didn't want her falling behind, and it hurt to see her looking so glum when I picked her up at the end of the day. I couldn't get her talking about anything, let alone her feelings, but I could see she wasn't doing so well making friends. She was new to the school, and she wasn't the type to take the initiative talking to kids her age. Most of her classmates lived in different towns. I told her I'd drive her anywhere she wanted to be, and she could always have friends over, but Dinah never had anything to say to that. I didn't want her to be lonely so I helped her with her homework and some days I surprised her by taking her to the movies or over to the Wetlands National Park to walk the trails after school. It was weighing on me that soon, I wasn't going to have the time to spend with her, once my book tour took off.

Speaking of which, Rafe called me frequently with encouraging news. After that starred review at *Booklist*, my novel got another starred review at *Kirkus* and the preorders were doing remarkably well. Rafe had convinced the editor of the *New York Times Book Review* to include a featured write-up the first week of March. It blew my mind that the book wasn't even in stores yet, but the galleys were being read by editors from newspapers and magazines all over the place. I hadn't fully appreciated until then how well-connected Rafe was.

I was jittery as hell when it came time to fly up to the Literary Writers Conference in New York later that month. Rafe had gotten me on a panel of début authors, where I'd be expected to say something intelligent. After mulling it over for weeks, I still had no idea what that would be. I'd never been shy about public speaking, but it had been a long time since I'd done that as a teacher, and for the conference, I really had to impress an audience of experts in the field. I briefly considered leaving the kids behind, but I felt in my heart I'd be calmer having them there with me, even if I'd be tied up a lot of the time. Sophie was excited about making the trip, and she had lots of ideas about things to do with the kids. It would be a nice break for Dinah in particular, who'd been struggling at her new school. So we packed up and flew into town the day before my scheduled appearance and got settled at a suite at the Peninsula Hotel.

The Literary Writers Conference was held at the Marriott Marquis Times Square, and they got one thousand authors, editors, agents and press people attending every year. For the panel, I was sitting between a woman who'd written a memoir short listed for the PEN award about escaping the Bosnian War, and a fellow who people were calling the next Chuck Palahniuk. I'd picked out a new outfit for the conference, and I was sweating in my shirt, tie, light wool sweater, and sports jacket. Suffice it to say, I was just hoping to get through the program without making an ass of myself.

Five hundred people or more were crowded into the grand ballroom. The moderator was a seasoned agent from the Curtis Brown Literary Agency, and he read our bios and started off a conversation that mainly involved my fellow panelists. Then, he threw me a question about the dividing line between narrative nonfiction and literary fiction. I don't know where it came from, but all at once, I had a lot to say.

"Sylvia Plath once said writers are the most narcissistic people. I don't disagree with that, but I do think there's a difference between narrative nonfiction, or memoir, and literary fiction. One tells the truth, and the other doesn't. The problem is, nobody's ever figured out which is which."

That got the audience in that huge ballroom smiling and paying attention to me. I guess I caught a bit of stage intoxication in that moment. I followed up by saying how growing up in the middle of the AIDS crisis had influenced my story. I talked about being part of the post-Stonewall generation. We'd come of age with all the righteous indignation of our elders while having the added bonus of accumulating prodigious levels of guilt. You had survivor guilt and sex guilt and the kind of guilt that comes from fantasizing about homophobic rockers like Sebastian Bach. People laughed. I was on a roll. When we got to discussing the state of publishing and the moderator mentioned the idea of "access points," I said exactly what was on my mind.

"In my experience, when someone says the words 'access point,' you best run the other way. Because what they're saying is, do you have a story that'll sell to so-called mainstream readers? I reject that. I wrote a book that happens to be about gay people and AIDS, and if you want to call that gay literature, that's not a problem for me. I'm happy to reach readers who don't see their own lives represented in books or films or TV. But if you tell me no one outside of the gay community is going to be interested in my book because it's about gay people, I say that's censorship, plain and simple. It's an insult is what it is. It's saying the only stories that are accessible to the public are those that feature heterosexuals, and I think that's not giving the general public enough credit."

The audience clapped and cheered. Nobody was more surprised than me that I'd done so well. After the program, I had a line of people wanting me to sign my book. I met aspiring writers and people from the publishing industry and fellows I suspected were gay. Some were shy and awkward, and others looked at me like I was some kind of gay guru. When the crowd finally trailed off, Jonathan and our friend Henry came over to congratulate me.

"You stole the show," Jonathan said. "We were sitting by the arts editor from the *Village Voice* and a production manager from NY1, and the only time they were taking notes was when you were speaking."

He sounded excited. It was hard to believe I'd drawn attention from the local press.

"You've got some cajones, my friend," Henry said. "I think what you said about censorship in publishing was brilliant. Everybody's talking about it, and I say it's about time a queer author shook things up at this tired industry event."

Henry was the editor of the *Latin American Literary Review*, and he rubbed elbows with big name authors like Esmerelda Santiago and Oscar Hijuelos. I was humbled by his kind words. When I glanced at Jonathan, his expression was hard to read. We'd been best friends since boarding school and both dreamed about becoming famous writers. He had huge talent and was well-known in New York poet's circuit, though he hadn't achieved commercial success. I was worried he had feelings about me getting so much attention when he'd been writing for longer than me, but then he patted my shoulder.

"A group of us are going to Nowhere after the conference. You gonna be there?"

Before I could answer, I spotted a group of familiar faces headed toward me. My very pregnant agent, Janet Hughes, took the lead. She was a petite thirty-eight-year-old, looking fashionable in a patterned maternity wrap dress. Behind her came Rafe, and Sophie was bringing Chase over by the hand. Dinah was a few steps behind them.

Janet seized on me. Her face was glowing. "You were fabulous, Arizona. Intelligent, witty, charming." In a lower voice, she told me, "They ran out of copies of your book at the Random House booth."

I couldn't do anything but smile and shrug. Then Rafe stepped around her. He always put himself together in style, and that day was no exception. He wore a pair of Gucci eyeglasses, a Valentino pinstripe suit, and a bright pink tie. I could tell he'd been working his charms at the conference.

We hugged, lightly. Then I made introductions while Sophie and the kids stood off a little way. Janet knew Rafe, but neither of them had met Jonathan and Henry. Well, Jonathan and Henry had met Rafe briefly one drunken night about a year ago when we were supposed to be keeping our relationship on the QT. It only seemed right to introduce them properly. I was about to call the kids over, but Rafe cut me off with an announcement.

"I heard back from the networks. *The CBS Morning News* just confirmed they'll do a feature to air on March 3rd, and *Good Morning America* wants you the next day for a live interview."

I froze in shock. Rafe smiled and nodded. Janet looked at me with her eyes bulging out of their sockets, and Henry laughed exuberantly.

"They'll send an outline of the segment, including interview questions, and you'll have plenty of time to work with our media trainers," Rafe said.

He meant to be reassuring, but I was crippled by flashes of terror and disbelief. I was going to be on national TV? March 3rd was the day my book came out in stores.

"You'll be great," Janet said. "This is so exciting. You're going to get offers from Hollywood, not to mention a fantastic media tour across the country."

I couldn't wrap my brain around that. Meanwhile, I didn't want Chase and Dinah to have to stand around. I called them over, and I gave little Chase a high five and I stretched an arm around Dinah and gave her a peck on the head. They didn't understand what was going on, entirely, but it felt good that they were in my cheering section. Chase grasped my arm and leaned his silver-haired head against my side. He had to be bored out of his mind, but he was perfectly behaved. I pried a smile out of Dinah. I hadn't seen her so happy for quite a while.

"So what're you all doing to celebrate?" Janet asked. "I have to live vicariously these days." She rubbed her pregnant belly. "If I'm not home by six each night, I never hear the end of it from my husband."

I glanced at Sophie, trying to work things out in my head. "I bet these two have had more than enough of the conference." I smiled at Dinah. "But there's a Disney Store right down the street." She nodded enthusiastically. I stooped down to eye-level with

Chase and told him the news. "Sophie's taking you to Disney, and after, you all can order room service and have dinner in bed, watching movies. Daddy's catching up with his friends tonight." I gave Jonathan a wink.

Janet asked Jonathan and Henry about the night's itinerary. I felt a little bad about sending Chase and Dinah back to the hotel, but they had a whole suite at the Peninsula with games, movies, and anything they wanted to eat. Neither one of them looked disappointed about it. I reminded them I'd booked us a helicopter ride over Manhattan the next day.

Rafe stepped over close. "I told the editor from *New York Magazine* you might be free for dinner at Buddakan. Simon Armitage. He's eager to meet you."

I told him, quietly, "You think we can work around that? Jonathan invited us for drinks in the East Village."

"I can tell him nine. But some journalists are going to Toad Hall in Soho after things wrap up here. It would be a good place to make an appearance."

I was in a quandary. If I wanted to promote my book, I should follow Rafe's advice. But I really wanted to spend some time with Jonathan and Henry. I was only in town for a few days.

"How 'bout we start at Nowhere and see where the evening takes us?"

Rafe nodded. "I'll firm things up with Simon on my way back to the office. I've got a few loose ends to tie up. I'll call you when I'm headed downtown." He scratched the back of my neck and said his goodbyes.

Jonathan and Henry left to catch a poet's forum, which was one of the last sessions of the day. Then I kissed the kids goodbye, and they headed out with Sophie. That left me and Janet. She hooked my arm and said I was coming with her for a cup of caffeine-free herbal tea at the hotel café.

I didn't mind. I could use a comfy sit-down. I'd barely slept a wink the night before, and after all the excitement that day, my brain was fried. We took an elevator to the mezzanine, grabbed a table in the courtyard-style café, and Janet insisted on getting our order at the counter. A strawberry ginger tea for her and a mocha with whipped cream for me. The two of us had gotten close while we were working on getting a publisher for my book, and Janet could be a lot of fun.

She brought over our drinks, got herself settled in a seat, and gazed across the table at me. "So, how does it feel?"

I screwed up my brow. "How do you mean?"

She gaped at me like I was being flip. "How does it feel to have made it, Arizona?"

I scratched my ear. "It's a little premature for that, don't you think? The book doesn't go on sale for three weeks."

"It's got starred reviews. The preorders are better than Frank McCourt's book last year. And he didn't get a spot on *Good Morning America*." She smiled firmly. "You made it. How does it feel to achieve your dream?"

Emotions overwhelmed me. I tried to swallow them down, but I was real brittle all of the sudden. I shook my head and tried to smile.

"You should be proud. You wrote the book you wanted to write, and people love it, Arizona."

I winced and wept into my napkin. Call me a crybaby, but everything I'd been feeling before the conference, during the conference, and now after, it was bearing down on me.

Janet turned stricken and reached over the table to take my arm. "Those are happy tears, aren't they? Honey, you're getting me emotional, too. It's a lot. I know. But tell me you're enjoying it. You've had a hell of a year. You deserve to bask in your glory, don't you think?"

Janet knew about Preston and me splitting up, and I'd also told her the situation with Dinah. I guess my little breakdown had something to do with those things, but the bigger part was disbelieving I really had written a book that critics thought was good and tens of thousands of people wanted to buy.

I wiped my eyes and drew a breath. "I am enjoying it. It's just sometimes it doesn't seem real." I tried lightening the mood. "You know I've always been a basket case. I tear up from a change in the wind. Let's hope I make it through the TV interviews without looking like Jimmy Swaggart."

"You will. You were terrific today. A real natural. It must've felt great to have your son in the audience. And your niece."

I got emotional again. I guess it was kind of ridiculous. I just felt like a wealthy man what with my dream coming true and two beautiful kids who loved me.

"I'm glad you have such a great support team." Janet glanced down at her tea and smirked. "And Rafe is a marketing shark. I had no idea he was so well-connected. I mean, network television? The top PR managers are clawing to get their clients that kind of exposure."

I didn't know what to say to that. I was in awe of Rafe myself.

Janet took a draw of her tea, and I swallowed back some of my mocha. I had a feeling she was thinking about getting some scandalous details. Rafe and I were trying to be discreet, but our little bit of affection earlier was enough for people to put two and two together.

"This is a terrible segue," she said. "And I don't mean to imply anything. But how's it going balancing a business relationship with, well, whatever it is the two of you are doing on the side?"

I tightened up with a grin. "I had a good feeling about Rafe from the start. I guess you noticed."

Janet fidgeted with her paper cup. "I suspected. And honestly, I was a little worried. I thought he might be more interested in getting down your pants than selling your book or having a clue about how to do it. But he's the real deal, for sure. Does he sleep? A junior marketing associate typically has two dozen titles to juggle. I'm actually a little jealous."

"Jealous?"

"As in, I wish the marketing people working with my other authors put in one quarter of the effort." She eyed me playfully.

"So is Rafe the next Mr. Bondurant? Or do you have him under a spell until your book makes the *New York Times* bestseller list?"

I frowned back at her, deadpan. "Now Janet, I'm beginning to think you've got a vested interest in our relationship. Especially once your cut of royalties starts rolling in."

"I do. So, don't go screwing things up."

I chuckled.

"And how'd you find an au pair who looks like a young Catherine Deneuve and has your six-year-old trained like a British royal?"

I cocked a glance at her. "Why're you giving her all the credit? I'm the one who taught Chase his Southern manners."

"I'm sure. Well, I'd steal her from you if I wasn't worried about Howie developing a wandering eye. Our daughter is hell on roller skates. We'll be lucky to enroll her in a public elementary. She got sent home twice this year from Montessori for biting classmates and refusing to share toys. When her little sis comes along, we're seriously considering locking the nursery room at night."

I kidded her that the apple doesn't fall far from the tree. Janet could be real forceful herself in a conference room with a group of editors. We laughed about her trials with parenting, and I shared my own with Miss Dinah. She was doing better in her new private school, relatively. She hadn't busted anyone's teeth. Still, I was concerned she was holding a lot in. I hoped she'd finally warm up to that psychologist I found her.

"I'd never have guessed she had any problems." Janet hesitated. "She looks up to you a lot. I was sitting in the back near the three of them during your panel. She didn't blink the whole time you spoke."

I wasn't sure what to expect bringing Dinah to the conference, but something had a positive effect on her. She'd told me once she wanted to be a writer when she grew up.

"How do the kids get along with Rafe?" Janet asked.

"Don't know yet. They haven't spent time together." I squeezed my wadded napkin in my fist. "It feels kinda soon. Y'know, they've still got a relationship with Preston. Dinah especially, as a matter of fact. She took to him since she was four years old. The only time she's well behaved is the third weekend of the month when he picks her up."

"You've got a complicated situation. Half of my friends are divorced with the kids shuffling back and forth from one parent to another. It's hard on the kids, and I'm sure you want to protect them. But at some point, you have to move forward with your life, don't you think? If you're serious about Rafe..."

I don't know why I was squirmy, but I was. "We haven't defined things. Y'know, it's been long distance. This week I'm in town will be the most time we've spent together in a while, and between having the kids, catching up with people, and all the promotional events he's got on my calendar, it's not a lot of time."

"You've got child care. You two could make the time, couldn't you?"

I frowned at her again. "I know why you're playing couples' counselor. You want the two of us committed so you can pay for those renovations on your kitchen you've been talking about."

"That's icing on the cake. Arizona, I hope you know, you're more than a client to me. Christ, we spend more time talking about our families than your book. I really care about you. I hope you feel the same way about me."

In the past, Janet and I had our ups and downs. We started out real well when she offered to represent my book, and we had long conversations about the story and hit it off when we shared more personal things. Then we locked horns about how to sell my book. She actually was one of the people I was referring to when I spoke up on the panel about the pressure to de-gay stories for mainstream readers. But Janet was good people. We'd worked through all that, and I told her I absolutely did care about her and considered her a friend.

"Good. Then, as a friend, I want to see you happy. Does Rafe make you happy?"

I skipped a beat, and then I told her declaratively, "He does."

Janet's eyes sparkled. I think she was looking for one of those vicarious experiences again. "He's ridiculously handsome. And charming. And he's got incredible taste. How does he feel about kids?"

"He says he likes them. But I don't know if he understands all it entails." I held back for a moment. There was something I hadn't mentioned to my New York friends because I didn't want to get their hopes up while I was still figuring out how it would work with the kids. Then I just told her. "I've got a lot to figure out. I've been thinking about whether I want to stay in Louisiana or move up here."

Janet could barely contain her enthusiasm. "You're moving in with Rafe?"

Hairs shot up my neck, and I glanced around to see if anyone I knew was in earshot. Luckily, I didn't recognize anyone.

"Actually, Rafe's not offering, and I'm not buying. I'd appreciate if you'd keep that under your hat." Her eyes widened, and I threw my head back with a snicker. "I'm just saying I'm considering the move for myself."

"Either way, you'll love living in New York. You'll have so many opportunities. You could teach a course at the Gotham Writer's Workshop. Rub elbows with the literati at the Algonquin. And there's great schools for your kids"

I slowed her down. "It's just something I've been thinking about. I want what's best for Chase and Dinah. They could go to good schools up here and meet other kids with gay parents. I'd like for them to grow up around more diversity, and in Louisiana, gay families barely have legal rights. The problem is, New York is a long way from all their cousins and aunts and uncles."

"An urban environment has a lot to offer. And Louisiana isn't *so* far away. There's school breaks and summers. I don't mean to pry, but do you have a custody agreement with Preston?"

"There's no such thing as a custody agreement for gay parents. We couldn't get married or have a domestic partnership. Preston couldn't legally adopt Chase." That came out kind of hot, and I noticed Janet had turned pale. "We made our own agreement. Preston gets Chase at least one weekend a month."

"I'm sorry. That's horrible. I'm sure I've been naive. Or ignorant would be more accurate."

I waved her off.

"How would Preston feel about you moving? Have you talked to him about it?"

"We talked about it. It was part of the reason things fell apart. Preston's never going to leave his little corner of the world. It works for him." I scratched my ear again. "He also understands I've got different priorities for my life. We'd need to hash out how things would work, but I think he'd be okay so long as he still got to see Chase a few times a year." I fidgeted with my hands under the table. "He needs to move forward with his life too."

"I think it's outrageous the courts don't recognize you as a family. This evangelical movement in the country is disgusting. But it's better in New York City, isn't it? I have a good friend from college who's a lesbian, and she and her partner adopted their son together. They had a commitment ceremony at a synagogue in Park Slope. There's lots of gay parents like them all over the city, and we have elected officials like Deborah Glick and Tom Duane. You deserve to live in a place that's moving in the right direction at least."

I didn't disagree, but I was still working out the pluses and minuses. I could afford to bring Sophie to New York so I'd have help with the kids. She'd been excited about our trip, and I had a feeling she'd love living in a more cosmopolitan city, too. But my daddy wouldn't be happy about it. He thought New York was a dirty, crime-ridden place, and there was no reasoning with him. Chase and Dinah wouldn't get to see Preston and his family as often. I had a lot to think about.

5

LATER THAT NIGHT, I strolled into Nowhere and got a chorus of cheers from Jonathan, Henry, and some dozen of their friends. It was a divey, basement bar I'd been to before when I'd come up to visit Jonathan. They got a young, artsy crowd, but it wasn't pretentious. It was just a neighborhood place you could go to any night of the week and pass a good time. I'd been missing places like that and missing my friends.

Jonathan lined up tequila shots for me and his pals, which in addition to Henry included Russell Thorne. He'd gone to boarding school with Jonathan and me, and he and Jonathan had been seeing a lot of each other over the past year. Despite the fact they were polar opposites, I'd been rooting for them. Now, Russell stuck out like a sore thumb in his Brooks Brothers suit. He was a corporate lawyer, and he'd probably come straight from work. Jonathan always underplayed their relationship, but for as long as we'd known each other, Russell was the only guy he'd ever stuck with for more than a few months.

Russell got chummy with me right away. "It's great to see you. Congrats on your book. I heard it's taking off. I can't wait to read it."

"Thanks, Russell. How you been?"

"Good. Y'know, crazy busy with the law firm, but I can't complain." He looked at me with a grin. "Jonathan told me your book is semi-autobiographical. Does that mean any of us from Middleton figure into it?"

"Your secrets are safe with me, if that's what you're worrying about. It's not a tell-all type of book. It's just based on some of my experiences." I remembered our good times in school, and it hit me that I should tell him something. "But I did dedicate the book to Dale."

Russell nodded somberly, looked away, and sipped his drink. Dale was one of our best friends from Middleton, and Russell had known him the longest. Dale died of AIDS at twenty-three. Six years had passed since we all got together for his memorial. I almost couldn't believe it had been that long.

I was about to ask Russell how he was feeling since he looked a little blue. But someone pressed up close behind me and wrapped his arms around my middle. "How's our star author?"

I turned. It was Henry. He could get a little extra friendly, especially when he was drinking. Generally, I didn't mind, and truth be told, one drunken night, we'd made out pretty hot and heavy at a bar downtown. That was after Preston and I split up, and Rafe and I had started our "undefined" relationship. Though we weren't putting labels on what we were doing, I never mentioned that night to Rafe. I gently disentangled myself and faced Henry.

"Now Henry, that's kind of you to say, but I'm nobody's star author, yet."

He scowled, and then he threw an arm around me and raised his voice. "Listen up. This is Arizona Bondurant, the author of *When Fallen Angels Fly*. He's going to be bigger than Gore Vidal, so you better buy his book."

The room of fifty or so gay boys quieted for a moment and stared at me. You may have noticed, I was no shrinking violet, but all that sudden attention had me feeling like my head was too heavy for my neck. Someone hollered drunkenly, and a few people muttered half-hearted congratulations. Then mercifully, everyone went back to their private conversations.

"Fucking New York queers," Henry said. "Their idea of good literature is the back pages of *H/X Magazine*."

I snickered. "Now those back pages were quite educational in my formative years."

"They're sex positive. I'll grant you that," Henry said. "But the gay community can be so one-dimensional. We need more story-tellers like you. Gay culture is losing its soul. We don't support the artists who have something to say about being queer beyond hypermasculine adoration and orgiastic circuit parties."

I couldn't help glancing at Russell. He was far out of his element. I could talk to Henry all night about gay culture, but I didn't want Russell to feel out of place.

Jonathan came over and steered conversation to more general topics, and we alternated ordering rounds of drinks. I was flying high and enjoying the vibe of men flirting with each other while funky hip-hop throbbed from the bar's speakers. We joked around and Henry put his hand on my behind, which I don't think anyone saw. I'm not going to say I minded getting that sort of attention, but I wasn't looking for trouble. I eased away from him and joined in on a conversation some of Jonathan's friends were having about Mayor Giuliani's policing of Black neighborhoods.

Nobody was keen on the new mayor who had vowed to "clean up" the city, which was code for making it more hospitable for straight, white folks while doing nothing for other communities. I'd missed being part of spirited New York political conversations. Back in college, I'd been involved in ACT-UP and participated in marches and demonstrations. I chimed in when I could, and then a popular hit blared from the speakers, and we all headed over to the dance floor to get our moves on. I loved the freedom of dancing with men, and getting some attention from Henry and a few other boys wasn't bad either.

Later, Rafe showed up and found me in the crowd. I gave him

a big hug, during which he muttered, "I called three times. I got delayed at the office and wasn't sure you were still down here."

I realized I'd left my mobile in my jacket, which I'd thrown on a chair when I first walked in. I explained that to Rafe and said I was sorry. He was never big on hanging out at bars so I wouldn't have been surprised if he'd gotten himself delayed on purpose. Anyway, I grabbed his hand to lead him over to say hi to Jonathan and Russell. Rafe didn't budge.

"It's ten to nine," he said. "We've got to get over to Buddakan to meet Simon."

I glanced at my watch and jolted. I had no idea so much time had slipped by. The restaurant was just crosstown, but with New York traffic, ten minutes to get there by cab was cutting it close.

"How much trouble are we looking at if we keep him waiting fifteen minutes or so?" I tried prying out a smile. "You just got here. Have a drink. Jonathan rounded up all of his friends to celebrate with me."

Rafe looked a little flustered. He'd cleaned up and put on a new tie, a slim-fitting button down, slacks, and pointed leather shoes. I thought he might argue with me, but in his usual way, he reset to neutral. He brought his phone out of his trench coat.

"I can call and cancel. I'll say you're fatigued from your trip."

I felt like a villain. He'd worked hard to get me that dinner with the head of *New York Magazine*. "Just fifteen minutes. What do you say? You can blame it on me. Tell him I've got my son with me and got held up at the hotel."

He shrugged and lowered his phone.

"What do you want to drink? I swear, it'll be quick."

"I don't need anything."

I gave him a crooked glance.

"If we must, I'll take a bottled water." He pulled his hand away from mine. "Let me go make this call to Simon outside."

I watched him go out the front door. I supposed I should switch over to bottled water myself. I pushed up to the bar and got the bartender's attention.

While I was waiting for my order, Jonathan appeared at my side.

"I saw Rafe. Everything okay?"

"Yeah. He's coming back." I peeked at Jonathan, feeling guilty. "He lined up a meeting with Simon Armitage at *New York Magazine*. I'm going to have to cut out, and I feel real bad about that."

"Simon Armitage? Don't feel bad. That's amazing."

It was nice of him to say, but I still felt lousy. I settled up with the bartender and turned to him. "I'd rather spend the night with you. We've been best friends since we were sixteen years old. It meant a lot to me for you to come to the conference and invite all these people tonight."

Jonathan clasped my shoulder. "Listen cabroncita, you don't have to apologize. Go to that meeting and sell your book. A write-up in *New York Magazine* is fucking gold."

I patted his hand. "Thanks for understanding." I remembered the look on his face back at the conference. "You know you were my inspiration. How's your writing going?"

"I've got another chapbook coming out from a tiny, independent publisher."

"That's great."

"I'll be lucky to sell a hundred copies. It is what it is. But I've come to terms with my career. I'm writing from my soul, and if that means I'll be working a day job for the rest of my life, I'm fine with it."

"It shouldn't be like that. You're an amazing writer." I rubbed his back. "You know, I kind of stumbled into this situation. Maybe because of who I am. But it's writers like you who ought to be getting more attention."

"Don't apologize, Arizona. You wrote a great book, and you deserve to have your moment."

I studied him because I still wasn't sure how he was feeling. "Jonathan, I remember having a conversation with you when I was considering selling my book to a publisher that wanted to make it more mainstream. I was complaining about how hard it is to be a gay author, and you said, try being a gay, Hispanic poet." I saw his eyes shift from the recollection. "I just wanted to let you know I appreciate that, and I hope that doesn't sound stupid to say."

"Arizona, I'm not jealous. If any gringo was going to get a big publishing deal writing about being gay, I'm glad it's you." I watched him. "I'm serious," he said. "Just promise to use your platform for good and go impress the shit out of Simon Armitage."

I pulled him in for a big hug to let him know how much I appreciated him. Then I took a draw of my water and wondered if I had sobered up enough to make a good impression. I had no clue what I was going to say to a man who headed a premiere magazine.

Jonathan glanced at me, curiously. "Before you go, tell me, how are things going with Rafe? I mean, besides his crazy media blitz."

"He's fine." I averted Jonathan's gaze.

"He seems kind of stiff."

"He's driven. I'll say that." I took another sip of my water. "We'll find another time to get together when he's not in marketing mode."

"Okay. So long as you're happy."

"Why do I have a feeling you've got more to say on that topic?"

He blushed a little and peeked around. "Henry's a great guy, and he's really into you. Rafe just doesn't seem like your type."

"Jonathan, didn't we agree a long time ago to not give each other dating advice?"

"I only said that so you'd stop lecturing me about Russell."

"Well, it goes both ways, doesn't it, cabroncita? I'm figuring things out and taking things slowly."

He smirked. "Since when do you take things slowly?"

Jonathan knew me too well. He'd seen me jump into relationships throughout high school and college. "It helps that we live in separate states," I pointed out. "I think it's what I need right now. You know, a relationship that's uncomplicated. It hasn't been easy getting over Preston."

"You think you're over Preston?"

I couldn't answer him right away. Jonathan always did cut to the chase. It was additional stress I didn't need right then. I clasped his shoulder.

"Darling, you've always known I'm a work in progress."

"We're all works in progress. I'm not judging who you date. I was just curious, I guess. Everything in your life seems to be coming together. Your writing career for sure. I guess I wondered what it's like to find your happiness, y'know, all around."

Our eyes met for a breath, and it was one of those moments that stays etched in your brain. Like, it was the last time Jonathan and me were going to see each other the way we were. Two queer boys who hadn't belonged in an elite boarding school. Now I was becoming something more, and I wasn't sure I was ready for it, but it was happening whether or not I wanted it to.

"I'll let you know if and when I find it," I told him with a grin.

"Now you promise me the same. 'Cause I want to be there when you're accepting the Pulitzer Prize for poetry and settling down with your Prince Charming. Whether or not that's Russell."

Just then, Rafe came back and looked at me impatiently. I gave Jonathan another hug, and then I took Rafe around to introduce him and say goodbye to Russell, Henry, and the rest of Jonathan's friends.

6

THAT DINNER WITH Simon Armitage got me a full page article in *New York Magazine*, and for the next three months, Rafe had me running from TV studios to book signings and a whole lot more in between. It was like how people say your life can change in an instant. I'd gone to bed as a regular person and woken up as a famous author.

Later in February, Rafe lined up an interview and photo shoot for *Vanity Fair*. That same month, we had a lunch meeting with Jann Wenner, and he put me on the pages of *Rolling Stone*. Rafe also landed me the April cover of the *Advocate* with a sexy photo and the headline, "The Literary Sensation Bares All." I'm not complaining. Lightning struck when my book came out. People were talking about it like it was a cultural phenomenon. I did events in Boston, Chicago, Philadelphia, Raleigh-Durham, Atlanta, Miami, Austin, Denver, San Francisco, Seattle, Los Angeles, and places I don't even remember. People waited hours outside of bookstores just to get me to sign their book and take my photo.

I was feeling mighty important, but when I could set aside my ego, I understood part of the reason I'd become a big deal had nothing to do with my book. There was a certain strain of fetishization of Southern boys who'd dignified themselves by doing some good. Those magazines had nice things to say about my writing, but they seemed to be more interested in showing me off as some kind of highbrow sex symbol. I posed for photos with my shirt unbuttoned, and for the *Advocate*, I stripped down naked for the famous photographer Herb Ritts. He told me if I wasn't a writer, I could've been a model. I won't lie. I didn't mind him saying that. Would you?

I'll say it also helped that I was the heir to B&B Sugar, and my daddy was a US senator. All of the sudden, I got invitations to A-list charity events, film premiere parties, and even the Met Gala in New York. *Jane* Magazine asked me to be on their most eligible bachelor's list for 1998. I was the first openly gay man to be in that kind of feature. They called me "the thinking girl's dream best friend." I received a lot of fan mail from that.

From February to the middle of April, I was barely home for more than two-day stretches. I did my best to keep up with the kids, but I'll admit the thrill of being famous got to me that year. Every morning, I picked up the *New York Times* and *USA Today* to see how I was doing on the bestseller lists. When my book debuted in the top twenty, I cried tears of joy, and then it crept into the top ten and hit number two the first week of April, which got me hyperventilating.

Being number two was great, but being number one would've been even better, so I said yes to every interview Rafe lined up and yes to every social invitation to keep up my public image. We made our rounds at exclusive LA clubs where paparazzi were crowded by the entrance. We went to New York parties where socialites and entertainment moguls recognized me and gushed about my book. Rave reviews kept coming out in the papers, and my book's success felt like a vindication. It was as queer as could be and in the front display cases of bookstores across the country. I felt vindicated as a writer. After fifteen years of dreaming, writing, begging agents to take me on, and putting it all on hold for other people, the world was recognizing me for my talent.

Random House cut back on the other authors Rafe was

working with so he could devote his time to me, and he was my bedrock those couple of months. We were pretty much sewn together, whether I was traveling around the country or doing events in New York. He kept my schedule, got me prepped for interviews, negotiated my media appearances, arranged the car services, and even helped me pick out what to wear and pack my suitcase. I needed that. I was on the top of the world, but at the same time, I didn't know the hour of the day or the day of the week. I'd been taking care of myself for years, but it was like I'd lost my ability to manage the simplest thing without his help. You could say we were living like a married couple, and we did go to bed together most nights of the week. But the main thing that fed our relationship was making me a superstar. Like people say, I was the flower, and he was the gardener. I got lost in that for a while.

Anyway, the truth is, I let a lot of things slip while I was chasing after fame and validation. I saw Chase and Dinah maybe a half dozen times in three months. Sophie was raising them, along with Preston. We arranged a car service to get Dinah back and forth to school, and I asked Preston to take the kids on weekends until my schedule cooled down. I had to call my daddy for his birthday because I was tied up on the West Coast doing events and couldn't get to Washington. I didn't see Jonathan once during that time, and the couple of times he called, I had to call him back a few days later because I was so busy.

When I remembered, I phoned the kids before they went to bed. Chase was always sleepy and didn't have much to say, and a few times, Dinah wouldn't even get on the phone. I had pangs of guilt. It's not like I completely forgot about them and my responsibilities as a father. But I'd hang up the phone and have Rafe briefing me on our next flight here or there and the big opportunities awaiting me the next morning. I told myself I just had to put my all into making my book a success, and I'd get back to being a father real soon.

It was exciting, getting all that media attention and meeting famous people. Rafe said I was a natural celebrity. I didn't get shy around journalists or celebrities, and I always came up with something clever to say. I guess I just always loved sitting down with people and having a conversation no matter who they were, and for the first time in my life, I was reaping rewards from doing something I really believed in. I couldn't pass up any media opportunity because I was worried about slipping down those bestseller lists and losing everything I'd accomplished.

I was also worrying about my next book. I didn't want to be a one hit wonder, but with my media tour, I never had time to write. That was weighing on me while I was being a big shot, getting myself in newspapers and TV and going to A-list events. I guess I was afraid I'd be forgotten in a few months unless my next book was even better than the first.

By the end of April, Rafe's promotion schedule was beating the hell out of me. Three months non-stop, I'd been putting on the charm for this or that interview or appearance, nearly every day, sometimes two or three times a day, not to mention worrying about what outfit to wear and if my hair looked just right and what more I should be doing to whiten my teeth. I started to feel like I was on a hamster wheel I could never step off. As soon as I was done with one event, I had to get myself ready for the next, and the questions people threw me were repetitive. I was getting sick of airports and hotel food and meanwhile feeling lousy about being away from the kids so much. Particularly Dinah. She'd just been settling into a new routine, and I'd left her on her lonesome. Things all came to a head when I was doing a spot on a morning show in NOLA for the local ABC affiliate station WGNO.

I'd flown into town the night before, traveling from the Savannah Book Festival where someone asked during the Q&A if I considered myself a writer or a cultural provocateur. That put a bee in my bonnet for the rest of the day, and I told Rafe I was taking a break from public appearances and to cancel my interview in NOLA. Rafe assured me it was a softball segment in a city that loved me. Well, it was true, I'd had a profile there before anyone knew me as a writer, and I'd gotten a lot of positive local attention since my book came out. That year, I'd been King of the Orpheus krewe at Mardi Gras and a featured speaker at the Tennessee Williams Literary Festival. I came around to changing my mind about the local TV piece.

That morning, the fellow interviewing me stopped by the green room to say hello. He introduced himself as Clive Mangano, as though the name should mean something to me. I think I'd seen him on air before, but I wasn't impressed. He was your typical, silver-haired news anchor who'd been around for decades. Keep in mind, my tank of charm and equanimity was running low. But right away, I sensed he was the kind of heterosexual who wasn't comfortable in the company of gay men, and that never sat well with me. It felt like he was compensating too much by commenting on how good I looked and trying to get chummy with me.

Once we sat down in the studio, the interview started in the typical fashion. Clive introduced me with a short version of my bio and mentioned I was the son of Senator Bondurant and grew up in Darrow. Then he asked me to describe my book.

By then, I could do the twenty second description in my sleep. I explained it was the story of a poor boy growing up in Acadiana and dealing with a broken family and discovering he's gay. Then he uproots his life to live in New York City where the AIDS crisis is devastating the gay community.

Clive looked down at his notes. "Most of our viewers know you from the society pages. And an honoree at this past year's Mardi Gras parade. Where did the inspiration for the book come from?"

I suppose that was a standard question, but that morning, it hit me the wrong way.

"Well, Clive, it's what you call a novel, which means it's a fictional work. But as a matter of fact, I spent most of my child-hood in one of the poorest parishes in the state. It's true, my daddy took me in, and I've been privileged since I was fifteen. But I know something about being poor, and I also know about being gay, so the story I wrote wasn't such a stretch."

Clive gave me a tight smile. "You've been called a bold writer. The *Times-Picayune* said you 'write like Tennessee Williams if he'd had the courage to write characters who are overtly homosexual.' These topics you touch on, like homosexual rights and AIDS, do you consider them part of a larger agenda?"

I looked at him twice. "I write about things that interest me. And if you want to call it an 'agenda' that my point of view is that people should be treated like human beings, I guess that counts as a 'larger agenda.'" I added, "People don't use the word homosexual anymore, Clive. We prefer gay or queer."

His eye twitched. He recovered smugly. "So, would you say it's a political book?"

"George Will and James Fallow write political books. I wrote a story that speaks to our essential humanity."

He waited for me to say more, but I didn't.

"Your father is Louisiana's junior senator. Do you have political ambitions of your own?"

I rolled my eyes.

He chuckled. "You've been involved in politics. While your father represented Louisiana's 18th district in the state senate, you ran his district office. He appointed you as a liaison to, as you say, the gay community. Do you see your novel as an extension of that work?"

"I don't have political ambitions. I wrote a book about real people and situations that get overlooked in mainstream literature."

"That sounds like an argument. Are you hoping your book changes how people view the homosexual community?"

I faced him squarely. "I don't know. Did *you* read it?"

Clive fumbled for a moment. "I read the press kit. I think many of our viewers would consider your book provocative. How have you been addressing that?"

"This is bullshit." I ripped off my microphone, stood, and pointed my finger at Clive. "You wouldn't be asking a heterosexual author if he was promoting an agenda or going out of his way to be provocative. I've been on the *New York Times* bestseller list for sixteen weeks and got the début novel award at the *Los Angeles Times*. And you wanna say it's some kind of political stunt? You're a small-minded man, and I'm not wasting my time. I've been dealing with idiots like you all my life."

I stormed out of the studio, trailed by a pair of production assistants. Rafe was calling us a car, and I was getting the hell out of there. Then I ran into Rafe in the hall. He must've come out of the camera room where he was watching the interview.

"He don't know shit about my book," I railed at him. "Why'd you agree to the interview? He just wanted to embarrass me."

Rafe held up his hands. "Let's take a break. This is live, but they've got the option to cut out and reset the interview. You're overtired. Take ten, fifteen minutes. I'll get you a cup of coffee. They just need a four minute segment."

I glared at him. "You think I'm going back there? I've had enough of this. I'm leaving."

Rafe gave me his be-reasonable look. "They've got two minutes of usable interview. I'll talk to the producer about modifying the questions. You'll be out of here before you know it."

I stomped my feet. "How's this helping me? He doesn't want to talk about my book. He hasn't even read it."

"We've been over this before. Local news stations are just looking for a personal angle."

"It's personal all right. That old has-been wants to paint me as a radical homosexual. You know what? This whole thing is a set up. This station has always been the first to give bad press to my daddy and B&B."

After that, Rafe gave up. He ran off to make his apologies to the producer, and then he called a car service and we drove to Hotel Monteleone where we were staying for one or two days. I'd lost track of my schedule. Heck, I couldn't have even told you what day it was. Anyway, the two of us didn't talk in the car.

We got up to our hotel suite, and I threw off my suit jacket, loosened my shirt and tie, and went to the bar to get a bottle of sparkling water. I lit up one of my Camels and plopped down on an overstuffed chair. I was aware Rafe had entered the room. I wasn't sure what I had to say to him.

He wandered over. "How about taking a hot bath and a little nap?"

It wasn't even ten in the morning. I hadn't slept much the night before, but I wasn't going back to bed so early.

He looked at my cigarette. "This is a non-smoking room."

"Why the hell did you book it then? You know I smoke sometimes."

"I wish you wouldn't. It's only for the night. We fly to Toronto tomorrow."

I vaguely remembered having some bookstore event up there. I felt like I was living in a nightmare, chained to a treadmill every minute of the day.

I looked up at him fiercely. "I'm sitting here, and I'm having a cigarette. I might even have two."

"I'm not your keeper. I'll leave you be. I set up my computer in the other room. I need to call the concierge about printing services." He turned to leave.

"I'm not doing this anymore," I called after him.

Rafe halted and turned to me. "What do you mean?"

"I've been on the road non-stop since February. I'm over it." I had a long ash hanging off my cigarette, and there was no ashtray in sight, which ticked me off some more. I plodded over to the bar and filled a tumbler with water.

Rafe stepped near. I wasn't in the mood to be placated like a child, but naturally, that's what he did.

"You had a rough couple of days. That's all it is. You've got all day and night to relax. We can order in tonight. Go to bed early, if you want."

I shook my head. "I want to see my kids. I want to *spend time* with my kids."

"Are you sure you're in the right state of mind for that?"

I fixed on him with venom. "They're *my* kids. I've got a right to see them any time I want."

"I was just saying—"

"You're going to lecture me about my state of mind? How 'bout this? You're a shit marketing manager. What kind of fool puts a client through what I went through this morning?"

Rafe's face reddened. "I wouldn't have booked it if I knew you'd behave like a five-year-old."

I coughed out a laugh.

"The interview was fine. You overreacted." He crossed his arms in front of him.

"Well, I'll just overreact my way out of the whole media tour. I'm done."

"Okay. So, that'll be your career. Three months. A year from now, no one will even remember your book."

"My book's selling. It's making you a pretty paycheck. It's making everyone a pretty paycheck, and what do I get out of it?"

He snorted a laugh. "You know what's happening? You're still upset one person had something critical to say about your book back in Savannah, and you can't let it go."

I dunked my smoke in the water and gripped the counter. My stomach burned, and I was enervated all of the sudden.

"There's not an author in the entire history of the world who hasn't faced criticism. You *know* that. You can't take it personally."

My voice shook. "You're pushing me too hard."

"I *am* pushing you hard. Because you wrote a goddamn amazing book. Arizona, it's broken sales records. There's never been a gay novel that's gotten this kind of press. It's the number one book in the UK. Number five in fucking Japan. We've got four Hollywood studios in a bidding war for the film rights."

Cold sweat beaded on my forehead. "Then why can't I take some time off? I can't keep going like this. I feel like I'm losing my mind."

"The media is what sells the story to Hollywood. And it doesn't stop there. They could shelve the project indefinitely if we don't show there's an appetite for it." I felt his hand on my shoulder. "Don't you want your story to be as big as it can be? The trade book market is five hundred thousand readers. With a film done the right way, you could have millions of people seeing it. Do you realize what a difference that would make to gay people around the world?"

I shirked away from him and collapsed back on the lounge chair. When he put things that way, I felt real bad about myself. Like I didn't have a right to complain, and I ought to be stronger. I just hadn't known what it would be like having to promote myself day in and day out. It wasn't enjoyable anymore. I was spending all my time with people who only saw me as a commodity to help them sell newspapers and magazines or sell tickets to a conference or raise money for their charities. I barely saw my family or friends. I had no time to work on my next book. When was it going to end?

Rafe stooped down next to me. "After Toronto, we have *The Late Show with David Letterman* in New York, and then we have three days before we fly to London. We can take things easy that week. Meet with some real estate agents. Take a look at apartments. It'll be fun."

We'd talked about me buying an apartment in New York. I'd been thinking it would be nice to have a place in town since I was up there so much, and I could afford it. That morning, I couldn't work up enthusiasm for what Rafe was saying. Three days in New York wasn't much of a recuperating period, and then I had that trip to London. It was non-stop press events, media interviews, and staged appearances at trendy nightclubs.

He rubbed my arm. "I know it's stressful. Maybe after London, we can spend some time in Europe, just as a vacation. I'll move some things around. Push them into June. We could visit Paris." He looked for some reaction on my face. "Or Amsterdam, or the Amalfi Coast, or Barcelona. Wherever you'd like to go."

"I need to feel like me again. I'm no good to anybody like

this." I looked at him sincerely. "I didn't mean what I said before. I'm sorry. I appreciate everything you've done for me. But when I say I'm breaking, I'm not trying to be a prima donna. It's how I feel."

"I know. And you're doing spectacularly. I'm here to take care of you. I won't let you break."

I wasn't so sure about that. Rafe meant well, and I didn't doubt he cared about me, but he'd dug his teeth so deep into making my book a sensation, he'd never let it go. We couldn't have these conversations without him bringing up how the book was bigger than the two of us, and I always ended up feeling ungrateful. But if the book was bigger than us, when was I ever going to matter? It also made me wonder what we were doing as a couple. Everything we did, everything we talked about revolved around my book.

His mobile rang. He was always getting calls. At least one every half hour from early morning to midnight. He hesitated to bring it out of the pocket of his jacket.

"Go on," I told him.

Rafe stood, took a few steps away and answered the phone. I stared off, unfocused, not paying attention. Then Rafe strode back over to me.

"It's Sophie."

I searched his face. Sophie had his number for emergencies, and of course she had mine. I realized my mobile was somewhere back in the bedroom. It might've even run out of battery. I grabbed the phone from him.

"Hello? What's going on?"

She was tearful and hard to understand. But little by little, I got it out of her. She was at a police station in Lafayette. Dinah's principal had called to say she hadn't shown up for school, and then Sophie had gotten a call from the police. Dinah got locked up for shoplifting.

\

7

LAFAYETTE WAS A two-hour drive from NOLA. With Sophie using my Beamer, I needed to take a town car, and Rafe hopped right to it, calling a limousine service to pick me up. I told him he didn't have to come along, but when he said he thought it would be best to join me, I didn't argue. It wasn't the way I pictured Rafe getting to know my family and vice versa, but the truth was, I was a wreck, and he'd been taking charge of my travel itinerary for so long, I'd become helpless without him.

On the drive over, I sure felt like a crappy father. We were lucky as hell I was in town, and there was no reason for Sophie to have to go through the stress of not being able to reach me. What if Chase had gotten sick and ended up in the hospital? What if the house had burned down? I fidgeted with my mobile, cursing myself. From now on, I was going to make sure the damn thing was strapped to my side around the clock. I would've looked like a real fool if Sophie had to resort to calling my daddy. She probably would have if it had been something to do with Chase.

We got to the police station, and I shot straight inside, several steps ahead of Rafe. The lobby was crowded with people, but after a glance around, I spotted Sophie's blond hair. Then I saw Preston sitting in a bucket seat with Chase. They were playing with Chase's

GameBoy. Sophie must've called Preston since he was close by. I stumbled over to them.

Sophie got up first. She looked pretty crumbly, and before she could say anything, I took her in my arms and gave her a hug. Then Preston stood and Chase hugged my midsection. I lifted him up and gave him a kiss on the forehead. He should've been in school, but I guess Sophie had no choice but to bring him along.

I looked at Preston. "So, what the hell is going on?"

He glanced at the barred counter. "They goin' to release her since she a minor, but they say they can only do that wit' a family member."

Preston was wearing his mechanics suit and his Merle's baseball cap. He must've left his shop in the middle of the morning, hoping to help spring Dinah from jail. We hadn't seen each other since Dinah's custody hearing. I felt like I'd never been happier to see anyone in my life.

"Thanks for coming," I told him. I looked down at Chase. He'd taken hold of Preston's big ring of keys and was jangling them around. "How's this rugrat doing?" I asked.

"He fine. He happy to be out of school. Thinks this is some kind of adventure."

I glanced around the dingy lobby. A gruesome looking woman with one hell of a black eye was sitting in a corner. A big scruffy fellow was arguing loudly with the officer across the counter. It was no place for Chase to be.

I also noticed Rafe was standing by the door. I caught his glance and nodded for him to come over.

"Preston, this is Rafe. Rafe, Preston. And you know Sophie and Chase."

"Pleased to meet you," Rafe said.

Preston shook his hand a little guardedly. Then Rafe said hello to Sophie. He liked using his French around her, so they got into some sort of conversation. That gave me and Preston a bit of privacy.

"What's she charged with?" I asked him.

Preston rubbed his face. "She try stealing some things out of a Walgreens. Stupid stuff. Lipstick. Hair dye. Makeup."

My brow perspired. "How'd she get all the way up here?"

"Hitching, prolly. Sophie say the car service dropped her off at school at eight thirty as usual, but her teachers say she didn't come to class. I don't know what Dinah was thinking."

It was over ninety miles from her school to Lafayette. I guess it was a good thing the police had picked her up, but I was terrified and spitting mad.

"She done this before?"

"No, Arizona. I mean, you can talk to Sophie, but I sure you woulda heard. Sophie, she real broken up 'bout it."

Breaths rushed through my nose. I felt like I was reliving the turmoil and pain I'd been through with Dinah's mother.

"You go talk to them, and I can drive Sophie and Chase home," Preston said. "You got your car here."

"I'm not promising I'll bring Dinah home in one piece."

He eyed me steadily. "We could do things the other way 'round. I can drive Dinah home, if you and Rafe wanna go with Sophie and Chase."

I didn't like that idea either. I had questions and words to say to that girl. I didn't know how it was going to come out, but I wasn't going to wait to have that conversation back home with Chase, Sophie, and Rafe in the house.

"You want me to stay here wit' you when she come out?" he said.

I felt better about that plan, and I thanked Press for offering. Then I explained things to Sophie and Rafe. Chase didn't need to be in that miserable place any longer. I told Sophie to take my car, and I told Rafe to tag along with her. I said we could all have dinner back at the house.

Rafe tried to catch my gaze. He might not have been happy about the arrangements, but it was a private family matter. We said goodbye, and I went up to that barred counter with Preston to work through the procedure for claiming Dinah.

AN HOUR LATER, we walked out of the station with the little thief and a summons for a court hearing in three weeks. Dinah wouldn't look at me. She stuck close to Preston, which wasn't helping my mood. I stopped us short of piling into Preston's pick up and pointed her over to a picnic table on the side of the police station. I sat on one side, and Dinah sat on the other while Preston stood off a little. Dinah looked like she'd been crying, but that didn't soften things for me. She also had a backpack that was too full to just be carrying her school books.

I fixed my gaze on her. "I've never been more disappointed in my life. This how things going to be from now on?"

She stared away from me defiantly.

I pounded my fist on the table. "I'm talking to you, Dinah Fanning. You best snap to attention."

In the corner of my eye, I saw Preston watching me with concern. But I had to get some things off my chest. Gradually, Dinah faced me.

"You're going to be thirteen years old next month. You've got one job. That's going to school." She covered her face and started crying. "Those better be tears of remorse. You've got people who love you, and you scared us to death. You've got a little brother. How you think he feels? How you think he'd feel if you never came home or ended up getting killed out here?"

Preston sat down next to her. He gave me a look to back off a bit and turned to Dinah. "You gotta tell us what happened so we understand. We worried 'bout you."

Dinah sobbed. Preston put an arm around her. Now, I know she was just a kid and she'd lost her mama and her granddaddy last year, but I couldn't be gentle with her. It was a miracle from heaven she'd been picked up by the police so soon. She could've run away and never been found.

"You've got a good home now. For crying out loud, if you wanted money for makeup, all you had to do was ask. What do we got to do to get you to behave?" She wouldn't answer. I pounded my fist again. "Goddamn it, Dinah. You explain yourself right now."

She croaked through tears. "What do you care? You're never home anyway."

Now, I had a lot of guilt about that, but I wasn't going to backpedal when she'd done something wildly reckless. "I'm working, Dinah. So you can go to a private school and get chauffeured back and forth. But you can bet I'm going to be home twenty-four seven now since you can't be trusted with a little independence. So let's try this one last time. What the hell were you doing packing a bag and running away from school?"

"I wanna live with my mama. Louie said she's living in Oklahoma. I was going to find her."

An icy shock passed through me. By the look on his face, Preston was dealing with the same thing. He took his arm away from Dinah and sat up straight. Dinah spent time with his cousin Francine's son, Louie, when he took her for weekends.

"Dinah, I'm your legal guardian—"

"You made my mama run away," Dinah shouted.

I winced for a moment and came back at her with fire. "Your mama didn't need one ounce of encouragement to run away. She left, and she doesn't want to be found."

"Then I wanna leave, too. I'm no good, just like her. Like belong with like."

"Who say you no good?" Preston said. "If it's Louie, he gonna hear from me."

"Louie just wanted to help me," Dinah sobbed. "Because I don't belong anywhere."

It might sound heartless, but I just had to pound some sense into her. "You know what I had at your age? A drunken father who beat my mama and beat the tar out of me when he was in the mood. That's where your mama came from, too. That's what made her what she is. But I gave you a good home. Better than I had at your age. Things don't have to repeat themselves, Dinah. I've been trying to set an example for you, and you want to run off to live on the street?"

"You made my mama leave," she squealed. "You make everybody leave 'cause they're not good enough for you."

Now I was itching for a spar. All last year, we'd sat down with social workers to help explain Dolly abandoning her and how not all kids have a mama who can take care of them. How Dinah had lots of family who loved her and would always be there for her. We'd taken it slow and gentle, and I'd been real careful to not say a bad word about Dolly. I'd taken her to a child psychologist so she could talk to somebody about how she felt being adopted by me, and she refused to participate in that. Moreover, I'd treated her like my own and given her every ounce of my love, same as Chase, more than Chase to be honest. She wasn't going to turn out to be a disaster like Dolly.

"Here's what we're gonna do. You're coming home, and you're not leaving unless it's going to school or talking to that psychologist. You're apologizing to Sophie, and I swear Dinah, if I hear you giving her one word of lip, I'm sending you to one of them nun schools where they lock you in your room at night and get you up at five a.m. to wash the floors with a toothbrush. You're not going to see your cousins again until you earn that privilege. You hear me?"

"You're not my daddy," she shrieked. "You're not even my uncle, and I'm not related to Chase either. I should be with my mama. Louie says the same thing."

We'd covered that territory many times before, too. I cocked an eye at Preston. He had a shadow of humor on his face, and maybe it wasn't nice, but I was suddenly feeling some humor as well.

"Well, we should have Louie over for Sunday dinner. I'd like to hear his opinions about where you belong. Why, we could invite your probation officer, too. Make it a party." I eyed Preston playfully. "What do you say?"

"Sound good to me. And if you want, Dinah, we can take you

over to the Dollar General first. You can steal some Alka-Seltzer case anybody get heartburn from Arizona's cooking."

Preston and I busted out laughing. Dinah glared at each of us hatefully. Maybe it wasn't the best parenting in the world, but I think it made the point with her. She was brooding instead of crying, and that was fine with me. We stood and headed over to Preston's pickup.

8

WHEN WE GOT to the house in Thibodaux, Preston and I walked Dinah inside. I'd made her promise to apologize to Sophie, and she did, though it came out like it was her only reprieve from water torture. Then she hustled upstairs to her room.

Sophie was cooking a beef bourguignon that smelled delicious. She asked Preston if he was going to stay for dinner, and he thanked her and said he had to get back to Franklin to check on his garage. Rafe peeked out from the living room to ask if everything was okay. I told him yes, and then I said I'd walk Press out to his car.

Along the way, I pried out my pack of Camels and offered him one.

"Y'know, I been cuttin' back, but after today…" He took a cig, and I lit him up and lit up mine.

"Thanks again for everything," I said.

He waved me off. "I'd do it anytime for Dinah." He leaned against the door of his pickup and took a draw. "I jus' hope she gonna be okay."

"Me too." I gave him a lopsided glance. "You know, this is usually the time when you tell me I was too hard on her. Well, too hard on someone from the Fanning side of my family, I mean."

"You had your moments, Arizona, but she need to know this was serious. I was freakin' after Sophie call." His face darkened. "And Louie…I don't know where he heard Dolly was in Oklahoma. I'm gonna swing by Francine's after work and get that sorted out."

I took a drag and let my thoughts settle. "It's high time I shuffle things around a bit. I've got to be home more." I shifted my weight. "Dinah needs to be talking to that counselor. I'm really worried, Press."

"If it make you feel any better, I can't get her to talk to me neither. This all hit me out of a clear blue sky. Dinah loved hanging out with Louie, Gracie, and Stella, but something happened there. I gonna figure it out."

"They're kids. Don't take it out too hard on them. If anyone's to blame, it's me. I should've been around more. You know, if this had been any other week, I might've been in New York. San Francisco. Dinah would still be in that jail till I came home."

I could see that sinking in on his face, and it made me miserable. There was no reason he shouldn't have been able to sign for Dinah at the police station. No reason except for homophobic laws.

"I ain't saying that's a bad idea to be 'round more," Preston said. "But you can't take the blame. Any girl Dinah's age is gonna miss her mama. She going through things, but she gonna come out the other end." His eyes passed over me. "And you, you got a big career now. You must have a lot to do keeping up with that."

It felt funny he was looking at me like I was a big deal. Besides my daddy, he was the one person I thought I could count on to not let me get a swollen head. Then he started smiling, and I realized I was in for some grief.

"My aunt Eugenia, she cuts out every article about you from the newspaper and magazines. She got video cassettes of every time you on TV, too. And you'll get a kick outta this. I come over to my parents' house last week, and my père was reading your article in *Rolling Stone*. Aunt Eugenia must've left it over. Anyway, he say to me, what I do to make you break things off?" He smiled wistfully. "Ain't nobody believe it was a mutual decision now."

I had mixed feelings about that story. I could see it made him happy, and it was pretty funny that his père, who probably couldn't say the word gay out loud, was feeling nostalgic about our relationship now that my face was in magazines. But us breaking up hadn't been a "mutual decision." Preston was the one who wanted to call it quits. He didn't sound bitter, but I thought he should be given the credit from his own folks.

"Over at Lucky's," he went on. "They got your photo spread from the *Advocate* in a frame up on the wall. I gotta see that every time I go."

I broke out in a blush. Lucky's was the only gay bar in a sixty mile radius. "I didn't know they wanted to take those kind of photos till I showed up for the interview."

"You looked good, Arizona. It just funny, ain't it? A year and a half ago, you was worried you wouldn't sell your book. And look at you. You all over the place now."

"I got a good publicity team. I'm grateful for that. But after today, I'm thinking all the success has come at a cost. What am I supposed to do with Dinah? Put a deadbolt on her room and bar the windows so she can't run off again?"

"Dinah gonna straighten out. She been through a lot, but she got a good head on her shoulders. You remember Annie? The girl my cousin Darlene adopted? She went through all kinds of things with wanting to know 'bout her mama. Lying and skipping school. Darlene was even thinking for a time she'd have to put Annie back in foster care. We all showed that girl some love, and I ain't sayin' it happened overnight, but Annie, she settled down and you wouldn't even know she ever went through a phase of fightin' and talkin' back. She a cheerleader now and getting good grades at school."

That reminded me of Janet saying she never would've guessed that Dinah had any emotional issues. I was starting to feel just a little more hopeful.

"I'm trying to find some balance in my life," I told him. "You know, before I had to start hustling for my book, I could spend all my time with the kids and never worry I wasn't giving them enough. And I'll tell you something, Press. I worked real hard on that book. I'm not complaining that people want me on TV and magazines. I'm not complaining that the book is getting good sales. But it's work. Harder work than even writing the damn thing. Don't get me wrong. I understand, it's a privilege. But something's gotta give. I guess I'm thinking this situation with Dinah is a wake-up call."

"I read your book." Press skirted my gaze, looking bashful. "I don't know why, but I didn't want to for the longest time." His face blossomed. "I loved it, Arizona. I kinda knew I would. I guess I worried there'd be things I wouldn't understand. Y'know, the way you writers write. But I understood everything, and I dunno, it jus' made me kinda proud, knowing your book was in every bookstore in the country."

I felt warm inside, hearing him say that.

"Anyhow, I happy for you. I know that book been your dream, and if you need time doing what you need to do, it ain't a problem for me to help out wit' the kids mo'."

"I appreciate that, Press. It's not easy for you either since you've got your shop."

He waved me off. "I got a little repair shop in Franklin, Louisiana. That's not the same as all you've got going on."

"It's something you did all by yourself."

"I suppose." He scratched his ear. "It's my first time meetin' Rafe. He seem all right."

I'd been hoping to avoid that topic. "He's a good marketing manager." I peeked at Preston. There was no use pretending there was nothing going on between us. Preston knew I'd been traveling with him and staying over at his apartment in New York. "We spend a lot of time together, and it turned into something. I guess you figured that out."

"He met Chase and Dinah 'fore today?"

"New Years Day, we spent a few hours together. And when I

took them up to New York back in February. I only told the kids we work together."

I don't think he liked that, but he gave me a playful grin. "If it ain't my place to ask, you can tell me, but how long you two been knocking boots?"

"Press, you called it quits on us over a year ago, so you haven't got a reason to be mad about it, do you?"

"I'm pleading the fifth on that. How long we talking 'bout?"

I fiddled with my hair. "We, well, it's not like you and me. The boot-knocking part, yes it is. But we don't call it a relationship, exactly."

"Who don't call it a relationship? Him or you?"

I gave the smart aleck a crooked look. Then I got to thinking, and I finally admitted Rafe and I met and fooled around in October of 1996 when I was in New York, meeting with Random House. I'd covered that up for a lot of reasons, including the fact my brother Duke had come along with me that weekend. I guess, technically, Press and I were still together, though he was sleeping in the downstairs bedroom. I didn't think he'd had an inkling, but I was getting the impression he did. "You knew about us back then?"

"I guess you could say. I picked up little things. Duke was really jumpy 'round me when he came back from that trip. Then you got that message from Rafe on the answering machine 'round the holidays."

I remembered all that. "Why'd you never confront me?"

He balked. "That my job to get you to tell me you seein' someone else?"

"No. But it might've made a difference." I heaved a breath. "Press, I'm sorry I lied to you. That's on me, like you said. I'm just saying how I feel, and I was feeling like you gave up on me, *before* I met Rafe. I'm not looking to rehash the past, but that's how it happened."

Our conversation fizzled for a moment.

"Well, I got regrets too," Preston said. "Maybe it all happens for a reason. Look here, we having a conversation and neither of us is bawling or cursing the other out."

I dropped my gaze and scuffed my shoe on the pavement. "What about you? You met anyone special, over at Lucky's?"

"Nah. I only go there to shoot pool."

I peeked at him. We hadn't been together for over a year, but it still would've broken my heart if he had taken up with someone else and fallen in love.

"You're a good father to Chase and Dinah," I told him. "I can bet it hasn't been easy."

"I just pick them up on Fridays, and they running with their cousins all weekend."

I knew it was more than that. He loved Chase and Dinah like they were his own, and he had to feel out of place sometimes. Not just because we'd broken up. If the world wasn't so ignorant, he'd be recognized as their equal guardian. I told him that, and Press just kind of scowled.

"Well, anyway, I'm gonna see to being around more," I said. "That's a promise."

Preston glanced at his watch, took a final toke on his cigarette stub, and stomped it out on the street. "I should get over to the shop. You let me know how Dinah's doing."

"I will." He hugged me lightly, and I watched him climb into his pickup, start the engine, wave goodbye, and drive off.

I WENT BACK into the house and found Chase in the kitchen paging through a school workbook at the dinner table while Sophie was cooking. I sat down next to him and told him to show me everything he was learning in school. Chase was such a good boy. I'd been an absent parent, but it was like I'd never been gone at all. We went through his reading workbook, and then I took him up to his room so he could show me his math and social studies notebooks. He'd gotten As or double plusses on all his homework, including naming all fifty states and writing something unique about each of them. He was my angel *and* my little genius. He probably could've skipped ahead a grade. I told him I was real proud, and I loved him all the time, no matter if I was on the road.

Around six thirty, dinner was ready, and I went to Dinah's room to make sure she came down and joined us. She dragged her heels, but eventually, we all sat down to eat, including Rafe. It was one of those quiet dinners where everyone around the table was in their own world, but I was determined for us to sit together peaceably, like a family. We hadn't done that since the start of the year.

By the time we finished, it was getting late for Chase. I told Sophie I'd make sure he finished his homework and get him settled in bed. By god's grace, Dinah spontaneously cleared the table and rinsed plates to put in the dishwasher.

Chase did a worksheet of addition and subtraction, and then I got him in the tub and made sure he washed his shaggy, silver hair. I was impressed how well he followed a routine of flossing and brushing his teeth and stepping into his pajamas. In his bedroom, I found *Treasure Island* on his bookshelf. I'd bought it for his sixth birthday, and I'd never gotten around to reading it to him. I read him the first chapter while he was in bed. He fell asleep toward the end, and I clicked off his night lamp and stepped lightly out of his room.

In retrospect, I suppose I should've been a better host to Rafe. I'd left him on his own in the house, and we'd barely said a word since earlier in the afternoon, back at the police station. I found him downstairs, sitting in the dining room with his mobile and his notepad while Sophie was packing up lunches for the kids in the kitchen. I stepped over to help her finish and told her to take off for the night. She thanked me and went to her room.

I drifted over to Rafe. "How you doing? This has been one disorientating day."

He glanced at me briefly. "I didn't know if I should wait. But I'll give you some space now to spend with your family. I'll just call a car to go back to the hotel."

The wall clock read nine forty-five. I looked at him. "It's getting pretty late, and it's an hour drive to NOLA. Why don't you stay over?"

He stood. "No need to worry about me. I don't really have a purpose here. I'll only get in the way."

I watched him. Seemed to me he wasn't happy about that, and I felt bad, but then again, I couldn't see the wisdom in persuading him to stay. It wasn't a good time for the kids to get to know him, and he'd probably be happier having his privacy at the hotel. He was always either on his phone or on his MacBook.

"Thanks for coming to Lafayette with me," I said.

"I don't know that it was such a great idea." He packed up his notebook in his briefcase. "Oh, I canceled the Toronto event. Take the week to catch up with your family. I'm flying back to New York tomorrow morning. When I get back in the office, I'll have Jen rework your travel plans for next week. We've got Letterman on Tuesday night. You can let me know what you want to do between that and the trip to London."

I'd forgotten about those engagements. For the first time in probably six months, I'd forgotten for a little while I had a book to promote. Tough as things had been that day, that had been a big weight off my shoulders. Part of me wanted to tell Rafe to cancel everything he'd booked for the rest of the year. I needed to spend time with Dinah and Chase and take a break from all the nonstop promotion. Though Letterman was too steep for my principles, I guess.

"I'm going to need to be here for a while," I said. "I can fly up for the show on Tuesday, but after that, I'll have to play things by ear."

"What does that mean? You're backing out of London?"

I stretched my neck to work out a knot. "I'm going to have to. I need to be down here more."

"That's extreme. But if it's what you want. I'll have to run interference with Julian. Unless you want to call him yourself."

I suppose it would've been a sticky subject even if we only had a business relationship, but it felt like navigating a glue trap with barbed wire since we were sleeping together on a regular basis. I'd signed a contract saying I'd fulfill Random House's marketing plan. If I reneged on that, maybe Julian, the executive editor, wouldn't hold Rafe responsible exactly, but it would reflect poorly on him.

"I'll call Julian," I said. "I'll let him know you've been doing an amazing job, but I've got to slow down for personal reasons."

"Right. Let me know how it goes." He punched the number for the car service in his phone and stepped along to the living room. I let him be.

9

I WENT BACK to my daddy routine that week. Dinah needed my attention, whether or not she would say so, and while Preston was optimistic about her straightening out, I didn't trust her to stay out of trouble. I drove her back and forth to school myself.

I wanted to make things up to the kids after being away for so long, so I told Sophie I'd pay her full salary for the week, and I'd take care of the kids when they came home from school and over the weekend. I hadn't cooked in a long time, but I knew my way around a kitchen. One night, I had Chase help me make pasta from scratch and a sausage ragù. Another, we decided to have breakfast for supper, and we made pancakes, bacon, and a potato hash. I sat with him while he did his homework and picked up reading *Treasure Island* to him at night. I'm not sure what Preston was seeing. Chase was perfectly behaved with me. He got clingy sometimes, but little kids were like that. He certainly didn't seem like a spoiled brat. I could barely get Dinah to say two words to me, so Chase and I spent a lot of time together that week.

While the kids were in school one day, I called Annette Dougherty to see if she could help with Dinah's legal trouble. She told me she only dealt with family law, but she put me in touch with one of her associates who dealt with juvenile court. The woman said she'd be happy to take on the case. We scheduled a meeting at her office in NOLA on Friday.

Though Miss Dinah steered around me most of the time, she attended school, did her chores around the house, and didn't complain about being grounded. I made a call to the psychologist she'd seen at the start of the year, and we scheduled an appointment for the following Thursday. One day, I asked Sophie to fill me in on any problems she'd had with Dinah.

I could see on Sophie's face there'd been issues. I liked her a lot and thought we'd established a personal relationship, but she was being careful and polite. She said she sometimes had trouble getting Dinah to do her homework, and then she mentioned she found some of her jewelry and makeup hidden in Dinah's room. I apologized and said I'd replace whatever needed to be replaced if Dinah did any damage. Then Sophie brought out that she was going to have to put in her notice.

"I'm sorry, Mr. Bondurant. I have tried, but this cannot be done. I am trained to care for little children. Dinah needs more than I can give." She broke into tears. "She calls me names. She will never accept me because she misses her mother. I'm sorry. I love Chase. He is a little angel. But I cannot take care of both."

I was horrified, and it wasn't only due to her anguish. I couldn't fathom replacing Sophie. Chase was going to be devastated, and I worried about Dinah, too. I understood a bit about emotional problems, and as much as Dinah was acting like she hated Sophie, she had abandonment issues. She was going to be real hurt if Sophie left.

So, I pleaded with her. I asked if she could wait out the decision for just a little while. After my quick trip to New York the following week, I'd be home to take Dinah off her hands. I told her she'd be working with a counselor. I even threw in that I'd fly her to France to visit her family for a week or two so she could take a break.

Thank God Sophie came around to say she'd delay her decision for two weeks. I'd hit the jackpot finding her, and maybe she was too young and modest to realize it, but she could have her pick of jobs with other families that didn't come with so much drama. Now, I had fourteen days to get my niece to stop being such a terror. I called Preston to share the dilemma with him. He didn't have much to say about that at first, but he filled me in on his talk with his nephew Louie.

"Louie swear he never tol' Dinah her mama was in Oklahoma. He say that come from her. Something she hear Dolly's boyfriend Bobby talking 'bout. Must've been over a year ago when they was livin' in Gus's house. Anyhow, Louie tol' me up and down the only thing he say to Dinah is he sorry she can't live with her mama. I think he telling the truth."

"Probably he is, but it doesn't matter either way," I said. "He wasn't the one skipping school and taking rides from strangers."

"I know. But I told him and Francine, I don't want to hear he been talking 'bout anything what concerns Dolly. Not 'round Dinah. That go for Gracie and Stella too. I can take Dinah and Chase this weekend if you need. I ain't got nothin' special planned."

"I appreciate it. I thought I'd spend some time with the kids, though. I've gotta get up to New York for a few days next week." I scratched my ear and decided to tell him the news about me being on *The Late Show with David Letterman*.

"David Letterman? Get out of here."

The way he said it made me grin.

"I gotta tell my aunt Eugenia. What night? That on Channel 4, right?"

I gave him all the details. It felt good sharing that with Press, but it had taken us on a detour from the situation with Dinah.

"The lawyer told me Dinah will probably get off with some kind of court-mandated education about shoplifting. On account of her age. But I've got to figure out something so she can get along with Sophie. It's going to break Chase's heart if she leaves, and where am I going to find another nanny as good as her? I'll have to go through interviewing strangers."

"I don't know, Arizona. Now that you a celebrity, I bet you'll have a line of girls down the street wanting to be your live-in babysitter."

I could feel his humor over the phone. I told him to knock it off and get serious. I was worried Dinah would refuse to talk to that psychologist who was supposed to help her come to terms with her mama leaving her.

"I sorry. I know you serious," he said. "Well, I ain't ever known a psychologist to help anybody, but I s'pose it can't hurt. I think what she need is friends, and that goin' to take time. But she be real happy when she can see Louie, Gracie, and Stella again. They been spending every weekend together."

I was glad Dinah had become close with Preston's nephew and nieces, but I'd told her she was grounded for one full month. I needed her to earn back my trust.

"I think it go a long way you being back," he said. "I know she don't show it, but she look up to you."

I snorted. "She looks up to *you*. She thinks I'm Lucifer, scaring everyone away."

"Arizona, she couldn't stop talking about that conference in New York you took her to. She say she want to be an author and live in New York. Now Dinah and I get along real well, but at the end of the day, there no doubt 'bout it, she *your* girl."

I felt that deep down. Dinah had been sewn tight to Preston when she was younger, but over the past year, the two of us had grown really close. I just didn't know how to get through to her that she needed to respect Sophie. If I couldn't do that, I was looking at some dark days ahead with the kids.

THE FOLLOWING MORNING, I woke up to an even bigger disaster. Jonathan called me at 7:55 a.m., and I picked him up since he never called that early. I was one hour behind New York time, but even so.

He wanted to know if I'd read the *New York Post*. Of course I hadn't. I'd never paid attention to that right-wing tabloid even when I lived in New York. Jonathan explained he always picked it up on the way to work so he and his editor colleagues could have a good laugh about the sensationalism over their morning coffee. He wanted to give me a heads up about some potential bad publicity, and the gist of it was my interview with that local anchorman Clive Magnano exploded into a mess. His station never aired it, but someone gave the story to a writer at the *New York Post*.

"Did you really tell off that guy from *Good Day New Orleans?*" Jonathan said.

I heaved a breath. "Now, it might be true I walked off the set and said a few words. How's that news?"

"I guess it depends on the words."

"How 'bout you give me the benefit of the doubt? We've been friends for fifteen years."

He laughed. "That's why it's believable. In addition to the fact you've been on a nonstop press tour. I was just wondering if you might've had a diva moment."

"Jonathan, I'm not saying I haven't been a little caught up in getting publicity. But that Clive Magnano is a world-class asshole. He was on mission to trip me up so I'd look like a political opportunist. What's the *New York Post* saying about me?"

"It's a dishy article and not so flattering." He hesitated. "But look at it this way. They only cover people who are going to help them sell their trashy paper. You've entered a new phase of celebrity."

I was pretty sure I wasn't going to like that new phase. I asked Jonathan to fax me the article, and since he was in the office, he did so no more than five minutes later. When the page churned out of my machine, I read the headline.

Literary It-Boy Bondurant Throws Hissy at Local News Reporter

The article was one hundred and fifty words of garbage with a homophobic slant. They called me "a foul-mouthed Southern belle" who "bared all for his homosexual fans" and thought he was "too big for his hometown." Initially, I laughed out loud. It was a small piece and surely nothing an intelligent reader would take seriously. Like most of the reporting in that rag, it was filled with phrases like "an anonymous source" and "allegedly." Then Rafe called.

He said the press department at Random House had just been contacted by *A Current Affair*, the evening gossip show on FOX. They were running a segment that night about my interview at *Good Day New Orleans*. They even had videotape from the station. I was carving a gutter into the floors pacing back and forth while he spoke.

"They can't do that. Can they?"

"The station must've given them permission."

"What about *my* permission? Or Random House's permission? We backed out of the interview. You said that took away their right to run it."

"They're not running it. They gave it to another outlet to run. The legal team here says it's probably actionable, but they wouldn't get a court order for weeks."

My blood pressure spiked. "So, what can we do to stop it?"

"We can't."

"Are you fucking kidding me?"

"You're a public figure. The tabloids can run whatever they want and count on no one taking the time to sue them."

"Well, did somebody talk to *A Current Affair* and issue a statement in my defense?"

"They're not going to say anything until they see the video for themselves."

"Why do they need to do that? Rafe, you were there. If they're going to make me out like a hopped-up Sean Penn, throwing punches at the paparazzi, we ought to tell the other side of the story. It was a shit interview with a biased reporter."

"They want to see how it plays, and the word from PR is no comment. This is important, Arizona. If someone from the program contacts you, you hang up."

As things sank in, I was falling to pieces. The only thing that gossip program was interested in was making people look bad, and they got millions of viewers. Coast to coast, people were going to see me teeing off on that reporter like an entitled celebrity, including, in all likelihood, some of the kids' teachers, neighbors, Preston's family, and my friends. I was trying to show my kids I was a good father. I also remembered Jonathan's words to me: just use your platform for good. When people saw how I behaved, I'd have no credibility as a gay rights advocate. I'd be letting down my entire community.

"The good news is *Letterman* hasn't canceled. They must be waiting things out as well."

That gave me some hope to hang on to. I wasn't sure I could live down being canceled from the biggest media opportunity of my life. It could be my book was finished, and I'd never have another publisher willing to take me on. I thanked Rafe for letting me know, and then I had to drive Dinah over to that lawyer's office in NOLA. It wasn't easy, but I tried to put the whole thing out of mind for the rest of the day.

Then, after dinner that night, I asked Sophie to take Chase out for frozen yogurt. Dinah had already shut herself up in her room for the night, which gave me a little time to myself. I went to my bedroom, locked the door, and turned on the TV.

Foolishly, I thought there was a chance they'd decided not to run my segment. They had stories about Meg Ryan, Tommy Lee and Pamela Anderson, and the usual crap about the Monica Lewinsky scandal. I was nobody compared to those big names. Then, my piece came on toward the end of the half hour program.

I stared at the TV like I was watching a ten car pileup on the highway. They'd put together a photo montage with a shot of me on stage with my daddy at a campaign event, my racy Herb Ritts spread, a hair-tossed and glazed-faced photo of me coming out of Club USA that went back four years, and a shot from Mardi Gras on the Orpheus float where I was wearing a sequined suit and cape that made me look like a queer ringmaster, at least to Middle America.

"The twenty-nine-year-old heir to B & B Sugar was having a great year with the success of his début novel *When Fallen Angels Fly,* a *New York Times* bestseller. But that all changed when he sat down with a reporter from WGNO in New Orleans earlier this week. Witnesses described Bondurant as 'arrogant,' 'belligerent,' and even 'verbally abusive.' We have exclusive video of the young media star and reporter Clive Magnano."

They ran twenty painful seconds of Clive pitching his last question and me tearing off my mike, cursing him out, and storming off. They'd caught the audio and enhanced it. Apparently, one of the cameramen had followed me while I bumped past people and went out the door cursing. It was gutting. My boasts about my book made me sound like an egomaniac and an asshole. I wanted to be swallowed up and buried beneath the ground for the rest of my life.

A short while later, my phone started ringing. First Janet, then Rafe, then some number from California I didn't recognize. I felt like such a jerk, I was scared of talking to anyone. But Rafe kept calling. I finally picked him up.

"Did they cancel my contract?" I said.

"No. I just wanted to check in on you."

"Any chance there's a ball game going on that preempted airing the segment on the East Coast?"

"No. I watched it here in the office with Julian and the rest of the team."

I paced my room. "You know it wasn't that bad. It was taken out of context. They're looking to tear apart my character is what it is."

"They're looking to get viewers and sell ads. Try not to take it personally."

"How the hell am I supposed to not take it personally? That was me in that video, and I didn't give permission to use it."

"You're a celebrity now. It comes with the territory. But listen, we spoke to the producer from *Letterman*. They're not canceling. As a matter of fact, they want you moved up the program. It's going to be a full seven minutes. During Sweeps Week. Those idiots at WGNO actually helped you."

He was giddy. Giggling like a fool. I couldn't believe it that night. I mean, I'd heard the expression there's no such thing as bad publicity, but this was all happening to me. People who saw that segment on TV were going to hate me.

"Listen, we think it's best to assign you a press agent," Rafe went on. "Margaret Croft works with celebrity authors, and she's the best in the business. I'll continue handling your schedule, but Margaret will take care of talking to the media moving forward. She's available to meet next Tuesday when you're in town for the show."

I told him I'd take any help I could get. I was sweating bullets. My phone was red hot the next few days. I screened out any number I didn't recognize, and I caught up with Janet, Jonathan, and Preston. I apologized for my behavior, and I ended up having some laughs with all three of them. Janet agreed with Rafe that the piece on *A Current Affair* could be the best thing to happen to my career. Jonathan gave me plenty of grief about the drama, and I let him get his jokes in about me being the next big literary diva. Preston told me his Aunt Eugenia was furious, and she was organizing a boycott of both FOX TV and WGNO.

Meanwhile, just to be safe, I told the kids we were staying in that weekend while Sophie took some time off. I'd been planning to take them over to Lake Palourde and rent a motorboat, but I was antsy about being out in public just yet. It was late spring, so the weather was nice for hanging in the backyard. I grilled hot dogs and hamburgers, and we filled up water balloons and squirt guns and chased each other around the yard. Dinah came out of her funk, and we passed a good time. We made s'mores at night, played board games, and stayed up late watching movies.

The next week, I had my appearance on *The Late Show*. I hadn't been so nervous in my life. I'd grown up watching that show and never dreamed of being on it. Now, I was stepping on to the fancy set with an audience, a band, and cameras pointed at me from all angles. I was fresh from one of the most disgraceful moments of my life being broadcast across America, and since then *Star Magazine* and the *National Enquirer* had picked up the story. You can bet neither one of them gossip pieces was flattering.

I'd met with my new press agent, Margaret Croft, and gotten coaching from a media team. They all wanted me to be contrite and to use my sense of humor. Still, when a production assistant called me out of the green room of the Ed Sullivan Theater, my legs were wobbly and my brain froze up. She cued me to walk on stage. I managed to do that while a mixture of applause and snickers blew up from the audience.

I said hello to David and answered his warm up questions. He got right into the piece on A *Current Affair*. They even ran a few minutes of it. Then David asked me, "So, what happened?"

I glanced at the studio audience. People were grinning ear to ear and hanging on my reply. I was scared, but somehow, just like at that Literary Writers' Conference at the start of the year, a braver part of me showed up.

"Dave, I'm just a young man from Louisiana, and the part you don't see there is I was having my integrity questioned. Where I come from, we don't take kindly to that. I think it's due to the heat and all the Jesus billboards."

It took the audience a second, and then some laughter bubbled up. I relaxed. Dave threw me some lighthearted questions, and we just fed off each other like we'd been working comedy routines for years. I admitted I hadn't been on my best behavior, but I'd never had anyone judging my behavior before besides my daddy and my ex-boyfriend.

That got Dave red-faced and giggling, which made the audience laugh more. I managed to get a bit more serious, telling him how I felt like I'd been fighting all of my life, from being poor, to coming out as gay, to going to schools up north that weren't supposed to be for people like me. I said that's probably where my feistiness came from, and maybe I should work on turning it off sometimes, particularly when I had the privilege of good folks inviting me to be on their show. We ended with the band striking up a jazzy number, and me showing Dave how to dance a fais-dodo. The audience roared while I hammed it up.

I walked off the stage during the commercial break feeling like I just might have redeemed myself. Rafe found me backstage, and he looked happily shell-shocked.

We got into a town car, and I had so much adrenalin pumping through me, I howled out the window to the New York streets like a teenager on his first night getting tipsy.

"How the fuck was that?"

Rafe pulled me back inside the car with a chuckle. "You were great. Dave loved you, and you're electric with a live audience. And think about this: if they hadn't leaked the story to the *New York Post*, your spot wouldn't have been half as good."

I grabbed him for a big wet kiss, and then I pulled my mobile out of my jacket.

"Who are you calling?"

"Jonathan. He and Henry watched the show at their apartment. We said we'd get drinks at Hell afterward." I tapped in the phone number, and Jonathan and I shouted back and forth triumphantly. I told him to get his butt over to Hell because we were on our way. Then I got the driver's attention to point out we needed to head downtown. When I sat back, I could see something was bugging Rafe.

"I thought you'd want to spend a quiet night at my place," he said.

"After appearing on *Letterman*? No sir. We're celebrating."

"You've got a flight first thing in the morning."

"As a wise man once said, I'll have plenty of time to sleep when I'm dead."

Rafe sat back, pulled out his Blackberry, and scrolled through it. "Fine. I'll drop you off."

I looked at him twice.

"The guest room is made up for whenever you get in," he said. "There's coffee in the kitchen if you want it before you have to leave out for the airport." He was trying to sound casual, but he was giving off one ice cold draft.

"Now c'mon, Rafe. This is a big night for me. You're not going to come out for a drink?"

"It was a big night for both of us."

We sat in silence for a moment. I wasn't quite sure what I was dealing with.

"You're right. It is a big night for both of us." I clasped his leg. "Aren't you pumped up? We just did live late night TV."

He pushed my hand away. "I thought we were going to spend the night together. Seeing as you're in town for all of twenty-four hours. But if it's not a priority for you…"

I sighed. "Look, don't be like that. Of course I want to spend time with you. So, come out with me and have a drink. It's not every day a person gets on the *Late Show with David Letterman*."

"*I* fucking booked it for you."

The sharpness of his voice struck me dumb.

"But go out and have a great time with your friends." He went back to looking at his Blackberry.

Now I was ticked off. "I always said I was grateful. Why am I on trial for wanting to go out on one of the biggest nights of my life?"

He didn't answer.

"I asked you to come. I *want* you to come. I know we didn't talk about it, but isn't celebrating what people do after being on the top-rated talk show in the country?"

"Arizona, I have no interest in going to a noisy bar at one in the morning. I've been working since seven thirty."

"And I've been up since five to head out for my flight. We only live once, don't we? We're twenty-nine years old."

Rafe ignored me again.

"You know the reason I had to make this a quick trip," I said. "I've got a niece with some serious problems. It'd be nice if I could've spent more time in town, but I need to be with my kids."

"Of course. It's always your family first. Then your friends. Let's just forget it. I'm sorry. I shouldn't have made any assumptions."

I sat back in my seat and rolled my eyes. "You're not going to make me feel guilty about wanting to celebrate tonight. I've been through hell since that *New York Post* article came out. If you're not happy about me going out for a drink, that's on you."

"Celebrate, Arizona. Get shit-faced. Fuck as many guys as you want. I'm just your marketing manager. I really don't care."

I stared at him. "It's one goddamn night."

"Of course it is. You do whatever you want. I never asked for anything from you."

He was making me feel like a real shit, and it wasn't fair. Rafe had a way of doing that a lot of the time. He said he never asked for anything from me, but he meant I was taking him for granted. It was complicated with us working together so closely. I did have feelings for him, and I didn't like being the cause of him being hurt. But I was only asking to celebrate my biggest TV appearance with friends. I didn't know how else to explain it.

"When you have time later this week, we should discuss getting you back in circulation," he said. "Now that you have a profile on network TV."

I drew a breath of courage. "Rafe, I'm thinking what we should make time for is discussing you and me."

He smoothed out his jacket. "What would you like to discuss?"

"What's happening right now. You can't be happy the way things been going. Maybe it's the stress of working together, but you've got to admit, this undefined relationship of ours hasn't been going so well."

"Are you getting back together with Preston?"

I coughed out a little laugh. "No."

"I just thought I'd ask. You could tell me if you were."

"Rafe, I'm trying to talk about you and me. If you want to

know the truth, I'm hurt you won't come out tonight. Feels to me like some kind of punishment, and that's not fair. I've been trying to give you as much as I can, but if that's not enough...well, we ought to accept that and figure out how to move on."

"Don't be so dramatic." He placed his hand on mine. "We'll spend some quality time the next time you're in town. I'm just beat tonight. It has nothing to do with you."

He smiled at me. It was like we were speaking different languages. I didn't know what to say, and then he leaned over and kissed me.

The town car pulled up at Hell. Rafe straightened out my tie and jacket and told me to have a great time. I decided to just let things slide. I stepped out of the car, and it drove off.

10

AFTER THE *LATE SHOW*, I was invited to do a call-in segment for Howard Stern, and then came an article for *People* magazine. Rafe was exactly right. Those sons of bitches at WGNO did me a favor by leaking that video. My book was hotter than ever. The first week of May, it reached number one on *USA Today*'s bestseller list.

I was hotter than ever. My press agent, Margaret, was fielding calls from daytime talk shows and speaking opportunities across the country. I'd made a decision to spend time with my family, so I rang up Julian to explain I was fine with doing a radio interview over the phone here and there, but I had to turn down anything that involved travel. I might sound fat-headed, but he wasn't in a position to make demands of me while my book was breaking sales records. Well, I made one exception to travel to Chicago for a daytime show that begins with an O. Besides that, I held firm about cooling down my schedule. I needed to give my attention to Dinah and Chase, and I was hoping I could fit in time to work on my next book.

As for my relationship with Rafe, that car ride after *Letterman* felt like a defining moment but sometimes it felt like nothing at all. When I got back to Louisiana, he sent a huge flower arrangement to apologize, along with framed photo stills from my interview. I called him up to thank him and said I was sorry too, though I wasn't sure what I had to apologize for. It was easier to let things go while we were communicating long distance, and I guess I was giving him the benefit of the doubt. He'd done so much for my career and dealt with plenty of my bad moods. It seemed like I owed him a pass for bad behavior. We'd both been through a lot of stress.

I kept on top of Dinah, and she pulled up her grades. She was being more civil with Sophie, and a big bright spot that year was Sophie agreeing to stay. But I was still concerned about Dinah. The way she ducked around the house, like she didn't want anyone to notice her, I knew she was carrying a lot of pain. She didn't have a single friend at her new school, and when I tried asking her about that, she got angry or weepy and closed herself up in her bedroom.

I became even more concerned when she said she didn't want to go to Preston's on the weekend any more. Just on the turn of a dime, she didn't want to see Preston's cousins and nephews and nieces. Those weekend visits were the only time she socialized with kids her age. I called Preston, and he had no idea what was going on. Dinah wouldn't talk to him about it either.

I kept taking Dinah to weekly appointments with that psychologist, but that went nowhere whether we met with the woman together or Dinah sat with her one-on-one while I was in the waiting room. One day when we were driving home from the psychologist's office, I was feeling so low about it, I pulled off to the side of the road and turned off the ignition.

"Honey, if you don't want to go back there, you don't have to. Every week, I feel like I'm putting you through torture, and I'm not sure it's doing either of us any good." I rubbed my mouth. "Here's the thing, though. You've *got to* tell me what's going on. When I see you looking like you've got the weight of the world on your shoulders every day, it breaks my heart, darling. And more importantly, I know your heart is breaking, too."

As usual, she crossed her arms and looked out the window.

"Dinah, I was exactly your age when I lost my Mama Lou. It's not the same thing as with your mama, but well, in the end, I think it is. Keep in mind, my birth mama died before I knew her. I didn't even know who she was till I was fifteen, and that got me feeling like crap all over again." I gazed at her. "There were times I was so angry at the world for taking away my mama, I just wanted to curse everyone out. There were times I wanted to disappear 'cause I thought no one was ever going to love me and I'd never belong anywhere. And I know I wouldn't have gotten through it without talking to people and saying what was on my mind. It doesn't make all the pain go away, but it makes it easier. Little by little."

She finally looked up at me. "My mama didn't die. She just never wanted me."

"Dinah, your mama was thirteen years old when she had you. That's the same age as you in a couple of weeks. Could you imagine having a baby yourself? When you don't have your own mama to take care of you?"

"If I had a baby, I'd love her. I'd never give her away."

"Well, that's how you feel. When you were born, that's how your mama felt about you, too. But Dinah, you're old enough to understand your mama wasn't ready to be a mama. She was searching for love herself. Same as you. Same as I was back then. And I can tell you I wouldn't have been able to do right by a child when I was your age."

Her face darkened, and she shook her head. "I'd love my baby. No matter what. 'Cause she'd be mine, and she'd love me."

"I'll tell you something, honey. I think your mama was counting on the same thing. But babies aren't for making you feel loved. They need love. They don't give it."

"I'd never give up my baby. I know what it's like to be thrown away. I'd quit school and do whatever I needed to give the girl a good home."

"Well, maybe you're stronger than your mama could be. I don't know. But Dinah, we've got to find a way for you to put this in the past. I know it's not easy, but you're not doing yourself any good holding on to this grudge with your mama."

She turned away from me again. I wasn't sure if that was the wrong thing to say, but I just had to let out what had been on my mind for over a year now. Dinah's grief was tearing both of us apart.

"When you hold on to a grudge, it can make you do bad things," I went on. "Like blaming your cousin for something *you* did. And stealing things that don't belong to you."

"I apologized to Louie and Sophie. What you bringing that up for?"

"Well, there's apologies, and then there's understanding when you've done wrong."

"I know I done wrong." She stared out the window. "What's it matter? Nobody cares anyway."

"Your family cares. That's me, Chase, Preston, Sophie, Louie, and all the Montclairs." I made her look at me. "You don't need a mama to belong somewhere. You don't need a mama to be a special person. Why, I bet you know plenty of people with mamas who are nothing special. It's not a nice thing to say, but there are people with mamas who are just plain idiots." I glanced at her. "Maybe you know some people like that at school?"

Her face compacted bitterly. "They all fake. When I started, some girls wanted to be friends with me, but that's 'cause they heard you're my uncle. They just wanted to know what you were like 'cause they saw you on TV. When they hear I'm not a Bondurant, they start asking me why I talk funny. They say I'm low class."

"Then I think you know what I'm talking about. I bet those girls have mamas, and what good is it doing them?"

I hoped that would make her smile, but she shifted in her seat and looked away. "One of them said if you don't have a mama, God doesn't love you either, and you're not going to heaven."

I rolled my eyes. "Dinah, I'm no theologian, but everybody knows Jesus loved everyone. It didn't matter who you were or where you came from. If they're not teaching you that at that school, we'll see about a better school for you."

"I hate it. They all look down on me like I'm trash."

I was taken aback. I mean, it could've been she was so depressed, she got it in her head everyone was thinking that way about her. But if her classmates or teachers were treating her mean, I was ready to yank her out of that school immediately. I'd have some words to say to the principal, too.

"It don't help you driving me to school every day," she said.

"How do you mean?"

"Everybody stares at me. The teachers too."

I drew a breath through my nose while I worked out what to say. "If you want, we can go back to you taking a car. But honey, if they're giving you a hard time about me being gay, I can't change who I am. We should talk about what people are saying."

"It's not that, Uncle Arizona. Some of the boys make jokes, but they're just stupid. They stare at me 'cause I'm a freak. I'm the ugly, dorky girl who got taken in by her famous uncle and still turned out to be a loser."

I didn't like that boys were making gay jokes around her, but I was starting to get the bigger picture. I did get some attention when I pulled up at her school. Mothers materialized out of nowhere and told me they were fans. Even some of the teachers came out of the building. Sometimes, they asked to take my photo. I could see how that would be embarrassing for a girl going on thirteen.

"Dinah, let's get this straight. You're not ugly, and you're not a loser. Now, I know something about going to school with small-minded people. The more you try to steer clear of them, the worse they're going to make it for you. How 'bout just being yourself and showing them you're the better person? You could invite them over after school. Why, you've got a birthday coming up. What do you say to having a party? We can invite the entire sixth grade, and they can see who's got class."

"Sure. They'd only come to meet *you*. I don't want them at my birthday anyway. They're all stuck up snobs."

"There must be one or two you get along with."

She shook her head.

"Well, how 'bout inviting Louie, Gracie, and Stella?"

"*No.*"

"Okay then." I scratched my chin. "I see what you're getting at. Birthday parties, they're for common people. What you should do is take a birthday *trip*. So, what're you thinking? The Caribbean? Mexico? There's some nice places to see in California."

She told me I was corny, but gradually, I got a smile on her face.

"Nothing corny about it. Where do you want to go?"

She laughed. "Where am I supposed to go?"

"I don't know. You name it."

"Okay. New York."

I chuckled. "You really want to go to New York for your birthday?"

"Yes, Uncle Arizona."

"All right. That's settled." I looked at her again. She had a tiny grin, which made me smile. "We better get back to the house so we can figure out what all we're going to do when we get up there." I revved up my car.

IT TURNED OUT that conversation was what you'd call a breakthrough with Dinah. She stopped going straight to her room as soon as she came home from school and spent time with Chase like she used to do. I loved seeing her teach him games and help him with his homework. That was the amazing side of Dinah. She was a great big sister to Chase, and it warmed my heart to see her acting like she was part of the family once again. A few times, she even asked Sophie if she could help get dinner ready and practiced speaking French with her. The following week, I rebooked the car service to get her back and forth from school since she had earned that privilege.

Most importantly, she started opening up to me. We got into a routine of taking bike rides through the campus of Nicholls State University nearby the house. Now, she'd complain I looked ridiculous in my sleeveless shirt and peach shorts and bucket cap I'd taken to wearing when I was bumming around, but we had our best talks on those rides. Dinah liked to race me around the track, and afterward we'd pedal at a lazy pace and she'd tell me about the books she was reading and all the places she wanted to visit in the world.

She told me she wanted to be a travel writer, so I asked her how she'd describe the places she'd been. I'd taken her to my daddy's vacation house in St. John's. She'd been to New York and Washington, DC, and we'd gone to NOLA a bunch of times. I asked her to tell me about all that, and she told me stories like a real travel journalist. Once you got her talking, she had a lot of insights on topics from local history to regional foods and cultures, and she could express herself real well. The fact she loved New York so much amazed me too. She was real mature that way, thinking about wanting to be in a place where people came from all different cultures and backgrounds. I realized my niece was the kind of person who'd grown out of Louisiana just like I had. It would be great for her to be with people who had more in common with her, whether it was their creative aspirations or their openness to difference or just that fact that not all kids had traditional families with a mama and a daddy.

Things were going so well, I should've been prepared for the world to throw me a curveball. Three days before Dinah's birthday trip to New York, I got a call from Margaret. What she said was so far-fetched, I couldn't believe it was true. Some woman was claiming I stole her daughter, and Margaret was being contacted by news outlets asking for a statement from me.

I thought it had to be a mix-up until Margaret said the name Dolly Haulker. She offered to fax over the tabloid article she was talking about. The kids were in school for another three hours, and that sleazy rag was in every checkout aisle of the local grocery store. I told Margaret I'd pick up a copy myself and get back to her.

I hopped in my car, drove to Rouses Market, and picked up a pack of Camels and the latest issue of the *National Enquirer*. I lit a cigarette and read the article in my car right in the parking lot. The headline was: *Arizona's Secret Baby Swindle.*

I stared in horror at a lousy photo of me smiling deliriously on *The Late Show with David Letterman* with an insert photo of my stepsister cringing in tears. I guessed she'd gotten married since they gave her last name as Haulker.

Hot author Arizona Bondurant, 29, is hardly the nice guy he makes himself out to be. According to his stepsister Dolly Haulker, 27, he used his fame and money to pressure her to vacate custody of her daughter. She says it was a calculated ploy to take attention away from his homosexual lifestyle and build his image as a self-sacrificing "family man" to sell more books.

Haulker, who grew up with Arizona until he was removed from the home at fifteen years old for assaulting her father, says her brother was always obsessed with fame. "He's ruthless," Haulker says. As soon as he found out his birth father was a millionaire, he sucked up to Gaston Bondurant and dropped his siblings like yesterday's news, including Haulker who was pregnant at the time and living in a foster home. But having money wasn't enough for her brother. "He got his rich daddy's lawyers to get my baby back from her father, but all along he just wanted to adopt my girl so people would look the other way when they found out he was gay," Haulker says.

Haulker's daughter Dinah, 12, is presently a ward of Arizona, along with his six-year-old son Chase. She lives with her media-hungry step uncle in Thibodaux, Louisiana when he's not jet-setting around the world to promote his book. Haulker is desperate to get her daughter back. *"My girl belongs with me. She's not a pawn in my stepbrother's scheme to make himself respectable," she says. Haulker doesn't have her stepbrother's connections and clout, but she plans on fighting him in court for custody of Dinah. "Money shouldn't be the reason he gets to raise my daughter," she says. "I'm her mama. Arizona is just collecting children to prop up his image while he's got the media's attention."*

I was so disgusted, I thought I might heave right there in the car. That tabloid was hardly a reliable new source, but lots of people read it. It hit me, it was going to be impossible to shield Dinah from hearing about it.

I drove home, and I was barely in the door when Sophie let me know I had some messages. Rafe. Janet. Jonathan. Preston. I handed Sophie the tabloid and drifted around the house, trying to figure out what to do. I'd just cleared my name in the media, and in a blink, I was being smeared even worse. My biggest fear was that Dolly would try to get custody of Dinah like she'd said in that article. I couldn't put Dinah through that. I couldn't lose her. It felt like I would die.

I rang up the only person who would understand. Luckily, Preston picked up right away at his shop.

"You seen Dolly's article?" he asked.

I threw myself down on the living room sofa and told him that I had.

"Aunt Eugenia tol' me 'bout it," he said. "She heard it from her friend Charmaine. This the first you hearin' from Dolly?" He didn't let me answer. "What kinda way is this to have a relationship with her daughter? She pull some stunts in the past, but this gotta take the cake. You think Bobby put her up to it?"

I was falling apart and couldn't answer him.

"Well, they not gonna get away with it, I tell you that. I given Dolly a lot of chances o'er the years, but whether this was Bobby's idea or hers, I ain't giving chances no' mo'. Earl say he heard she married Bobby Haulker last year. You remember his older brother Phil? I was in vocational classes with him, and he came over to the house for family get-togethers sometimes. Anyhow, Bobby was a real hellraiser, worse than Earl. He went to juvie in eighth grade, and he spent two years in prison for stealing cars. Earl say he heard they living in a trailer outside New Iberia. Now I don't know that's true for a fact, but if it is, she only been forty-five minutes away this whole time, and she couldn't bother to visit Dinah?"

I appreciated that he was pissed and outraged. I felt the same way too, but I had darker emotions pressing down on me. What if, after everything I'd done to give Dinah the stability she needed, family court said she belonged with her mama? I was a gay man with no rights in Louisiana. Had I been selfish, chasing after publicity for my book? If I'd kept a lower profile, Dinah wouldn't have to be dealing with this drama.

"Arizona, you still there?"

I broke out of my thoughts and wiped my face. "Mm-hmm."

"What you thinking you gonna do? If you need character witnesses, you got at least two dozen of them from my family. I'll talk to the *National Enquirer* and any other newspaper that needs to hear it. Dolly's a deadbeat mama. You want me and Earl to track her down and talk some sense into her, you jus' say the word."

"Thank you, Press." I dabbed my eyes with my shirt sleeve. "I've got to talk to my lawyer and a bunch of people at my publisher. I just don't know what I'm supposed to say to Dinah."

"She thirteen years old on Saturday. I think she understand."

"I don't know. She already hates all the attention I brought on her. Press, I've done selfish things. I've been trying to fix that lately, but I haven't been around for her as much as I could this past year."

"You a good father, Arizona. Everybody know that, including Dinah. If you want, I talk to her wit' you. Chase gonna need somebody to explain things too, but he come around. You just tell me what you need."

It surprised me he mentioned Chase. I hadn't thought about the situation affecting him. It seemed like he was too young to pick up what was going on. I just wanted to circle the wagons around both of my kids and shield them from the embarrassment I'd caused. I didn't know how to have a conversation with them about the terrible things being said about me, and I guess I wasn't ready to give it a try, even with Preston's support. It just felt like it was only going to upset them. So, I told Press I'd let him know and thanked him again for being on my side.

11

THE NEXT CALL I made was to Annette Dougherty. I filled her in on Dolly's tabloid article and soon enough I was rambling in near hysterics. For a lawyer, Annette was a real sweet lady. She calmed me down and got me telling her what happened bit by bit.

After, she explained we would've been notified by family court if Dolly had contacted them. She said she'd make an inquiry, just in case, and in the meantime, she assured me Dolly had a tough hill to climb if she truly intended to get back custody of Dinah. She hadn't shown up once for court hearings over eleven months. Instead, she'd chosen to sell a story about her daughter to a tabloid, which wasn't going to be looked upon favorably by a family court judge.

That was reassuring, but then Annette got to mentioning things that made me antsy. She was aware I'd come out as gay on national media and said if Dolly raised the issue with the court, it could send Dinah's case into review. Under Louisiana law, I was considered a sex offender based on a 1992 state statute. That law was being arbitrarily enforced, but it still scared the heck out of me. Being gay made me a criminal in the state where I'd been born. In the place that I called home. That hadn't truly sunk in until that conversation with Annette. Dinah and Chase could be taken away from me at any time. It got me thinking, moving to New York wasn't just about it being better for my career or better for the kids. I needed to move to ensure my own family stayed intact.

Meanwhile, Annette said I should get ahead of Dolly's insinuation that I was an absent parent and make sure Dinah was keeping to an appropriate routine. She advised against taking Dinah out of school for her birthday trip that coming weekend. Dinah had already missed ten days of school that year, along with committing a juvenile offense, and that was the kind of thing that would be scrutinized. Annette was from a firm that had worked with my daddy for years, and she told me, in order to avoid media attention, I'd be best off moving myself and the kids into my daddy's estate in Darrow, just temporarily. Daddy had gates around the property and better security than at my house in Thibodaux.

I didn't like that idea. My daddy's house was far from both Dinah and Chase's schools, and we were all more comfortable at my home. But I was also reeling from the possibility of news cameras showing up and people harassing me or even harassing my kids. So, I tried calling my daddy and finally reached him while Sophie was getting the kids to sit down for dinner. It turned out he was already aware of the situation.

"You all should pack up and head over to the house tonight," he said. "I've been telling you, you need better protection. Now the shit hit the fan, and you're lucky you've got options. I can get down there Memorial Day weekend and make sure things get sorted out."

I'd been knocked down pretty bad, but I wasn't so low as to not have certain feelings about what he'd said.

"It's only going to be for a few days, till things blow over. Daddy, I'm handling this. I've got a publicist to manage reporters. Dinah's finally doing well at her new school, and the last thing she needs is a security guard accompanying her when she's trying to fit in with her classmates."

"I told you, you'd be better off up here with me. They've got schools for senators' kids where you don't have to worry about the paparazzi following them around."

"I'm a writer, Daddy. I'm not John F. Kennedy, Jr.. Nobody's going to be interested in me for that long."

"I'm not talking about you. I'm talking about me. The news is going to make a big deal out of this. Republican donors control three-quarters of the media, and that's a fact. They're going to want to smear me just like they smeared Bill Clinton and Dick Morris. Chase needs to be protected."

Gaston Bondurant had one big ego, and being elected senator clearly hadn't helped. I considered letting things pass, but that had never been my strong suit.

"Daddy, the issue here is *I'm* getting smeared. You understand, I could lose custody of Dinah?"

"Seems to me taking in that girl is what led to this big mess in the first place."

My eyeballs rolled into the back of my head.

"Son, I warned you something like this was going to happen. Now, I've been thinking, if you insist on trying to rehabilitate that girl, Chase should move up with me. He needs a healthy, stable home, and that's not something he's getting right now."

"There's nothing wrong with Dinah." I rounded myself and practically got tangled in the phone cord. "Now, there might be something wrong with you. You can't acknowledge that Dinah's part of my family?"

"I know you see it that way—"

"I see it that way because it *is* that way. Chase grew up with Dinah. She's spent more time with him than you as a matter of fact." I caught myself and lowered my voice. "Let's make two things clear. You're not taking Chase, and you're not lecturing me about my parenting. I'm the only son you ever raised and to say you did it on a part-time basis would be generous."

He shut up after that, and I ended the call. The truth was, I was an emotional wreck. I had people saying I wasn't fit to raise my niece, and my daddy saying I ought to let him raise Chase. I fought against it, but part of me was starting to feel like maybe they were right.

I WASN'T IN a good state to talk to Dinah that night, but I knew it had to be done. I caught Sophie while she was cleaning up after dinner and asked her if she could keep Chase occupied while I took Dinah aside. I could read on Sophie's face that I didn't have to explain things more than that. She'd read the article in the *National Enquirer*, and she might have overheard me on the phone. The poor girl hadn't realized all she'd signed up for when she agreed to stay on.

It was a mild May evening, so I brought Dinah out to the back deck and shut the sliding glass door behind us. The sky was lighting up with stars, and it wouldn't have been a bad time to just enjoy the peaceful night with the crickets and toads droning in the brush that hemmed in the sodded lawn. But I had itchy business to deal with.

I sat down with Dinah in the glider loveseat and got straight to it before I lost my nerve. I told her about her mama appearing in the *National Enquirer*. I gave her the highlights and said she could go on and read it herself since she was old enough. I explained I'd made a decision, and we were moving into my daddy's estate just as a precaution. Then I asked her how she felt about all that and tried to pretend I was the adult in the situation, steady and prepared for any reaction she might throw my way.

"Why's she going to that paper instead of talking to me?" she said.

I'd always felt like I could speak to her on the level, so I told her I'd wondered the same thing. But if her mama took things to court, she might be asked how I was taking care of her and who she preferred living with.

Dinah drew up a scowl on her face. "That's stupid. I want to live with you and Chase. She can't say she's got a right to be a mama when she's never done anything to show she wanted me."

She rested her head against my side, and I stretched my arm around her.

"It wasn't so long ago you were skipping school to find your mama." I lightly brushed the top of her hair, which was fine and reddish-brown just like Dolly's. "It would be okay if you had mixed feelings."

"That was dumb. She never looked for me, so why should I look for her?" She snuggled closer. "Why're you bringing that up? I'm over it, and you should be too."

"That's good to know." I still had some tough things to talk to her about, but I was relieved that she was taking the news real well so far.

"Honey, we're going to have to postpone your birthday trip to New York. With all this swirling around, I can't take you out of school. I'm sorry. You know I'll make it up to you."

She didn't look upset. I soldiered on.

"When that article gets spread around, kids might give you a hard time. I want to have a talk with your principal. Make sure he looks out for you in case somebody mouths off. You be all right with that?"

"I can take care of those kids myself."

"I'm sure you can. But honey, we don't need any bad attention. It shouldn't be your burden, but I can't have people saying I'm not raising you right. I don't want to lose you 'cause people got opinions about me being gay."

"Okay, Uncle Arizona. If you feel like you have to talk to my principal, fine."

I gave her a squeeze. "It's not like I have to do it in an embarrassing way. I was thinking, I'll wear my bucket cap, my turquoise shorts, and a cutoff T-shirt. You think Mr. Baldi will like that?"

She elbowed me. "You're too old to dress like that."

"Y'know, I can't wait till you're twenty-nine. Old and decrepit."

I chuckled. "I'll be sure to share my opinions about what you wear."

We laughed. I gave the glider a push, and we sat together quietly for a spell, cozied up while a breeze sighed through the oaks and pines around the house and a spectacle of stars shone above us.

12

I LEFT RETURNING phone calls for the next day, and then the following morning, while I was having breakfast with the kids, Sophie asked if she could speak with me. I followed her to the den, and carefully, she drew back a portion of the curtain at the window that looked out to the front yard. A tan Buick sedan was parked across the street. As I squinted, I saw the driver holding a camera with a telescopic lens pointed at the house.

I told Sophie we were packing up the kids for a few days and going to my daddy's house. I called their schools and said they weren't making it in that day due to a family emergency. Then I phoned my friend, Katie. I explained my situation and asked her for a big favor. Katie was a real lifesaver. While Sophie and I were throwing clothes into suitcases and pushing Chase and Dinah along to grab whatever toys they wanted to bring, Katie drove over in her minivan and harassed the photographer to move along. We loaded up my car, got the kids buckled in, and I hauled ass to Whittington Manor.

That old plantation estate had more than enough room for the four of us. The main house had twelve bedrooms on the second floor and a ballroom for one hundred people, and it was on one hundred acres of lawns, horse stables and trails, woods, a lake, and even a family chapel and a cemetery. It wasn't homey, but Chase and Dinah had stayed over many times before, and they loved it. They thought they were on vacation. I told them to mind themselves when they were upstairs and steer clear of my grandmother's room at the end of the hall. I hadn't seen Virginia Bondurant in over a year. She'd practically been an invalid, so I assumed she kept to her bedroom. Anyway, the kids ran off to the game room that Daddy had furnished for Chase. It had a big screen TV with Nintendo, an electronic dartboard, foosball, and a pool table.

Meanwhile, I had a talk with the house manager, Mr. Wainwright, who was a snooty old pain in the ass. My daddy had let him know we were coming over, but he hadn't expected us so soon. I told him the kids would need breakfast, lunch, and dinner for the next few days and said I'd be using my daddy's study to make some calls. Mr. Wainwright didn't look happy about it, but he took his marching orders and left me alone. Then I got on the phone with my New York people.

Talking to Jonathan was easy. He just wanted to make sure I was all right, and then we joked about all my busted family drama coming out in the press. Jonathan assured me the gays were on my side while I was feuding with my sister in the tabloids, and I told him for my next act, I was dredging up "my uncle Bubba," who was going to accuse me of giving my cousin a handjob behind the shower house of their trailer park. Not that there was anything wrong with that, I told him.

We had some laughs, and then I rang up Janet. She was stressed out and mostly concerned about how Dinah was taking everything in. I assured her we'd all get through it and said I had material for my next book and she better start pitching it to Hatchette, which had recently signed Anna Nicole Smith to write her biography. When the earth is shaking under you, sometimes all you can do is find some humor in it.

That left me with two return calls I needed to make. Margaret and Rafe. I wasn't in the mood to speak to either of them. Margaret would probably have more bad news, and Rafe, well, I'd

thanked him for the flowers and accepted his apology. I was trying
to keep an open mind. But that last time we'd seen each other had
left me wary. In the end, I dialed his number and hoped for the
best.

He picked up right away and voiced his shock about the
National Enquirer article, and then we went through the same
questions I'd been fielding for the past twenty-four hours. No, I
hadn't heard from my sister in over a year. No, I hadn't been
contacted by any reporters. I told him about the photographer
who'd been staking out the house and explained I'd taken the kids
to stay over at my daddy's place. A tabloid reporter would have to
scale a ten foot wall and trek across two football fields of wooded
land to get close enough to try to snap a photo of us.

"I'm glad you're safe," he said. "You must be a wreck. I don't
understand why your stepsister would do this. Do you?"

I plopped down in my daddy's leather executive chair and
fiddled with one of his gold-plated pens. "I don't. I suppose she's
thinking she can get some money out of it."

"Do you know how much the *National Enquirer* pays for
stories, on average? Five hundred dollars. Maybe she got seven
hundred if she gave them exclusive rights."

I hadn't even thought about that. Five hundred dollars was the
price that made it worth Dolly's while to hurt her daughter and
slander me.

"Did Margaret tell you she called the office here?"

My heart stopped beating. "No."

"She didn't get past the receptionist. One of Julian's junior
editors called her back. She told him she had a tell-all book and
wanted Random House to publish it. She put some man on the
phone who claimed he was her 'agent,' and they were asking for
one hundred thousand dollars. Of course, everyone is treating it
like a joke, but I thought you should know."

I ran my hand through my hair. "That's my sister for you."

"How are you doing?"

"I'm getting by."

"I'm glad you called. When I didn't hear from you yesterday, I worried I did something wrong. Is that crazy?"

It didn't feel like the right time to have a conversation about where we stood. I didn't need the stress when I had bigger problems on my hands. So, I said I'd had a lot to deal with when Margaret broke the news to me the day before.

"Of course. All I wanted to say is, I've got your back. I told Julian yesterday he has to respect however you want to handle the situation. I won't let this jeopardize your standing. You're a brilliant writer, and your book is making Random House a *lot* of money. Most of all, I wanted to let you know I care about you, so much, as a friend."

That lifted my heart. Or maybe it was my ego. I'd been so caught up in other things for the past month, until he said that, I hadn't thought about how important my writing was to me. And we'd been more than friends, though I appreciated him putting it that way to take the pressure off the conversation.

"Thank you. That means a lot." I scratched the side of my face. "I'm hoping to get up to New York with Dinah real soon. Her school year finishes in two weeks. It would be nice to see you."

"I'll be here whenever you can make the trip. Whether it's for a cup of coffee or you have the time to spend the night. Just let me know."

I told him I'd be sure to do that, and we said goodbye.

I SPENT THE rest of the day working out logistics with the kids' schedules. They'd both need drivers to get back and forth to school. I couldn't have them being absent if there was a chance Dolly was going to make a complaint to family court. Fortunately, my daddy kept his chauffeur, Buck, working year-round. He could take Dinah to her school in Vacherie, and Sophie could take my car for the shorter trip to Thibodaux.

Dinah gave me some grief because she'd have to get up earlier in the morning, but I told her this was no vacation, and I meant business. Chase was quiet while we were talking about it in the game room. Sophie had put on some cartoon show for him. He looked a little blue, so I asked him if he'd like to take a walk down to the stables to see the horses. He had a Chesterfield pony he'd named Missy. Chase shook his head and told me Sophie was going to teach him to play the piano that afternoon.

I didn't like that answer. It was a beautiful, sunny day, and I was asking him to spend some time with me. Chase wouldn't budge, and then Sophie entered the room. He shot up from his seat and threw his arms around her, looking away from me.

Dinah grabbed the remote control and clicked on *The Price Is Right*. I gave up on both of them and decided to take a walk by myself. I was thinking I could have a smoke along the way to the stables. Then my daddy called.

I couldn't be so heartless as to ignore him when I was staying at his house. I picked him up while I was crossing the south lawn toward the stables.

"Good morning, Daddy."

"You give more thought to moving into my place?"

"As a matter of fact, we're here." I stopped short of telling him about the photographer. I didn't need him getting bent out of shape about that.

"Good. You all hunker down and enjoy yourselves. There's plenty of things for the kids to do right on the property. Mr. Wainwright will have to get the kitchen stocked and call in Mrs. Gundy to make your meals. I'll ring him up. He's also going to need to get them folks from Allied Security patrolling the grounds."

I pried a cigarette out of my box of Camels. "Daddy, we don't need to be locked in here like FBI informants. You've got plenty of security already. The kids are taking the day off today, but they're going back to school tomorrow."

"You're letting Chase go off the property by himself?"

My jaw clenched. "I'm not blindfolding him and sending him

out the gates to play in traffic. He's got two more weeks of school to finish up."

"The school year's practically over. What's he gonna miss? You just call up his teachers and find out what he can do from home."

"He needs to get back to a routine. Dinah too."

"This is a crisis we're dealing with."

"Which is exactly why the kids need to be back on a routine. I'm not budging on this, Daddy."

"I don't see the wisdom in that with all this going on. But if you say so. You talk to Buck about getting Chase back and forth to school?"

"He's driving Dinah. Sophie's taking Chase."

"Son, that doesn't make any sense. Buck should be driving Chase."

"Sophie can stay at the house in Thibodaux while she's waiting for Chase to get out of school. Dinah's school is in the other direction. That's how it makes sense."

"You want to entrust the safety of your son to a girl who's five-foot-four and one hundred and ten pounds soaking wet?"

"I could drive him myself if you'd prefer that."

"Don't take a tone with me. I'm the one signing Buck's paycheck. I'm saying Chase should be chauffeured to school. Dinah's thirteen. He's only six years old."

"Daddy, I'll get a car service for Dinah if you're going to make this an issue. Why, we could all stay at a hotel, and you won't have to worry about the driving arrangements at all."

"There's no need for that." I heard him heave a breath. "Listen, I'm running late. They're waiting for me over in the senate chambers. The reason I called was to let you know I worked out a plan to handle Dolly." He lowered his voice. "I had some people look into it. They found her address in New Iberia. I was thinking I'll have Lawrence go over and have a talk with her. He can offer her some money to sign a gag order. The whole thing disgusts me, but if it'll get rid of the problem, it's worth it."

A shiver ran up my spine. I remembered Preston saying he'd

heard Dolly was living in New Iberia. I was wary of what my daddy was suggesting. He wanted to send a lawyer to intimidate Dolly and pay her off? That felt underhanded and extreme. Dolly lived the kind of life where she'd be moving on to another scheme soon enough anyway.

"Daddy, you've already been involved more than you need to be. She's real unpredictable. I don't think it's a good idea. I think we wait this out and see if it'll go away on its own."

"I've been advised, son. Maybe you can afford to wait things out, but I can't. From what I understand about Dolly Fanning, it won't take more than a couple thousand dollars to get her to leave you alone."

It still didn't sit right with me, and I let him know. Dolly was my problem. I had a press agent who could take care of the bad publicity.

Daddy didn't like it, but I got him to say he'd leave things be for now. He was flying down on Friday for the weekend, and we'd have plenty of time to discuss strategies for dealing with Dolly, if it even came to that.

13

I SHOOK AWAKE the next morning to the sound of screams. I threw off my sleeping mask and looked around. My bedroom was cast in pale sunlight filtering through the curtains of the balcony. It had to be early in the morning. I leapt out of bed in the Middleton T-shirt and boxer shorts I'd slept in, and I went to the hall to investigate the commotion.

I noticed Dinah and Chase first. They were both in their pajamas, and Chase was clinging to Dinah in terror. I had no idea what was going on until I glanced beyond them. A few yards down the hall, I saw a woman in a wheelchair who looked as spiteful as the devil himself.

"I told you filthy children to get out of my house."

Before I could intervene, Dinah faced her. "We were just tossing a ball around, and it rolled down the hall."

My grandmother, Virginia, had never been physically intimidating, especially now that she had aged and thinned and used a wheelchair. But she could strike a bear to stone with her haughty stare, and she fixed one of those looks on Dinah.

"Who are you, wicked child? You look like you belong in a cage with the chimpanzees."

Chase moaned and bawled. Dinah faced her defiantly. "You're the wicked one. You scared him half to death."

I quickly corralled the kids into my bedroom, told them to stay put, and shut the door behind me. My heart was racing from that violent exchange. I scooped up Chase's nerf ball from the hall and carefully stepped toward Virginia to try to smooth things over.

"I thought Mr. Wainwright would've told you we're staying over for a few days." I tried out a grin. "The kids are at that rambunctious age. I'm sorry they woke you up."

Virginia's eyes grew wide. She'd painted her face to make herself look younger, but I saw a tick of recognition beneath that heavy-handed mask of beauty. "Arizona? As I live and breathe. I thought we were rid of you."

"It's good to see you too, Virginia. I was about to say you're looking well, but there's no need for pleasantries, is there?"

She did look surprisingly well for someone my daddy had described as practically vegetative. She wasn't the elegant woman she used to be, but she'd put herself together in a black lace dress and what looked like a blond wig. She sure seemed to have her mental faculties.

"You crawled back home, did you? After making a fool of yourself writing some tawdry book. I read the papers. It's disgusting what you did to the Bondurant name."

I controlled myself, remembering she'd had a stroke. It wasn't easy, but I gave her a nod and turned around to get back to the kids.

"If you think you're going to live off your daddy's money, you've got another thing coming," she called after me. "I won't have it. And I won't have your illegitimate kids living here."

I swung back to her. "I make my own money now, as a matter of fact. And if you ever raise your voice to my kids again, I'll make sure you're locked up in a facility for the rest of your days. I'll find one of them run-down old folks' homes where they pay off the health inspectors. It'll be a real nice way to spend your last years." I stomped back to my room without another look at her.

I WAS DISTURBED on a number of accounts that morning. The way Virginia talked to Chase and Dinah was a big one, and maybe I shouldn't have expected anything better, but her recovery from her stroke hadn't changed her venomous treatment of me. That came from a grudge I supposed she'd never get past. My daddy had cheated on her with her own daughter, and in Virginia's eyes, I'd always be a reminder of that indignity.

But I was also out of sorts because my daddy hadn't told me she'd recovered. When I visited him in DC, he implied she was in bad shape and under the care of a live-in nurse. He could've warned me she was back to her usual self. Unless he didn't know. It seemed like something he should've known, but he'd been living in DC for the past five months. I had a lot of things to sort out with him.

I had a talk with the kids about what happened. They were both shaken up in their own way, and I probably didn't need to tell them they couldn't be throwing around balls on the second floor ever again. I also told them Virginia was an evil woman who spouted nonsense, and they should never take to heart anything she said. I made them each give me a nod to let me know they understood, and then I sent them off to get ready for their trips to school.

Not long after they headed out, I got a call from Margaret. I'd never called her back, though I figured Rafe had filled her in on my status yesterday. I picked her up and let her know I hadn't been swarmed by reporters with the exception of that photographer yesterday morning. Then Margaret eased in to the latest developments on her end.

She'd gotten some calls about the *National Enquirer* article. Not from any respectable news outlets. The *New York Post* was running a short piece about it along with *The Daily Mail* in the UK. Her most troubling call was from a producer at the *Maury Povich Show*. Apparently, they had Dolly and her husband, Bobby, coming to their studio on Monday, and they had invited me to tell my side of the story.

I needed no convincing that was a bad idea. I couldn't believe Dolly had the nerve to keep running with her BS. Margaret said she'd drafted a short statement disavowing Dolly's allegation that I'd coerced her to relinquish custody of Dinah. She wanted to fax it to me so I could look it over prior to sending it out to her contacts. I gave her my daddy's fax number, and we said goodbye.

I felt like I was living in a nightmare again. My name was being dragged through the mud, this time by my own stepsister. As well as Dinah had taken things so far, she'd be getting another round of attention when that sensationalized daytime program came out on Monday.

Well, I had no choice but to set that aside and try to focus on keeping things normal for the kids. Dinah's birthday was on Saturday. All we could do was have a little celebration at the house, so I caught up with Mr. Wainwright. I gave him some ideas for the menu and the décor. I figured the San Francisco room would be fun for the kids. It had an old jukebox and a dance floor. I would've liked to invite Preston's family, but with everything going on, I wasn't so sure about it. Around midday, I gave him a call.

I told him about the *Maury Povich Show*, and he got all wound up again.

"She swinging for the fences, Dolly is. How she getting there? That the kind of show that flies you up?"

They recorded in New York, so I supposed it was. It occurred to me she couldn't get it together to show up for an interview to recertify her food stamps, so maybe she'd wouldn't make it to the show.

"Press, I'd like your family to be here for Dinah's birthday, but I've been going back and forth about it. You know, I don't want anyone to feel uncomfortable."

"If you asking me, I've had my fill of big occasions at Whittington Manor."

"It's not going to be a big occasion."

"Is your daddy gonna be there?"

I told him yes and said I understood if he wanted to sit out the party.

"I'll give her a call 'morrow, and we can plan something with my family later this summer, if that all right with you." He hesitated. "My aunts and cousins will be happy to see her. But I was gonna tell you, I think I got to the bottom of why she don't want to spend the weekend wit' me. Louie, Gracie, and Stella been givin' her the cold shoulder since she say Louie tol' her to look for her mama in Oklahoma. I tell 'em Dinah's family, and they should give her a second chance, but you know how kids can be."

I could picture it and felt bad for Dinah. But short of getting them all together to talk things out, I couldn't see a way to patch things up before Dinah's birthday. It was looking like it was just going to be Sophie, Chase, my daddy, and me for her party.

"Earl say Duke's coming back in a few weeks," Preston said. "He got a break from the oil rig in June. You talk to him?"

I hadn't. He wouldn't have heard the news about Dolly while he was working offshore. There was a phone line for reaching him in the case of emergencies, but it hadn't occurred to me to call him.

"It prolly for the best," Preston said. "Nothin' he can do about it."

"You think so?"

"I do. We jus' all get together when he get back. Earl real excited to take the four of us out on his new boat. I tol' him you got a lot on your plate right now, but you might as well know he gonna be after you."

I smiled. "You tell him I can't wait. And Press, I understand you not wanting to come over here. I'm done defending Daddy. That caused you a lot of hurt."

"He's your daddy. I get it, Arizona. You gotta respect the ones who made you."

"I suppose that's true, but a grown man ought to make his own decisions. I think there were times I should've put you first and told my daddy to back off from telling us how to raise Chase. I've been thinking about a lot of things lately." I brushed my hand through my hair. "Anyway, I wanted you to know that."

"That sound like a conversation I wouldn't mind picking up at another time. But I gotta get back to the shop. When you think I should call Dinah tomorrow to wish her happy birthday? Late morning?"

I told him that was fine, and we said goodbye.

14

I WOKE UP Dinah the next morning to sing her "Happy Birthday," and I gave her the only present I had for her at the time. It was the latest book by her favorite author Octavia Butler. I'd had it shipped to the house before her birthday, and boy, did it make her smile. I'd planned to take her on a shopping spree at the famous Strand bookstore in New York, but with that trip shot to hell at the last minute, I was left a bit empty-handed. I told her we could do anything she wanted that day, starting with a pancake breakfast prepared by the best cook in the world, Mrs. Gundy.

We had that breakfast with Chase and Sophie, and Sophie was real sweet to Dinah. She'd somehow managed to buy Dinah a present, and it was perfect—a denim jacket Dinah had mentioned wanting and a bunch of iron-on patches to go with it. Then Chase gave Dinah a handmade card on construction paper that Sophie must've helped him with. I was happy to see Dinah brighten up. She wasn't getting the birthday trip to New York we'd planned, but she said it was her best birthday ever. She wanted to go riding and bring her book along so she could read in a shady spot for the rest of the day. I asked Chase if he wanted to join us, and he got moody again, saying it was too hot and he wanted to stay indoors with Sophie. For Dinah's sake, I didn't argue with him, but at some point, I was going to need to have a conversation with that child.

Dinah and I geared up, and I got her settled on one of the older, gentle horses. We did a full run of the trails, and then we laid out at a spot overlooking the lake. While she read her book, I scratched down some notes in my notebook for the novel I'd been working on.

Daddy had come home after we'd gone to sleep the night before, and I'll admit, it had been part of my plan to get out of the house with Dinah to avoid him. I didn't want anything to spoil Dinah's day, and we'd be seeing him soon enough for dinner. Around five, I headed back with Dinah, and we got cleaned up and dressed for her birthday dinner. With my daddy, you dressed for dinner, and it was a special occasion. I found a blazer and a madras shirt in my old closet, and I helped Dinah pick out her best sundress and a pair of wedged sandals. Sophie took care of getting Chase ready in a button-down shirt and slacks, and we all came down to the San Francisco room. Just as we'd gotten seated at the fancy table with flower arrangements, Daddy strolled in wearing a fine plaid summer suit, followed by a staffer carrying two wrapped boxes.

The staffer laid one down at Dinah's table setting and one at Chase's. The kids ripped their gifts open immediately. Dinah got a New Orleans sweatshirt Daddy probably picked up at the airport. Chase got a radio-controlled robot that had just come out that year. I held in my opinions, and we got through dinner okay. We had a strawberries and cream cake, and afterwards, Dinah got Chase jumping around and dancing to some Beach Boys songs from the old jukebox. Chase was spent by nine o'clock, and Dinah wanted to help Sophie put him to bed. I kissed the kids goodnight, and they went upstairs. That left me and Daddy alone in the room.

Daddy suggested we move over to the room's leather Chesterfield, and he had a staffer set us up with a pair of Johnnie Walkers on the rocks. I wasn't looking to spar with him, but I wasn't in the mood to be lectured either. Things started out okay.

"Looks like you might've been right about Dolly," he said. "I've got one of my aides with his ear to the ground, and he says he hasn't heard a peep from the media."

I didn't want to tell him about the *Maury Povich Show*. I rationalized that it might not happen, and I'd be getting him riled up for no reason.

His eyes brightened. "Chase is growing by the day. He showed me his school assignments. I think we should get him tested. He ought to be in one of them gifted schools. I don't think that St. Thomas's is helping him reach his full potential."

I tipped back my whiskey. Dinah was reading three grades above her level, but I didn't expect he'd have anything to say about that.

"The boy's bilingual," he went on. "We had a whole conversation in French this afternoon. I think he could pick up a third language. You know, at that age, they're sponges for learning. What do you think? Spanish classes? Japanese?"

I bit my lip and controlled myself for a second. "You know, it's Dinah's birthday, not Chase's?"

"I may be an old man, but I know my grandson's birthday. October 3rd."

I watched him take a draw on his drink. "Then what's with giving him a gift on Dinah's birthday?"

"He'd been asking about that new robot by Mattel. I didn't want him to feel left out."

"Dinah's got a mama who abandoned her and is trying to use her for money. But you're worried about Chase feeling left out?"

"As a matter of fact, I am. Chase would've spent the day alone unless I'd taken him out to the grounds. I took him to the shooting range and had him hold his first rifle. I got him started with a BB gun." He chuckled. "He's got a ways to go, but like I always say, the earlier you start, the better."

I was hurt Chase had gone along with him real easy when he had told me he didn't feel like doing anything outside. At the same time, Daddy teaching Chase to shoot a rifle didn't sit well with me. I looked at him firmly. "I don't want him handling guns."

"The boy needs hobbies." I kept glaring at him, and he shrugged in resignation. "If it offends you, there's plenty of other sports he could get involved in. What were you thinking?"

"Chase likes reading picture books and finger painting."

"Well that's just everyday things. He needs a sport. That's what gives a boy goals and helps his body develop."

"When were you going to tell me about Virginia?"

He cocked a glance at me but didn't say anything.

"She made an appearance yesterday," I told him. "Didn't seem like she was at the mercy of nursing care."

"She has her good and bad days."

"Well, she had a real good day yesterday. She laid into Dinah and Chase like they were looters broke into the house. Seems to me she's rehabilitated. You're going to tell me you didn't know about that?"

"Mentally, she's made progress. If you're saying she got mouthy with Chase, I'll have a talk with her."

"*Dinah* and Chase."

His eyes sparked. "If she got mouthy with the kids, I'll talk to her."

"Maybe she'd be in a better mood if you didn't keep her living like a shut-in."

He laughed that off. "Your grandmother is confined to a wheelchair. She gets the best medical care money can buy, and her nurse, Fabienne, takes her anywhere on the grounds she wants to go. I wouldn't call that a shut-in. She gets visitors. Her sister, Deirdre, came over just last month." He polished off his drink and waved to the staffer at the bar to bring him another.

I came real close to saying what was on my mind. He was a walking, talking, drinking hypocrite. He wanted to tell me I was endangering his reputation when any newspaper would have a field day with the fact he left his wife to rot in a wheelchair and had a steady stream of mistresses on rotation? I guess what held me back was that I was staying at his house with two kids. I had to protect them from the media, and I didn't have anywhere else to go. I was steamed. I hated feeling so helpless. I set down my drink and stood.

"I'm calling it a night."

Daddy looked at me funny. "It's not even ten o'clock. You sit your butt down. When's the last time we had a drink together?"

"I'm tired, Daddy. It's been a shit week."

"For you and me both. So, have a seat, son. We're commiserating. That's what family's for."

"The problem is, we're commiserating about different things. Just so you know, I made a decision. I'm moving to New York when the kids finish the school year. I'm done with living down here as a second class citizen."

"A second class citizen?"

"Yes, Daddy. Thanks to the good people of this state, they wrote it into the law that I should have to register as a sex offender and I'm a danger to children."

He tried cracking a smile, but I could see he understood what I meant. "Son, you're always going to be protected by my name. Now I'm working on overturning those petty state laws in Congress. There's no need for you to do something rash–"

"With one phone call to the court, I could lose custody of Chase. Have him taken in by strangers."

"Now you know that's not the case. He's got me as a second guardian. Not that it's going to happen, but even if it came to it, Chase would have a home with family."

I don't know if he meant to imply it, but I was feeling shaky about the possibility of him stealing my son away from me. I said goodnight, stepped out of the room, and went up to my bedroom.

I HAD A talk with Dinah the next day. I wanted to make sure she knew that both Daddy and Virginia were blue ribbon winning idiots when it came to kids, and she should never feel bad about anything they did or said. Dinah wasn't upset. Sometimes, she was wise beyond her years. She said she understood why Daddy would favor Chase over her since the Bondurant name meant so much to him. Then she told me I shouldn't let the issue bring me down or treat Chase any differently.

"You think I treat Chase different?" I said.

She shrugged and went back to reading her book.

"Now c'mon. You're not getting away with making a statement like that without giving me an explanation. Different isn't the same as equal, and it's not the same as unequal either. You're thirteen, and he's six. He's got Sophie to take care of him, and Daddy and Preston to spoil him rotten. I love both of you, but the fact is, you need different things from me."

"Just don't take it out on Chase because you're mad at your daddy."

I thought she was way off base, but it did give me pause. I wouldn't say I favored Dinah over Chase. It was more like I was trying to even out the playing field, and Dinah was at an age where we could appreciate the things we had in common, whereas Chase was shy and quiet. He was a good boy, and of course I loved him, but every child has a personality and his was becoming hard for me to navigate.

Later that day, when my daddy was headed to the airport, he said he'd been talking to Chase about spending the summer with him in DC and taking him on a trip to Europe when he had a break from Congress at the end of July.

"I think it would be good for him," he said. "He's old enough to be having some experiences. You're always talking about not having enough time to write, and if you're really going to move forward with this plan to move up to New York, you're going to need some time to get things settled up there. It'll be a win on all sides."

I was thrown for a loop. Overnight, he'd decided to support my plan to move to New York? I couldn't say he was proposing something that wouldn't help me out. It would be easier for me to deal with real estate agents and furnish a home without having Chase along, needing to be entertained over the summer. I could also use any free time I could grab to get back to writing in earnest, and Daddy was sure to show Chase the time of his life in Europe. But that conversation with Dinah was stuck in my head.

"I'll have to let you know. I haven't figured out the kids' plans for the summer."

My daddy never liked being told no, but he didn't make an issue out of it right then. We hugged goodbye, and he followed Buck out to his Bentley.

15

ON MONDAY MORNING, the kids headed out to school, and I got a call from Margaret that sent my world toppling again. She'd asked around about what was happening with that *Maury Povich Show*, and they were airing a live segment with Dolly that afternoon.

Luckily, the show came on at two, and the kids wouldn't make it home from school until four or so. I spent the day trying to tell myself whatever happened, I'd get through it. I'd been smeared by *A Current Affair*, and things had turned out all right. But by eleven, I was in a panic and needing to talk to someone before I lost my mind. I gave Preston a call, and he said he'd get his assistant manager to watch the shop if it would help for him to come over. I must've sounded really bad.

Preston got to the house a little before two, and I brought him to my daddy's study to watch the show on the little Zenith set he had in his wall cabinet. I was so antsy, I broke out cigarettes. Preston and I didn't say a word once the show came on. We were both fastened to the TV while Maury did his opening monologue. The theme of the day was mothers who lost custody of their children, and that got my brain knotted up for a moment. It didn't sound like a topic that favored my sister in her scheme to make me look bad and her look good.

My insides crawled when he introduced his first guests who came from a "celebrity family."

"She's the stepsister of best-selling author Arizona Bondurant, who you might also know as the son of Gaston Bondurant, a Louisiana senator and the CEO of B&B Sugar."

I watched Dolly and her husband, Bobby, shuffle out to Maury's sofa on the stage. It was surreal at first. Dolly Fanning, who'd never held down a job, got herself on network TV.

She and Bobby sure fit in on that show. Dolly was wearing a low-cut blouse that was at least one size too small. Her hair was teased and stiff with hairspray, and she'd overdone it with cheap makeup. Bobby looked like your typical good ol' boy in his trucker cap, baseball shirt and tattoos covering his arms and neck. Now as infuriating as it was to see that Dolly had turned up for the show, it was also depressing. I don't think she understood she was being used herself and looked like a fool.

The studio audience booed her when Maury asked why family court had taken her daughter away. He made her admit she hadn't had any contact with Dinah since January 1997.

Dolly shouted over the audience. "That's 'cause my big shot brother turned her against me. Not a day go by I don't miss my girl." She wailed with tears, though she didn't look too convincing.

Maury turned to Bobby. "Your wife is distraught. What have you done to try to get her daughter back?"

Bobby took a moment to answer. I wasn't sure he even understood the question, but eventually, he came around. "We ax'ed to see Dinah, but her bruddah won't let us. He too busy sellin' books is what he say."

"Our producers reached out to Mr. Bondurant, but sadly received no response," Maury said.

"He a phony and a [bleep]," Dolly burst out. She stood up from the sofa, waving her hands. "I say it to his face if he weren't a [bleep] coward. He tryin' to turn my girl into a lesbian just like his [bleep] [bleep] son."

It was hard to watch. Maury stirred things up by mentioning Dolly had a past conviction for prostitution, and Bobby had three kids by three different women and had been cited for failing to pay child support. The two of them couldn't come up with much to defend themselves.

Then Maury switched to taking comments from his audience. An elderly couple went on a rant about the sinfulness of homosexuality and how it was "infecting" children. They got a lot of applause, and another woman spoke out to say a child belonged with her mother, no matter what she had done in the past. Then a lady in the audience asked for the mike to tell Dolly and Bobby to clean up their act, and someone in the row behind her cried out in agreement, throwing in that it all seemed like a publicity stunt given that Dolly hadn't tried to fight for custody of her daughter when she had the chance. Then Maury did the classy gimmick of asking the audience if they thought Dolly's daughter belonged with her. She got a handful of people clapping for yes, and thunderous applause for no.

I don't know how to describe how I felt. I'd expected to be angry, disappointed, and embarrassed, but the reason for those feelings was a lot more complicated than I'd imagined. It wasn't from the hatred Dolly had spewed or her bold face lies. She was showing herself to be a country crackhead on national TV, and maybe that was the act she wanted to play, but it got me thinking about a lot of things.

After a commercial, Maury brought on another group of hard-luck women to make fools of them. Preston clicked off the TV.

"We don't need to see mo' of that."

I hadn't even been looking at the TV. I couldn't raise my head.

"I ain't a lawyer, but I pretty sure she jus' dug her grave," Preston went on. "Family court see that, they gonna give Dinah a restraining order. Tell Dolly she can't be in the same state."

I'd checked in with Annette earlier that day, and she said the court still hadn't heard from Dolly. I couldn't get the words out to tell him that. Preston slid closer on the couch and put his hand lightly on my shoulder. "How you feeling?"

I shook my head. We sat in dead silence for a while.

"This all gonna blow over now," Preston said. "I don't like to say it, and I hope you don't mind, but Dolly Fanning ain't gonna be able to show her face 'round Le Moyne Parish, let alone get herself in the papers."

I nodded, but I didn't feel relieved.

16

THAT TALK SHOW turned out to be a spark on a wet fuse. Dolly got a trickle of publicity the next few days, but it wasn't the notoriety she'd been driving for. *The Sun* ran a story titled: "Senator Bondurant's Family Secrets," that talked about her being a deadbeat mom and a former prostitute. My favorite morning TV anchor Clive Magnano from WGNO mentioned her in a segment, calling Dolly's allegations "low class shenanigans." That was the extent of things, and Margaret was happy as a clam. My book sales got a boost from the publicity, and she said Julian was eager for me to write a book about my family history to capitalize on the media attention.

I told her I had no interest in doing that. I was working on a novel that was focused on the AIDS crisis. Then Janet called. She was real excited because she'd been fielding calls with lots of opportunities for me. A bunch of magazines wanted me to write guest articles, and organizers of literary events around New York were looking to get me as a speaker. I had so much on my mind, all I could say was that I'd get back to her about those offers.

Dolly's tabloid spectacle had only made me a hotter commodity, but I was in a funk for three full days. I only started coming out of it when I moved back into my house with the kids, and life started feeling normal again. With that came a sense of clarity about what I needed to do. I told Preston first, and he agreed with me. Then I called my daddy and asked him for the address he'd dug up for Dolly.

"Why do you want her address?"

"Because I want to see her."

He lowered his voice. "What good is going to come of that, son? We gave her enough rope to hang herself, and that's what she did. Game over."

I told him I wasn't looking to give her hush money. It was just something I had to do. He asked if I was bringing someone with me, and I lied and said Preston was coming along. My daddy hemmed and hawed, but in the end, he told me he'd have one of his aides call me with the address.

The next morning, I drove to a trailer park outside New Iberia. It was a dusty, treeless lot that was pretty desolate. Number thirty-three was a run-down aluminum sided home with two beat-up lawn chairs and a gas drum for a barbecue outside. I remembered Bobby's junky sedan. It wasn't parked in the vicinity. Either he'd scrapped it, or he and Dolly were out and about, or he'd gone out and Dolly was home. I was praying for the latter. I'd come wearing a short sleeve polo shirt, jeans, and sunglasses, hoping I'd blend in. I stepped out of my car, took a careful look around, and went up to the door and knocked.

I was pretty sure I heard rustling inside, but it took three more knocks and a good two minutes until Dolly's irritated voice gained up on the door.

"Hold your horses. I'm comin'. You forget your damn keys again?" She threw open the door, and the sight of me turned her white as a corpse.

She looked like she was considering the option of slamming and bolting the door, or racing into the house to shimmy out the back window. So I didn't say a word while she got used to the situation. She'd come to the door in just a T-shirt that was big enough to cover her halfway up her knees. It was probably one of Bobby's. Some heavy metal band was emblazoned on it.

Dolly regained her composure and put on her charms. "What the fuck you want?"

"I want to talk to you."

She glanced outside. "You bring reporters? I know you been sendin' them to follow me 'round."

It was hard to believe she was being chased by reporters. As far as I could tell, her fifteen minutes of fame were over. The tabloids had moved on to newer dramas. "It's just me," I told her.

She crossed her arms in front of her. "You come to lecture me 'bout goin' on that show? You waste your time. It's a free country, ain't it?"

"Yes, it is. That's not why I'm here."

"Then what you want to talk to me 'bout?"

"You suppose we can have a conversation inside?"

Dolly had always played the tough act really well, but I saw some chinks in her armor. Maybe the negative media attention had worn her down. Maybe she hadn't turned cold to me completely, and being face-to-face had reminded her that there'd been a time when we loved each other as brother and sister. We had been close the first thirteen years of her life. Anyway, I'm not saying she looked happy about our reunion, but eventually she stepped back to let me in.

"You gonna have to make it quick. Bobby be back soon."

I entered her trailer. I had to control myself from covering my nose. It smelled like rancid grease and the bottom of a hamper mixed with some sort of sickly sweet air freshener. Thankfully, Dolly left the door open to let in some air. It didn't help that the aluminum house was baking under the sun in early June.

As I took in the narrow domicile, I got even more uneasy. The kitchen area was strewn with pots and plates caked with leftover food. A confederate flag covered the opposite wall. Empty liquor bottles were strewn helter skelter, every surface was gouged with cigarette burns, and I saw discarded thumb-sized plastic baggies on the counter. I didn't know a lot about drugs, but I'd seen those little bags tossed on the sidewalk in the East Village of New York. Jonathan had told me that's how they packaged heroin, cocaine, and crystal meth.

Dolly sat down on one side of the dining booth and swept aside some of the debris from the table. I carefully took a seat on the vinyl bench across from her, hoping that the grime wouldn't stick to my pants. Dolly found a pack of Salems and lit one up with a bedazzled disposable lighter. She exhaled in my direction.

"You braver than I thought, coming here by youself." She studied me. "So, what you got to say? This how I live. I can tell you think I'm trash."

"Nobody's trash."

She smiled in an unfriendly way. "You full of shit. I see you disgusted with me. You think I care?"

It had been a long time since we'd seen each other, but the older brother in me had never gone away, no matter how scary that trailer was.

"I think it's about time you stopped living like this, but I'm not disgusted."

She snorted a laugh and drew hard on her cigarette. "You always looked down your nose at me. 'Cause you got a rich family, and I got nothing. I don't give a fuck. I'm not gonna kiss your ass like Duke do."

Duke didn't suck up to me or ask for money. I had an urge to defend him, but I held it down. "Dolly, I came here with one purpose. I want to know, do you want to have a relationship with your daughter?"

She averted my gaze and held her hands under the table. "You tryin' to threaten me?"

"No. I'm asking you a straightforward question."

She took another pull on her cigarette and ignored me. Without her makeup, I could see the deep bruises beneath her eyes. Maybe she'd been up late partying. Her complexion was kind of washed out. I worried she might be on something. Her hand was tremoring under the table.

"Do you want to have a relationship with your daughter?" I repeated.

"Dinah know I always be her mama. You turned her against me."

I laced my hands together. "The fact is, you walked out on her less than one month after her granddaddy died. You cleaned out his house, sold Dinah's clothes and toys, and left her without even a note. So. I'm saying, all this telling stories to tabloids, was that your way of trying to get Dinah back or did you just want to make some money?"

In the silence that ensued, I saw a glimpse of the lost girl she'd been when we were younger. She'd hardened so much over the years, I hadn't seen her vulnerability very often. I thought she might start crying, but then her fraught uncertainty compacted into anger.

"I'm her mama. I'm the one who should be raising her. You ain't even related to her."

"So, what's your plan, Dolly? You're going to take responsibility for Dinah?" I frowned impartially. "We could go to family court right now and get a petition started."

"I could," she said. "She gettin' Daddy's disability. That should be goin' to me, not you."

Dinah received $700 dollars a month from Gus's survivor's benefit. I deposited it in a bank account she could use when she turned eighteen. Dolly was really testing my composure now. The only thing she had to say about Dinah was getting her hands on that monthly check?

I glanced around the trailer. "So, you're ready to take care of her? You want her living here with you?"

She stomped out her cigarette in a tin ashtray. "I need some time to work things out. Bobby want us to have a baby of our own. But when I ready, I be getting her back, and you won't be able to do shit about it."

"Dinah's thirteen years old. How long is that going to be, till you're ready?" She didn't answer. I cocked a glance at her. "Seems to me in the meantime, you could've had a conversation with me about visiting your daughter. Would've been more productive than airing your grievances to the tabloids. If you really want to repair your relationship—"

"Quit riding my ass." She lit up another cigarette. "I could get her back tomorrow if I wanted."

"Now, there's two problems with that. First is, I haven't heard you say you want her back. Second, no family court judge is gonna let you bring a child into this home." I tried to pry out eye contact with her. "Dinah's doing well. She's in a good school getting good grades, and she's surrounded by people who love her. I think it would be nice for her to have you in her life, but that's going to take some work on your part. She's hurt by what you've done, Dolly. I believe you can fix that, but it starts with having a phone call with her or at least writing her a letter."

She bowed her head. I wasn't sure what I was seeing. She was going through some kind of transformation, and it was scary. She was strung up tight, her face was twisted, and she couldn't lift her eyes to me. Then she shouted wildly, "It ain't my fault. You the one who ruined everything. If it wasn't for you, I wouldn't have been raped by that pastor and living on my own at thirteen. If it wasn't for you, Little Douglas would still be alive." Tears sprouted from her eyes. "So go ahead, judge me for what I done. You the one who made me who I am and went on to your rich family and your rich life."

I'd spent years blaming myself for what my stepsiblings went through, but I'd come to terms with all that. I didn't enjoy seeing Dolly tortured and weepy, but I was glad she'd brought it up so I could say a few things to her.

"Dolly, what your daddy, Gus, did to me, well, it's not exactly the same as what you went through, but he was hurting me. Both physically and psychologically. You might not have understood since you were younger, but I think you had an inkling. You remember how he treated your Mama Lou?"

She turned from me, but I could see her face was trembling. "That don't mean you had to break up our family. Gus was working things out. You just had to kick him when he was down."

I drew a deep breath. "Then maybe I wasn't strong enough, Dolly. I put up with it for as long as I could. Told myself, this is the family I have, and for the sake of you, Duke, and Douglas, I'd take my licks from Gus and hope he wouldn't hurt any of you. But the time came I couldn't take it anymore. Maybe you'd prefer I did. I can see why from your perspective. I'm just telling you mine. I don't regret sending Gus to the hospital and getting removed from that home. It saved my life. But I do wish things turned out different for you when we got split up."

Dolly huffed out a bitter laugh. "Oh, I bet you wish things turned out different."

I gazed at her earnestly. "Honest to god, Dolly. If there was one thing I could change in the world, it would be what happened to you."

I had to gulp back a lump in my throat. We were both quiet for a moment. Then Dolly lashed out again.

"You lied to me. You said your daddy was going to take us in."

"I was fifteen years old. That's what I thought, too. But my grandmother wouldn't allow it. She barely tolerated *me* living with them."

Dolly found a napkin to wipe the tears from her face. "So, you sayin', everythin' that happened to me is my own fault."

"No such thing. Nobody should have to go through what you went through. You ever talk to somebody about those things?"

"What? Like a social worker? They all full of shit. I take care of myself because you know what? Nobody else gives a rat's ass about me. So, you tell me why I should care about anyone else?"

"I don't know, Dolly. I guess because if you don't care about other people, people aren't ever going to care about you. Like

Dinah. Now there was a time when you were real proud to be her mama."

She stood up suddenly, covering her face with her elbow, and she pointed to the door. "Get out."

I hesitated.

"Arizona, I mean it. I not having this conversation with you."

I stood, but I didn't move to the door right away. She was breaking down in tears.

"You want to raise my daughter, go ahead," she said. "But you tell her, I didn't give her away." Her voice broke. "I tried to be her mama. I just never could catch a break. Not like you. Getting breaks all the time."

I couldn't think of anything to say. I just pulled out a check from my pocket, set it on the table, and gave her one last glance with all the emotions I felt for her pouring from my heart. Ten thousand dollars. Maybe she'd use it to straighten out or maybe it would be gone in a month, spent on things I didn't want to know about. It just felt like the only way I could show her I cared.

17

AFTER THAT CONVERSATION with Dolly, I felt real low for a while. I'd stopped blaming myself for what happened to her, and I'd forgiven her for abandoning Dinah and trying to make some money off my publicity. But it shook me to the core seeing her in so much pain. She was twenty-seven years old, and the way she lived, I wasn't sure if she'd make it to thirty. Even if she did, I was scared of what kind of shape she'd be in. I don't know if it's right, but I'd seen she'd made choices that seemed like the best for her at the time. I think that's what she was trying to say to me, and I couldn't do a damn thing to help her.

A few days later, I sat Dinah down and told her that I talked to her mama. I left a few things out about what I'd seen in her trailer since that wasn't important for her to understand. Otherwise, she was old enough to know the truth. Dolly couldn't take care of her, but that didn't mean she didn't love her, I said. Dinah wanted to know if her mama was going to be all right, and I said her mama had always been real strong, and we had to have faith in her. We both teared up, but in the end, it seemed like Dinah took it okay. She said she wanted to get back to helping Chase with his homework and strolled off.

Then, the next morning, no more than fifteen minutes after I'd gotten home from dropping her off at school, Sophie told me I'd just missed a call from Dinah's principal. As I was dialing up the school, I was thinking it was good timing. I hadn't gotten around to telling Mr. Baldi my concerns about how Dinah was treated at his school. He was cordial, but he got straight to the point. I needed to pick Dinah up because she was being dismissed for the day. I asked what for, and Mr. Baldi said we'd all have a talk about it in his office.

I hightailed it back to her school and come to find Dinah sitting outside the principal's office, hanging her head like a prisoner at the gallows. We didn't have time for her to tell me what was going on. Mr. Baldi brought us into his office right away.

I had flashbacks of being called into my own principal's office when I was sixteen. I had some authority issues back then, and those issues were coming back to me. Mr. Baldi was a frumpy fellow in spectacles and an unfortunate toupée. He was probably ten years older than me or more. He had a placating smile frozen on his oily face, which wasn't easing my nerves.

He started by asking Dinah to say what had happened. She kept her eyes down and shook her head. So Mr. Baldi took over and explained that Dinah had shoved a boy so hard, he fell back on his head and needed to be taken to the nurse's office. His mom had picked him up to get checked out by a doctor.

I turned to Dinah in disbelief. She hadn't gotten into a fight since she'd been at a public elementary school last year. "What did you do that for?"

"He been making fun of me all week," she muttered.

I looked from her to Mr. Baldi. Somebody needed to elaborate real quick.

"Their teacher Mrs. Albanese said Dinah and Montgomery had a verbal altercation in her science class," Mr. Baldi said. "She asked them both to cool down, and then Dinah shoved Montgomery, and he fell flat on his back. He came within an inch of bashing his skull against a desk."

That didn't sound good on Dinah's part, but I had questions. "What kind of verbal altercation are we talking about?"

"Mrs. Albanese only heard a few words, but she said they were calling each other curse names."

Dinah broke in. "He said: 'If it wasn't for my faggot uncle, I'd be living in a trailer park like my mama.'"

My eyes popped. I felt like shoving the boy myself. I'd been antsy about my legal status as a gay man, but that all went out the door. I fixed on that principal, waiting for some reaction from him. He looked pretty itchy.

"Montgomery and his parents will be advised about the code of conduct concerning name-calling. But with regard to Dinah, we take a hard line on fighting. Students who engage in physical aggression earn an automatic day's dismissal, a one week suspension, and the possibility of expulsion, depending on the severity of the offense."

I checked myself for a couple seconds, trying to peel my mind open to the school's point of view. But I was damn sure Mr. Baldi was missing a critical part of the context. Dinah didn't go around shoving other kids for fun.

"Mr. Baldi, I was a schoolteacher myself. I understand the importance of a zero-tolerance policy for fighting. But I've got a question for you. Dinah's been at this school for six months now. She's got no friends and says the other kids, and teachers, look down on her. I'm wondering what kind of insight you have into that?"

He hesitated. "To my knowledge, everyone's been welcoming to Dinah. We had some concerns about her acclimation to the school as she came in midyear, but I assure you, we've all pitched in to do our best."

I cocked a glance at him. "Would you say calling her uncle a faggot and telling Dinah she belongs in a trailer park is welcoming?" He fumbled for an answer, and I didn't wait. "We chose your school because you say 'you cultivate an environment where all students feel like they belong.'" I stared at him expectantly.

"That is our mission. But Mr. Bondurant, we can't ignore that you and your family have been in the public eye recently. I can only control what happens on school premises, not what's spoken about at home. To be candid with you, it's new ground for us."

I thought about all the mothers and teachers who had huddled around me when I dropped Dinah off and asked to take a picture with me. The school had never had a problem with that. Was everyone showing their true colors now?

"I am a gay man in the public eye, raising my niece by myself. I understand that, Mr. Baldi, but I also understand that homophobia and class prejudices are not 'new ground' for any school across America, with all due respect. I'm paying a lot of money so this girl can get an education in a place where she feels safe and supported. How is it possible that a boy in this school, under your direction, could think it was acceptable to talk about me and my niece like that?"

"No one is saying it's acceptable, Mr. Bondurant. But many of our students come from families with Christian beliefs." He smiled falsely at me. I noticed then a cross-stitch crucifix and dove hanging on the wall behind his desk.

"Which Christian beliefs would that be? Love thy neighbor? Judge not lest you be judged?"

"Well of course, our students come from good, loving Christian families. But I think you understand what I'm talking about. Traditional family values run deep in our community. This is Louisiana, Mr. Bondurant. I'm sure you realize it's not like up north where you went to school."

At Dinah's enrollment meeting, he'd fawned over me, real gushy, when I'd mentioned my education. I was about to hit back at him, but I thought better of it. If Dinah hadn't been sitting next to me, I would have, but she didn't need to be part of a heated argument.

"Okay. So, what's the verdict then? Dinah's on suspension for one week? What happens after that?"

"Seeing as the last day of school is next Tuesday, and Dinah already passed her sixth grade exams, she can go home early for the summer."

I nodded along.

"But the school would like to review whether Waldron Academy is the best setting for Dinah next year," Mr. Baldi went on. "We'll be putting together a committee of teachers and parents to discuss the issue, as a community. Montgomery's mother has asked for the pastor of her church to provide spiritual guidance as we consider the matter. I'll let you know the committee's recommendation, and we can take things from there."

I stood and told Dinah to run along and wait for me outside. When she was out the door, I looked at Mr. Baldi squarely. "You didn't have any concerns about this being the right setting for Dinah when I was here in your office writing a check for her tuition."

He smiled nervously. "I'm sure this is upsetting. If you'd like, I can have my secretary follow up with some recommendations for child specialists that help with behavior problems. I can't promise you anything, but having Dinah in the care of a Christian counselor could be looked upon favorably by the committee."

A snort rushed from my nose. "Save your time with that committee. I'm not spending one more cent on Dinah's education at your school. But I'll be filing a report with the state education department's Human Rights Committee, and making sure everyone I know hears about how you treated my niece. You're a small man with a small mind, and you've got no business saying you run a school that cares about kids."

With that, I walked out on him.

ON THE CAR ride home, I asked Dinah if she was feeling okay, and I told her she hadn't done anything wrong. I know, hitting or pushing somebody isn't the way kids should be taught to handle conflict, but in my experience, sometimes it's the only way to get ignorant bullies off your back. I might not have put that in a book I was writing about parenting, but it's the truth. The only way I'd gotten through high school was by fighting back. No teachers or principals ever stuck up for me. I knew Dinah was mature enough to understand I was only talking about standing up for yourself. She looked real pleased, and I think she was relieved she didn't have to go back to that school.

Then I shared with her some thoughts I'd been having. It was time for a fresh start for all of us. I told her I wanted to get up to New York and find us a new home there. I said I'd really like her to help me decide on the right place, if she wanted to take the trip with me next week.

Dinah's face lit up. "We're really moving to New York?"

"Darling, I hoped you'd say yes."

"I wouldn't have to go to school down here?"

I considered my words. "You'll still have to go to school. We'll need to find you one up there. And Dinah, while it's true that people in New York are used to kids from different families, kids are kids wherever you go. You're going to run into some blockheads, and I can tell you, they're not all friendly to people from the south."

"I know, Uncle Arizona. But if you could do it, I can too."

I glanced at her. "You'll also be far away from Preston and his family. You think about that?"

"I'll miss them. But don't you think we could visit him down here, and he can visit us sometimes?"

I nodded.

"Chase and Sophie are coming too, aren't they?"

"Of course they are. But listen, I haven't told them yet. I wanted to talk to you first to make sure moving would be all right with you. If we go up next week, it'll just be the two of us for a while. Chase is spending the summer with his granddaddy, and Sophie will probably be staying down here in the meantime."

I'd made the decision in my head, but I hadn't said it out loud. It wasn't going to be much fun for Chase to be up in New York while I was apartment hunting and getting a new home together. Having Daddy take him for the summer would also make the process easier for me. Over the next few months, I could write an article or two for the magazines that had contacted Janet, and maybe even do a speaking event while I was in demand. I could really start living my life as a writer in New York and not have to worry about my rights as a gay parent up there. Just thinking about it made me feel like a big weight had been lifted off my shoulders.

While the kids spent the weekend with Preston, I talked to Sophie to see if she'd be willing to spend the summer house watching instead of taking care of Chase. I explained my plans and said I'd eventually need her to move up to New York. I threw in that she could have two, three weeks off over the summer to visit her family in France. Thank god, she was fine on all scores. Actually, I think she was just as excited as Dinah. She said it had always been her dream to live in New York, and she was looking forward to taking Chase to all the museums and parks the city had to offer.

I smiled to myself. Sophie was the real deal when it came to professionalism, but having lived together for going on two years, well, I hoped she considered herself family too. "There's things to do for grown-ups, too. You could take a night off here and there and have your Sundays to yourself. You'll have a lot more options than living in a small town."

Sophie blushed and looked away. I was thinking there was no reason to not acknowledge she had a life outside of looking after Chase.

"I wouldn't know what to do," she said.

"I could give you pointers. Whether you like nightclubs or shopping or meeting people from other countries living in New York."

She didn't answer, but the expression on her face told me she was interested. So I mentioned some clubs I'd been to that were frequented by French ex-pats and told her if she was interested in taking a class at one of the colleges, I'd gladly pay for it and give her some time off during the day. She ought to have her own friends. Maybe she'd even meet a special someone. Sophie was just two years younger than me, and she wasn't going to be Chase's nanny forever. It made me happy thinking about giving her a chance to spread her wings in New York versus smalltown Louisiana.

After dinner the following Monday, I took Chase aside on the back porch to talk to him about the plans. He came along and sat down on one corner of the glider with his legs hanging off the bench and a pair of designer tennis shoes my daddy must've bought him on his feet. I was struck by how much he'd grown, in just the past few months it seemed. He was turning into a lanky boy in front of my eyes, and he had no interest in clinging to me like he used to. Well, in addition to noticing those things, I got a big dose of his developing personality.

I sat beside him, and he held out his hands, saying I didn't need to sit so close. I sat back a bit and told him he was spending the summer with his granddaddy while I found us a home in New York.

Chase wanted to know if Sophie was coming with him for the summer. I explained I needed Sophie to take care of the house while I was up in New York. I hadn't seen such a sour look on a child since Dinah's meltdowns last year, and I didn't see the reason for it. I'd expected an easy conversation, but I was having trouble getting one word answers out of him.

"Your granddaddy is taking you to Europe. Why, I didn't get to go to Europe until I was seventeen years old. Aren't you excited about it?"

"I don't want to go."

I was shocked, and I'll admit, I was a little disappointed in him. He was acting like a baby about a trip few kids his age ever had the opportunity to take. I asked him why he didn't want to go, and all he'd say was it was too far away.

"The world's a big place, young man," I said. "By the time you're in middle school, you'll have seen most of it at the rate you're going. Now that's not bad, is it?"

He turned from me and brooded.

"Well, you can take it up with your grandaddy if you'd rather spend the summer some other way. You're going to have a hard time convincing him, but like I said, you can try."

"Why can't Dinah come?"

"Honey, I told you, me and Dinah are going to be looking for our new home in New York."

"Do I have to live there?"

"Not right away, but eventually." I studied him. It would've been nice if he'd mentioned wanting me to come along on his trip.

"I don't want a new house. I don't want a new school."

"I know change is hard, cher. But you're a big boy. You'll get used to it."

He crossed his arms in front of him. "I don't want to."

I was losing my patience with him. The boy got everything he wanted, and he was going to live real well in New York. "You want to stay down here and live with Sophie? Or maybe you'd rather move in with your granddaddy?"

He sulked, avoiding my gaze. I felt a little terrible, but I was hurting too. *I* was his daddy. I'd put my career on hold to raise him for his first five years, and even now, I was turning down opportunities so I could spend quality time with him. Now I knew I was asking him to give up things. He loved St. Thomas's and had a lot of friends there. I tried to bring some words out, but I wasn't sure if I'd be putting them right.

Then he asked if his père was going to move to New York with us, and my heart caved in. That was what he called Preston. I told Chase that Preston's home was in Louisiana, and if he really wanted, he could ease into the move and even stay in Louisiana the next school year. That all came out of my mouth before I'd considered the logistics. I just hadn't expected Chase to get so upset.

18

I PUT OFF making the arrangements to take Dinah up to New York, and the next day around noon, I drove over to Franklin to pay a visit to Merle's Gas and Go. I needed Preston's advice, and I guess you'd say his blessing. It wasn't a conversation to have over the phone. I didn't even call to let him know that I was coming. I was nervous, and I couldn't slow myself down to give him the heads up.

It made me smile walking into the shop. I remembered all the times I'd surprised Press there during my breaks from school. He was always grumpy about me not calling ahead, but every time, I could tell he was real happy to see me. Over the years, he'd moved up from working the pump and covering the register to working as a mechanic, and since his uncle Merle retired, he owned the place outright. That shop was spic and span. Preston always made sure of that. I didn't see anyone working there besides a red-haired kid restocking the cigarette case so I stepped over to the cashier counter. I gave the young fellow a friendly how do you do and asked if Preston was around.

The kid turned my way, and his eyes went wide like I'd beamed down from outer space. He even glanced around to see if there were witnesses, but the shop was empty. Then he got goofy-faced and stuck out a jittery hand. "How do you do? Prolly you don't remember, but we met 'fore. I Uncle Preston's nephew. Stevie."

I shook his clammy hand. Now the memory came to me a little. He was Preston's cousin Darlene's oldest son. He'd only been eleven years old the last time I'd seen him, and he'd really shot up in height. That must've been four or five years back. I told him it was nice to see him again and asked how long he'd been working at the shop.

"It been a couple months. I work Tuesdays and Thursdays. Monday, Wednesday, Fridays, I in school. I in the vocational track. Learning auto repair."

"Good for you. You tell your mama and little Betty I said hello."

He stared at me again with a mix of terror and admiration. I could see he was going to need some help to move things along.

"You say your nonc's in the back?"

His face burned up in self-reproach. "Oh, I get 'im for you." He bowed his head, looking goofy again. "My friends ain't gonna believe it. Suppose I can get your autograph? I ain't got my mama's copy of your book, but we got extra copies of *People* magazine when you was in there." He rifled through shelves behind the counter and pulled out the issue. He set it down in front of me and flipped to the page with my article in two seconds flat. Then he scrambled for a pen though he had one behind his ear.

I signed at the bottom, and Stevie looked at my signature in awe.

"I ain't never met anyone from TV 'fore. It true you grew up in Le Moyne?"

"Mm hmm." I cleared my throat and glanced at the door to the back office.

"Oh, I get 'im for you." He stumbled in that direction then stopped. "You wanna cup of coffee? We got Slushies, too." He itched his head. "I shoulda asked 'fore. I just refilled the powder in the blueberry slushies. You mix the blueberry an' the lemonade, it taste pretty good. I can make you one."

"Thank you. But I just came by to see Preston."

He hurried into the back office, and I grinned to myself. I hadn't spent time in Le Moyne for quite a while so it had slipped my mind that I'd get that reaction. Giving Press advance notice might've been a good idea, I realized.

He came out in his cap and coveralls looking somewhere between peeved and mystified. "I didn't know you was coming by. Everything okay?"

I wanted to give him a hug, but he seemed on guard. "I was hoping I could take you to lunch."

Preston smiled to himself and stepped closer to speak quietly. "Arizona, I don't mean to imply I not happy to see you, but what this 'bout? You know I can't run off to lunch at the drop of a hat."

"If it's a bad time, I can wait."

He looked at me crossly.

"Or I can go over to Clemmons, get it to-go, and bring it back here."

He didn't look any happier about that suggestion. Then two men stumbled in through the adjoining door to the garage. They froze and stared at me. They were wearing mechanics suits, so they must've worked there. Beyond, Stevie peeked out from that door holding a phone with a long cord. While he hid from view, it was so silent in that shop, we could hear the conversation.

"I say, Mama, *Arizona Bondurant*. I ain't putting you on. Leave Little Betty with Mrs. Guillaume next door, and get yourself over here...I don't think he care how you look. You know he like men, not women."

I bit my lip so I wouldn't laugh. Meanwhile, Preston took things in and came to a quick conclusion.

"I'm running out for an hour," he called to his staff. "If Mr. Lefoy come by 'bout his Chrysler, tell him I be back real soon." He nudged me toward the door and muttered. "This better be real important, and it better be a real good lunch."

I DROVE US to Sonic's Drive-Thru off the highway since Press didn't have much time on his hands. It was also sentimental, I suppose. When we were teenagers, I'd picked him up in my old Corvette Convertible two dozen times or more to get burgers and shakes at Sonic's. Preston harassed me about showing up out of the blue and throwing his day sideways, and I let him take his digs because I did feel bad about it. I just really needed to talk to him. It wasn't something that could wait until the weekend when we had our weekly phone call. I knew he didn't like to break out of his routine, but I could also tell when he was genuinely mad or putting on a fuss just because he liked getting a rise out of me. That afternoon, it was feeling like the latter.

At the drive-thru, I ordered our burgers, fries, and shakes and sat back in my seat.

"Stevie's a little man now. I didn't even recognize him at first. He working out all right?"

Preston lit up a Salem with a Zippo lighter, took a puff, and held his smoke out the window. "He ain't the brightest Crayola in the box, but I tol' Darlene he could have some shifts while he in school." He gave me a sharp glance. "Half the town gonna be waitin' for us when we get back. What you thinking, Arizona? You just in the mood for attention?"

I hadn't bought a pack of cigs for a week, and his was looking good. "Suppose I could have one of them?"

Fussily, Preston pulled out his pack and handed it to me. I pried out a cigarette and glanced at him to light me up. He did so with the big Zippo flame nearly frying my eyebrows.

I batted him away, took a drag, and looked at him. "I'm sorry. I guess you could say it was inconsiderate of me, but I needed to see you."

A tender phase passed over his face, and he looked away, working on his cigarette. I felt warm seeing that, but I also worried about what I had to tell him.

"It's about the kids, and this idea I had. I guess I need you to tell me how you honestly feel, and if you think I've got a screw loose."

I proceeded to tell him about my plan to look for apartments in New York with Dinah over the summer. I had a hard time looking him in the face afterward.

"How that gonna work wit' Chase?" he said.

I told him my daddy was after me to take Chase for the summer, and after that, I was thinking about taking things step-by-step. I mentioned Chase wasn't happy about the move, and I said, regardless of how quickly Chase came up to New York, we'd always come down to visit some weekends, and Preston had an open invitation to come up to New York.

"What Dinah say?" he said.

"She's all for it. She hates her school, and she wants to give New York a try." I filled him in on last week's incident.

Preston lightly flicked the ash from his cigarette butt out the window. "You want to know the truth, I think it's a real good idea for Dinah. She always say she like New York. She been having a hard time down here, and it'd be great for her to have a fresh start where people don't know her from the newspapers."

I felt bad about that, and it must've been showing on my face.

"I'm not sayin' that's your fault. It just how it is. I had to wrangle her cousin Jean when we were over at Beau's house on Saturday. He was asking Dinah questions about that *National Enquirer* article."

I'd told him about my visit to see Dolly, and that I was pretty sure her days of getting tabloid attention were over.

"Dinah ain't been happy even before all that hullabaloo," Press went on. "If she be happier in New York, I'm all for it, too."

I studied him. "Press, I'm talking about moving to New York permanently. How you feel about that?"

"I always knew it was your plan to move to New York. You the main one supporting the kids, so what can I say?"

Preston didn't sound angry, but I was still feeling a little guilty.

He'd been a big part of Chase's life from the start and Dinah's life since she was four.

"Press, in the kids' eyes, you've been supporting them as much as I have. Especially Chase."

"Like I tol' you, Dinah *your* girl. She gonna want to be with you. I'll miss her, but I understand she need a fresh start."

I glanced at him while he was working out more to say. Then I remembered something that made me grin. "Chase wanted to know if you were moving up with us."

His face brightened, briefly. "I'm sure he come around to the idea of living in New York."

"It's not going to happen right away." I peeked at him. "You promise you'll come up to visit?"

"I will. When I can."

"We could work out something so Chase comes down on his breaks from school."

Preston nodded. I couldn't tell how he was feeling.

"Press, both Dinah and Chase are always going to want you in their lives. I just can't do it anymore down here. What happened with Dolly, well, it turned out to be a false alarm. But the fact is, I don't, *we* don't have any legal standing here in Louisiana. You know that always stressed me out. And it's not just affecting me. I told you what happened with Dinah's school. Same things could happen with Chase when he gets older. I just can't deal with living in a state that doesn't want us here."

"Plenty of people want you here. But I know what you mean." He lifted his cap to scratch his head. "You doing the best thing for the kids. I get that."

I sighed. "I hope so. You know, it never could be as easy as both of them being in good shape at the same time. Chase was behaving while Dinah was raising hell, and now it's the other way around. What does he say to you?"

"He don't say much when I take him for the weekend, and like I tol' you, he can get a little uppity 'round his cousins. He don't fit in as easily as Dinah does." He looked real pensive. "I think moving to New York could be good for him too. Francine said it, and I think I agree with her. He growing up to be like you and me."

I pointed my gaze out the window. I can't explain my reaction, but I didn't want to believe Chase could be gay. I guess it tapped in to a hidden worry that people would think I made him that way.

"Chase gonna be who he gonna be," Preston said. "I don't feel any better or worse 'bout it."

"He's six years old," I said. "Just 'cause he's quiet and doesn't like getting dirty playing with other kids doesn't mean he's one way or the other."

"Could be. I just saying he don't seem so comfortable with other boys. Maybe in New York, he be a little freer to be himself. I think he's getting to the age where he realize he different, and you know being different don't go so well in Louisiana."

I was surprised by how easygoing he was being about things. It got me worried again that he felt like I was making a decision without him and not giving him a choice. "Press, that may be true, but what I'm trying to say is, you're part of the family. Now, setting aside the legal issues, we could figure things out so it's not like you only get to see the kids a few times each year. Maybe I keep the house, and we go half and half between New York and Louisiana."

He gave me a sidelong glance, and then he took a puff and exhaled out the window.

"What?"

"C'mon, Arizona. Who ever heard of a celebrity living in rural Louisiana? You must have a lot more opportunities up there."

"I do, but I also want to do what's best for you." I scratched my ear. "Press, you know I never asked to be a celebrity, don't you?"

He smiled wistfully. "You always wanted to be a famous author."

"Authors don't usually get so much publicity. That hadn't been my plan."

"But it happened. It's not a bad thing, is it?"

I snorted. "Depends on the day of the week."

A waitress brought our food over to my window. I fished out a twenty and told her to keep the change. She looked at me twice as though she was trying to figure out where she had seen me before, but mercifully, she gave up and scurried away.

Preston grinned in amusement.

"What's so damn funny?" I chomped down a french fry. "You see? This here is what I'm talking about. I don't have any privacy anymore. I can't even get a hamburger without people looking at me."

"I think it's cute."

I gave him a beleaguered frown. Preston laughed at me.

"You could have a lot worse problems," he said. "But living in New York, you'd have an easier time, wouldn't you? Y'know, with all them people, it must be easier to blend in."

"You're sounding like you *want* me to move."

Preston chewed down some of his burger. "Honestly, it's the last thing in the world I want. But I knew I had to face facts last year. Trying to keep you pinned down here was only making you unhappy." He looked at me. "I want the best for you. Always have. It just been hard for me to let you go."

My armpits started perspiring. "Press, you never pinned me down. I stayed in Louisiana because of you. There's a difference."

He set down his burger, looking thoughtful. "I been going back to church. Not my parents'. It just been something I wanted to do after we split up. I didn't tell my family 'bout it." He took a sip of his Coke. "I heard about this church in Lafayette. They got a female pastor, and they're open to everyone, y'know? It helped me when I was feeling low, thinking 'bout the two of us and what went wrong, and what I'm doing with my life." He snorted mildly. "I know it ain't your thing. But I needed to understand how things happen for a reason. I truly do believe it is that way."

A shiver passed through me. "What're you saying? You think it's God's plan we split up?"

"Maybe. Or not exactly. But Arizona, I think he got a plan for you and me. And everyone. And you, you were never cut out to live a simple life in the country." He peeked at me. "You know that, don't you? Ever since we was in school, you were meant for bigger things. Now you got them things, and I happy for you. It took me a while, but I come to terms with it. 'If you love somebody, set them free.'" He smiled. "The pastor told me a famous writer said that."

I knew the quote. When I was teaching eighth grade English at a public school in Baton Rouge, I had the students read Richard Bach's *Jonathan Livingston Seagull*. What he was saying was bringing tears to my eyes.

"Guess that means I got to set you free, too." My voice got small. "I don't want to do it." I wiped my eyes and took some breaths.

Preston held my gaze. "You got a path, and I got one too. I can't believe we ever gonna wander so far from each other. We never have in almost twenty years."

I'd gone looking for his advice and approval and found myself a steaming pile of mush. I needed Press. I wasn't sure I could do anything on my own. But I couldn't turn back time to when things were simple, and just us loving each other was all that mattered. I respected what Preston was saying. I sat with him while he finished off his lunch, and then I dropped him off back at his garage.

I JUST HAD one sticky conversation to get through after I had Preston's blessing. I called my daddy one night, and I started off with the easy part, saying he could take Chase for the summer. Daddy told me he was glad I'd come to my senses. He couldn't wait to have his grandson up in DC and said he already picked out a two-week itinerary for their trip to Europe. London. Paris. Vienna. Capri, and so on. He was home and sounding relaxed, probably after a couple of Johnnie Walkers. Then he asked what I was planning for the summer and whether I could come up to DC as well.

Now he knew I was spending the summer getting settled in New York. He'd even used that as a rationale for taking Chase for the summer. But I told him again I was going to New York with Dinah. A silence ensued. I was pretty sure it was the calm before the storm.

"Son, you've got a house, not to mention Whittington Manor at your disposal. Why you need to buy a place in New York? You can always stay at a suite at the Peninsula when you want to visit."

"Because I'm not talking about visiting. Daddy, this isn't breaking news. You've always known I wanted to live up there, ever since I was in college getting my writing degree."

"Tell me this. How's it different writing in New York versus writing in Louisiana? Ernest Hemingway wrote from Key West, Florida, and he did all right for himself."

I heaved a breath. "It's not just for me. It's better for the kids." I told him what Dinah had gone through at her school.

"It sounds to me that girl's going to have trouble no matter where she goes. And what about Chase? You want a six-year-old living in New York City? I call that child endangerment."

"Daddy, I know, in your mind, six-year-olds are getting gunned down in the streets in New York, but that's not the case. In fact, he's going to be a lot safer living in a state where they don't have a law that says his daddy is a sex offender."

"I told you, you're making a mountain out of a molehill 'bout that law. It'll be struck down by the courts in no time. But if you're so concerned about the politics, come up to DC and live with me. They've got the most progressive laws in the country."

"Daddy, this is my decision, and I need you to respect that."

"I'll respect it when you're putting my grandson's needs first instead of your own. Chase doesn't want to live in New York. He told me himself."

I took a pause on my side of the line. I was sick and tired of his meddling. I was sick and tired of his lack of understanding. Soon enough, it all burst out of me.

"When are you going to listen to me?"

He didn't answer.

"Are you listening now?"

He chuckled nervously. "Son, I've been listening to you this whole time, and I'm saying you're not making any sense."

"Then listen again. I am moving out of Louisiana for the protection of my family. The people of this state don't want us here. They want me registered as a criminal. To have my kids taken away. A good number of them probably want me dead."

"You've got to look at things more broadly. It's one stupid law that's not even enforced. People love you in Louisiana. You're a famous author now, like you always wanted. Now, I know about the prejudice you're talking about. I hate it myself. But you're going to find prejudice of some sort anywhere you go in this country, and I think you know that."

"Daddy, every morning for the past month, I woke up terrified that Chase and Dinah were going to be taken away from me. Does that sound like a healthy situation to you?"

"So, you're going to trade out with me? You think I'm going to get any sleep at night worrying about something happening to you and Chase in New York?"

"It's not the same flipping thing. I wish you could put yourself in my shoes for one minute."

"What you need to do is put yourself in your son's shoes. Chase doesn't understand about laws and politics. You take him up to New York, he's going to have a lot of adjusting to do. You really want to put him through that?"

His words penetrated a little. I didn't want to hurt Chase in any way. With that bit of guilt circulating through me, I came back at him softer. "If he needs some time to get used to the idea, I'll take things at his pace. I'm not putting the house on the market right away. But I *am* buying an apartment in New York. That's the plan. I'm not risking getting dragged back to family court and putting Dinah and Chase through that. I'm not having them being called faggots by ignorant people raised in ignorant families. I would think that would be your bigger concern."

"I've got all kinds of concerns, but I can see you don't want to hear them."

I cut him off and told him I had things to do. We could work out Chase's travel arrangements later in the week. I didn't need his blessing to do what my heart was telling me, but it would've been nice for him to say he supported my decision for once.

19

LATER THAT WEEK, I flew up to New York with Dinah, and we checked in to the Peninsula. Our goal was to find a new home, and we'd be living in a hotel suite until that came together. We'd packed five suitcases to bring up all the clothes and necessities we wanted to bring. Prior to arriving, I let Jonathan and Janet know I was coming into town. They both were eager to see me. I wanted to see them too, but I had to explain I had Dinah with me and we had a lot to do with apartment hunting. I figured we'd have plenty of time to get together once I had a permanent place to live and got Dinah into a routine.

After I unpacked, I called Rafe with the news. I had to slow him down as well.

"That's fabulous. I'm shocked, really. You never mentioned you were moving up here."

"The decision came together kind of quickly. You know I've been dealing with my step-sister and things going on with the kids–"

"No need to explain. It's a great surprise. Can I take you out for a drink? Or a late dinner? There's a new caviar bar in Soho I've been dying to check out. We could make a night of it. The

Angelica is showing that new Todd Solondz film. It's supposed to be magnificent."

"Thanks for the offer, Rafe. The thing is, I've got Dinah with me."

"She can come along. Problem solved."

That might've been a solution if I'd had a chance to tell her about my relationship with Rafe. It felt too soon to have those two worlds colliding. To tell the truth, I wasn't sure I wanted to pick up with our dating relationship, if that's the right word. So, I was cautious about signaling to him that I was ready to go back to that.

"We're both pretty beat from the trip," I told him. "And first thing tomorrow, I need to find a realtor and start looking at apartments."

Rafe gave me the name and number for the "best real estate agency in New York City." I took down the information because I didn't doubt he was right. He knew the producers at the best talk shows, the editors at the best magazines, and the maître d's at the best trendy restaurants, so he probably knew the best realtors as well. Then I had to put him off again because he wanted to come along to view apartments. He could be bossy with his opinions, and I wanted Dinah to be involved with picking our New York pad. I thanked him and explained it was going to be a family decision, and I'd be in touch as soon as I was free.

The following morning, I rang up the agency he recommended and had a long conversation with a friendly woman, Mandy. She recognized my name and had nice things to say about my book. She asked about my "must-haves" and my price range. I explained I needed room for two kids and a live-in nanny, and I preferred living downtown. I said we could leave the price range off the table for now.

I think she was happy to hear that. She said she'd just need twenty-four hours, and she'd have a tour of properties to show me. I couldn't believe things were happening so fast. Two days later, Mandy picked us up at the hotel in a chauffeured Mercedes-Benz. She took us to a dozen places in Greenwich Village, Soho, and

Tribeca. When we came to an apartment on Fifth Avenue, just a few blocks from Washington Square Park, I saw Dinah's eyes light up.

We'd seen modern buildings of steel and glass and artsy loft spaces big enough to store a half dozen double-decker buses, but something about that Fifth Avenue apartment just felt like home. It was a prewar building with lots of character. Twelve foot ceilings, marble floors, and Venetian plaster finishes. The apartment was on the twenty-second floor and swept around three sides of the building so you had a downtown view overlooking the big arch in the park, a westside view where you could see the sunset, and an uptown view all the way to the Empire State Building and beyond. It had a ton of living space, three big bedrooms, each with private baths, and a "bonus room" that Mandy said could easily be converted into a suite for a nanny. It would cost me a fortune to furnish the place, but I told the realtor then and there I wanted it. The price wiped out every cent I'd made so far on my author royalties, but there'd be more rolling in from the second quarter of the year. Besides, Rafe was working out a three million dollar deal with Paramount for the film rights to my book, and Janet had gotten me a good size commission to write an article for *Esquire* magazine.

While I waited for the paperwork to go through, I told Dinah we were going to have new experiences every day. Some of that would be physical activities since I'd been slack with working out and felt like a bum.

One sunny day, I got us dressed in matching tracksuits, and we jogged along the Hudson River where there were freight and sailboats rolling along the waterway. On another, we rented bicycles and rode the big loop around the reservoir in Central Park. After that, I pulled her along to rent a paddleboat, and we cruised around the wooded lake.

Dinah was also open to try anything cultural. We went to plays and musicals, a walking tour of Jazz Age Harlem, cooking classes at a culinary institute, and some really offbeat film festivals. I told her I'd never taken her out for her thirteenth birthday, and she wanted to go to an authentic Chinese restaurant in Chinatown and then out to a poet's café to see Jonathan perform. She was a real precocious girl and more like a companion than a kid I had to look after.

In New York, we could both be ourselves. Well, every now and then, somebody would stare at me while we were out and about, trying to place my face from TV, but I just hustled us along. It took a lot more than spotting an author to get New Yorkers to stop and gawp. Meanwhile, we didn't get nosy looks from people wondering how we were related, and people didn't ask that question or ask where Dinah's mama was like they did in Louisiana.

Sometimes, Dinah and I took long walks around the neighborhood where we'd be living. We always ended up in Washington Square Park to see who was performing around the big fountain. We'd listen to a saxophone player do his set or watch a fellow doing magic tricks. We both loved people watching, and you saw all kinds of people in that park, from eccentric old ladies walking their dogs to rapping teenagers and every ethnic group under the sun. On Sundays, we stayed in and read the *New York Times* and did the crossword puzzle together over coffee and bagels. We'd talk about all kinds of things that interested Dinah, from global human rights to national politics to how people thought differently up north and down south and the reasons for things being that way.

I did some research on where she could go to school in the fall and rang up Janet to get her opinion. Unfortunately, she said it was too late to get an application in to a top-notch private school, but she told me about some Catholic schools in Manhattan with rolling admissions. Dinah could do seventh and eighth grade at one of those schools and apply to New York's finer academies for her last four years.

I talked to Dinah about it, and she impressed me again. She wanted to go to a public school. She said she'd had enough of Catholic education and didn't want to go to another school with a bunch of "rich kids." I liked her independent thinking, so we found a middle school just a few blocks crosstown from the apartment. I went downtown to the city's Department of Education, filled out some forms, and got her school records sent over so she could enroll in September.

I also wanted to look into schools for Chase, and Janet was helpful with that. She'd had her baby back in February and was happy to meet me for lunch one day. She told me her elder daughter, Madison, who was just one year younger than Chase, had been accepted to an A-list grade school on the Upper East Side. Apparently, she and her husband had been able to pull some strings despite Madison's poor track record in preschool. Based on Chase's testing scores and grades, along with my public profile, Janet said Chase was a great candidate for any top tier private academy. She shared all the research she'd done for her daughter, including the school where Madison was going. I ended up with a long list of options.

By late July, we moved into the apartment and had a flurry of workmen delivering and installing furniture. It was a crazy few weeks getting the place set up, and then I had the bright idea to have a housewarming shebang in August. Jonathan had been asking what I wanted to do for my birthday, which was August 12th, and I didn't want to do an all-nighter like we usually did. Still, it happened to be that August 12th was a Saturday, so I told Jonathan it was a good day to have people over, but I didn't want a birthday party. I wanted to make the occasion more about my new beginning in New York.

The planning quickly became a huge project. I needed to fly up Chase and Sophie just one day after Chase came back from his trip to Europe. Of course, that meant I had to invite my daddy too. Then I decided I wanted Preston there, and it turned out Duke was off from work that weekend, so I said I'd fly him up too. I invited Russell, Henry, Janet, and I couldn't leave out Rafe with a clear conscience seeing as he'd found me the realtor for my place.

I was excited to have all the closest people in my life together in my new apartment. Call me naïve, but I was thinking it was going to be the perfect start. I wanted to show everybody I loved how much I appreciated them and that they always had a place in my home. Moving to New York had already been real good for me. Dinah loved living in the city, and every day felt like a new adventure. I wanted everyone who meant something to me to see how happy I was and to know they'd helped me achieve my dream.

Meanwhile, I had sleeping arrangements to work out along with flights and pickups from the airport. Not to mention food and decorations and set up for the party. I wanted to do it in style and make sure all the guests enjoyed it from Chase and Dinah to Preston and Duke to my New York friends. I quickly realized I was in over my head, so one Saturday, when Dinah was at a conservation program for kids, I asked Rafe if he could come over and help me out.

Rafe and I had talked on the phone a few times since I'd come into town, but we hadn't seen a lot of each other. I'd been over to his office to talk about the Paramount deal and sign some papers. I had doubts about the future of our relationship, but I was hoping we could be friends. Anyway, when he showed up at my door, there was an awkward moment when he hugged and kissed me to say hello. I brought him over to the living room with its big view of Washington Square Park and started explaining what I envisioned for the party so far.

"This is a fabulous space for entertaining," he said. "How many people are you inviting?"

I counted in my head. "Twenty, I think. Janet's bringing her husband and two kids, and Jonathan and them might be coming with some friends."

Rafe stepped around with his Italian leather shoes clacking against the marble floor. The living room and adjoining dining room were nearly empty and echoed like a museum. I still needed to order more furniture to fill the rooms and get some area carpets for the floor.

"You could easily have forty or fifty," he said. "What about mixing up the guest list a bit? We know a slew of writers from

Vanity Fair and *New York Magazine*. And Herb Ritts? Anthony Sharpe from *Booklist* raves about you."

I'd met most of those people, but they weren't exactly friends. "I really want it to be more of a family occasion."

"This could be like your coming out party. To celebrate your arrival to New York. We can invite Michael Musto and fill the place with interesting people. Terrence McNally? Fran Lebowitz would come. She comes to everything. And people from fashion. Like Cynthia Rowley. Todd Oldham?"

I was thinking he'd lost his mind. Why the hell would I want all those people I didn't know in the apartment along with family and friends who meant something to me? Some of them were making the trip up from Louisiana.

"Rafe, I'm not looking to put on a party for show. You can invite anyone you want from Random House, but otherwise, it's just going to be the people I told you about."

He bustled over to me. "It's exciting, isn't it? You finally have your first New York apartment."

"I lived in New York for four years while I was going to Columbia."

"But you weren't living like this." He clasped the sides of my arms. "I'm just so proud of all you accomplished. I mean, look at this place. This is an apartment for a literary maverick."

I bowed my head. I wasn't looking for his praise, but I'll admit I didn't mind him saying that.

He grinned at me. "You're cute. You have all this confidence in public, but in private, you still look like it's the first time you ever heard you're a successful author."

I stepped away from him. "It's not that. It's just I'm not having a party to celebrate me. I'm bringing together the most important people in my life to welcome them to my new home. I'd like the focus to be on them, not me."

"Of course. That's the first rule for hosting a party." He stepped closer again. "I was just thinking about the people who helped you along the way. You don't have to go crazy with it. Michael Musto

was a terrible idea, but what about some of the authors and journalists who admire your work and put you on the map?"

"I don't want it to be that kind of party. I was looking for your
advice on the layout and food and decorations."

"Have you booked a caterer?" he said.

I shook my head.

He arched his eyebrows. "You want to have the party two
weeks from today? We might not find anyone who's available."

"I can do some cooking myself and tell people it's potluck."

He gave me a funny look. "Pot-*luck*?"

I explained what that meant. Rafe looked horrified.

"No, no, no. This apartment isn't meant for *that* kind of dinner
party. I know a great caterer. He does all of Carolyn Bessette-
Kennedy's parties." He pulled out his mobile. "I'll give him a call,
and we can pray he's available. You're also going to need a florist
and a deejay. You should have told me weeks ago. What were you
thinking? August is a tricky month. A lot of vendors take a business break because half the city clears out for the Hamptons."

I closed in on him before he made the call. "I don't need
Carolyn Bessette-Kennedy's caterer. I'm trying to explain, I'm just
looking for some suggestions to make it nice and comfortable for
everyone."

Rafe lowered his phone. "A caterer's a caterer. They'll follow
your lead. If you're worried about the cost, I'll help." He caressed
my shoulder. "It's exciting. The first time the two of us are
throwing a party together."

That made me queasy. I didn't know how to say I didn't want
him to co-host like we were a couple without hurting his feelings.
Though I guess it was showing in my body language.

"Maybe I misunderstood," he said. "I thought you wanted me
to be involved."

I sighed. "Rafe, I do want you to come, and I asked for your
help. But I'm just putting on a housewarming party for family and
friends. It's not an event for *Page Six* to scoop."

He lightly brushed the side of my hair. "You just tell me what you want from me." I could feel the heat from his body and smell his designer cologne. "You know how I feel about you. I'll do whatever you say to make you happy."

I gave him a grin and forced myself to ease away from him. It would've been as easy as falling off a log to start screwing around. I hadn't satisfied my physical needs with a man since the last time we'd slept together, all the way back in April.

"Rafe, if this is overstepping our relationship, maybe it wasn't such a good idea. I'll figure things out. I shouldn't have imposed on you."

"You're not imposing on me." He drew up close again. "I *want* to help. And make it an unforgettable housewarming. I'm looking forward to seeing your family again. And Jonathan and Henry."

I had doubts about his sincerity, but I'll admit, he was also getting me interested in pulling out all the stops. I had the money to live it up in style, and I wanted to show the people I loved a good time. We ended up making a list of caterers and florists, and I gave in to hiring a deejay.

20

THAT HOUSEWARMING WEEKEND came up on me so fast, my head was spinning. There'd been some cliffhangers with the preparation. Rafe called six caterers before he found the lucky seventh who was available. The florist's order nearly didn't happen because the person who'd taken down all the information quit out of the blue. Rafe had to beg a deejay to fly down from Montréal since all the local people were booked for that weekend. Some items from my furniture order only arrived at three o'clock on Friday, including the bar and the dining room chairs. I'd been working day and night for two straight weeks to get the place set up and watched the price tag for the party accumulate by the hour. Then, on Friday, I had the out-of-towners on my hands.

Sophie and Chase arrived at JFK first, and then we had to take a town car over to LaGuardia where Preston and Duke were flying in two hours later. Somehow, we made it through traffic, got everyone settled in their rooms, and showered and dressed before a seven o'clock reservation at a Texas barbecue restaurant Duke had liked the last time I'd brought him to New York.

Rafe met us at the restaurant, thirty minutes late. As much as he'd been talking about looking forward to spending time with my family, I have to say, he ticked me off. He turned up his nose at the menu, ordered a spinach salad and a glass of wine, both of which he complained about, and spent the entire meal just talking to Sophie in French. I was having second thoughts about inviting him back to the apartment, and then he beat me to it, saying his goodbyes while I was settling the check. He said he had some art gallery event to get to. It involved one of his clients, though it was the first I was hearing about it.

I don't think anybody missed him, and we passed a good time that night. Preston got acquainted with my kitchen and showed Chase and Dinah how to make an icebox cake. Duke wanted to watch a baseball game, so I found it on my new big screen TV in the living room and broke out beers from the fridge. Sophie joined us for a while, and the three of us got drunk and silly watching the game. Everybody was ready for bed by midnight. I had Preston and Duke set up in my bedroom and Chase on a cot in Dinah's since I hadn't finished furnishing his room. Sophie had her own bedroom, and I slept on the sofa bed in the den.

The next day, I took everyone out for breakfast, and I left Dinah in charge of sightseeing. I had the florist and caterer coming over before the party, and I'd paid the porter from the building to set up the lighting and move furniture around. Things were looking real good, and then Rafe swept in around five with the French-Canadian deejay in tow. They cleared some furniture out of the way in the living room and installed a dance floor and some kind of big projector screen.

Before I could ask questions, the Louisiana crew came back, and the apartment was a tornado of people wanting my attention. The chef didn't have enough room on the buffet table. Chase wanted to show me the dinosaur coloring book he'd bought at the Museum of Natural History. Duke needed me to help him pick out a shirt that matched his jeans. Sophie couldn't get her hair dryer to work. Preston thought the caterers had thrown out his icebox cake until we found it in the freezer, high up on top of bags of ice. Rafe pulled me over to say the floral archway should be closer to the door in the foyer so the photographer could catch people as they walked in.

I didn't remember having hired a photographer, but Rafe assured me I had and wanted to run a plan by me for getting staged photos and candid shots throughout the night. I don't know how, but I squeezed in a shower, threw on a pink, checkered dress shirt, a khaki suit, a pair of Gucci loafers, and a pink rose boutonniere that Rafe had bought me. I was running on fumes but not looking bad. I strolled out to the living space just in time to greet the first guests at eight o'clock.

Rafe had the lights dimmed more than we'd talked about, and the deejay's bass-heavy track was reverberating through my body. Jonathan, Henry, and three of their friends came in, so I had to delay reminding Rafe it was a housewarming, not a circuit party I was hosting. Jonathan and the gang thrust presents on me and said they wanted the royal tour. I told them to grab a drink at the bartender station while I put their gifts in a safe place, and I'd catch up with them real soon.

I'd overlooked needing a gift table for housewarming presents. Rafe came along and suggested we clear off the bar trolley in the foyer. While we did that, I asked him if he'd said hello to Jonathan and Henry. He said he was waiting for me to introduce them even though they'd all met twice before. Then an anxious cater waiter came over to say the chef needed another half hour because his rib roast had just come out of the oven. Rafe told me he'd try to speed things up and get some passed canapés going, and he hurried the waiter along to the kitchen.

I wanted to check in with Jonathan and his pals and steer them over to Preston and Duke who weren't going to know anyone else at the party. But the bell rang, and the dapper, nubile fellow Rafe had hired to coat-check jackets opened the door for Janet, her daughter, Madison, and her husband, Howie, who had their six-month-old Shauna in a papoose. I gave them a warm welcome, took a big wrapped box off Janet's hands, and directed them inside. I was fretting over how loud the music was and wanting to do something about it. I also needed to show Janet and Howie the playroom we'd set up for Chase and Madison in Dinah's bedroom, and an area in Sophie's suite where the baby could sleep. So I took care of that, and then I pointed out the bar to them.

Jonathan's gang had met Preston and Duke over by the big southside windows. I was just about to head over to see how all them were doing when the doorbell rang again. Rafe beat me to the foyer, and he was standing with three people I only knew from newspapers. The red-haired designer Patricia Field, the fashion photographer Patrick McMullan, and the drag queen Kabuki Sunshine. I was stunned and didn't know what else to do but thank them for coming. Rafe led the three into the living room while chatting them up.

Sophie caught up to me to ask what time I wanted the kids to eat. I glanced at my watch. It was quarter to nine. I thought I'd told the chef to fix plates for Chase, Dinah and Madison before the guests arrived, but Sophie said the waiters had brought all the food to the buffet table. I was about to go to the kitchen to straighten that out, and then I was distracted by a new group of guests coming in. It was Julian and a half dozen folks from Random House. Sophie picked up on my dilemma and said she'd just bring the kids over to the buffet to pick out what they wanted, and they could go back to Dinah's room to eat.

I said hi to Julian and chatted with him and his people for maybe a minute, then another group came through the door. Then another, and another, and another. I was caught in the foyer, having to greet everyone. I saw Russell and a pair of Jonathan's friends I'd hung out with before, but a lot of the newcomers I'd never met in my life. Guys in body-hugging, trendy T-shirts, short shorts, and baseball caps. Another group of artsy fellows with lots of piercings and complicated beards and mustaches. A brawny Adonis decked out in a leather harness and chaps. I had no idea where they all had come from, and then I recognized the play-wright Paul Rudnick, the artist Karen Finley, and the actor Alan

Cumming from Broadway. They walked into my apartment as regular as can be.

"Wow, Arizona. I thought Jonathan said it was a low key get-together."

It took me a moment to realize Russell was speaking. "It was supposed to be. C'mon, let's find Jonathan."

We waded through what had become a crowd in my living room. Now I'd always loved big parties, but I much preferred being informed I was hosting one ahead of time. As soon as I got Russell over to Jonathan and his friends, I was going to have a little talk with Rafe. But I didn't even make it that far because along the way, Duke pounced on me.

"I been lookin' all over for you 'cause I gotta ask you a question." Duke's face darkened, and he spoke in my ear. "You think it be all right if I ask Sophie to dance?"

I held down a laugh, and then I followed his gaze across the room. Sophie had thrown off her modest shawl and was looking rather stately in a black cocktail dress. She was fielding conversation from the few heterosexual men in the room, including Janet's husband. I spotted Dinah spinning Chase and Madison around the dance floor not far away.

I clasped Duke's shoulder. "You can do whatever you want, but by the look of things, you better be quick about it."

"You think I should get her a drink first?" he said. "I should prolly ask what she wanna drink. She ain't seeing that Rafe fella, is she?"

My stepbrother was one of the few people from Louisiana who knew I'd gotten together with Rafe while Preston and I were splitting up, but he didn't understand the whole gay thing so well. I suppose he misinterpreted why Rafe glommed on to Sophie at dinner the night before. "No. Duke, if you like her, go talk to her. It's as simple as that." I pushed him along. I wouldn't have minded the entertainment of seeing how that turned out, but I needed to get Russell over to the people he knew. I forged ahead with him toward a spot by the bar where I could see Jonathan having some laughs with Henry. Then Rafe intercepted me.

"Your father just arrived."

I glanced at him, but no words came out of my mouth.

Rafe smiled at my blank face. "You should greet him." He linked his arm and mine. "I've been looking forward to meeting him forever."

I had a queasy feeling building in my stomach. Then a few steps later, I was face-to-face with Daddy. And a young blond woman in an ivory slip dress and a big red lipstick smile. I was amused for a second, thinking Sophie was going to have a run for her money. Then the girl brushed his back, and I put things together rapidly.

He pulled me into a hug. "It's good to see you, son." He glanced around. "Looks like you're putting on one hell of a party." He squinted. "Is that Mr. Robin Leach from TV?"

I looked that way. It sure looked like him, though I had no idea how he'd gotten an invitation.

"It's good to see you too." I turned to his companion.

"This is a friend of mine, Vivian," Daddy said. "Viv, this is my son, Arizona."

She grasped my hand with both of hers. "It's so great to meet you. I'm such a fan. I read that they're turning your book into a film."

Normally, I would've taken that compliment with grace. But I was having trouble getting past the fact we probably graduated from high school the same year. Now I felt no loyalty to my grandmother. She'd been a viper for most of my life. But for my daddy to bring his mistress to my apartment, for all the world to see? Heat was rising up my neck.

"Vivian works in theater," Daddy said.

She gave my daddy a flirty, reproachful glance and turned to me. "I've done some modeling and a couple of TV ads."

"Well you're working on your stage career, darling, aren't you?"

Daddy fixed on me. "You two might know some of the same people. Viv knows lots of writers. She's done some writing too."

Rafe inserted himself. "I'm Rafe Mansoor. It's an honor to meet you, Senator Bondurant. Arizona has told me so much about you."

They shook hands, and my daddy didn't skip a beat. "I heard a lot about you as well. I figured you were handsome, but what do you say, Viv? My son has good taste, wouldn't you say?"

I was sinking into a nightmare. It didn't help that Rafe and Viv started gushing over each other.

"You have to see the apartment," Rafe told my daddy. "The southern exposure is spectacular."

"You set me up with a double scotch on the rocks, and I'll take you up on that offer," Daddy said with a wink.

"Of course." Rafe glanced at me in a nudging way.

"Why don't you take *Viv* on that tour?" I told him. "I've got some catching up to do with my daddy."

Rafe cheerily brought Vivian farther into the apartment. I gestured my daddy over to an alcove where the coat rack was set up, and no one was around.

"What the hell are you doing?" I said.

"I thought I was celebrating your new apartment with y'all."

I looked at him grimly. "You know what I mean. Bringing your mistress. Your grandson's here."

He put his big hand on my shoulder and looked at me in a not so friendly way. "You watch what you're implying. Is this how you welcome me to your home?"

I broke away from him. "I invited *you*, not her. Now I'm past weighing in on your infidelities, but aren't you the one always lecturing me about honorability and family obligation? Besides Chase, you've got Sophie, Dinah, and Preston here. Photographers and journalists too."

"Vivian's a friend. She's been keen on meeting you. She keeps on top of all the latest authors."

I gave him a crooked glance. "Anyone who sees the two of you is going to put things together. She's half your age."

"Listen here. I don't need to tell you I'm a grown man who can make his own decisions. I'm doing the honorable thing by sticking with your grandmother. Who I choose to go out with on a Saturday night is my prerogative."

"Okay. Go on and make a fool of yourself. You're making a fool of me and your grandson too, but I suppose you don't give a shit."

His eyes sparked red. "You're gonna talk to me like that when you invited me to your home? You're the one making a fool of yourself. I won't stand for it. Vivian and I are leaving. You've gotten too big for your britches is what it is."

For the first time that night, I was glad the music was loud because his voice was thundering. He pushed past me, and I watched him march into the living room, whisper in Vivian's ear and turn her around. Then he stormed out of the party with her like he was parting the Red Sea.

I needed a drink. People glanced at me as I entered the living room so I was pretty sure I'd created a scene. I caught Dinah and Chase looking at me uncertainly, which didn't make me happy. Then the lights cut out, the music built up to a big electronic flourish, and the projector screen lit up with fireworks and the message: Happy Birthday, Arizona.

People howled and cheered, and all them club-type boys started dancing up a storm. I wasn't feeling any of that. After that conversation with my daddy, I wanted some peace and quiet to clear my head. Then the screen started flashing with grainy images of men in various stages of undress. It was practically pornographic, right there in my living room.

Before I could charge over to the deejay to tell him to turn it off, Rafe seized on me.

"What happened with your father?"

Steam was coming out of my nostrils. I smiled at him angrily. "What the fuck you think you're doing?"

His face deflated. He took account of our surroundings and recovered coolly. "Why don't we step away for a minute to talk in private?" He tried to take my arm, but I pulled it away. It took every ounce of my forbearance not to lose it on him then and there. I spotted Sophie and Preston calmly gathering the kids to get them out of eyeshot of that racy screen, and I calmed down just enough to follow Rafe to my bedroom and shut the door behind us.

He anchored himself a few steps away from me in the dimly lit room while the music and commotion rumbled from outside. "I know you're angry. Did you have a fight with your father? You can talk to me about it."

"Cut the bullshit. I'm angry at *you*." I stepped over to a night table, scooped up Duke's pack of smokes and disposable lighter, and I lit a cigarette. I'd told him it was the only room where he could smoke.

Rafe stared at me, blamelessly. "You're angry at me? What did I do?"

I threw up my hand. "I said a little party with my family and closest friends. You know what you've done."

"We went over everything together. I told you I was inviting a few extra people."

"It's not a few extra people. It's half the crowd from the Roxy and frickin' Robin Leach from *Lifestyles of the Rich and Famous*."

He backed up a step. "You asked me to help with the planning. Everyone's having a great time. I wanted this to be the kind of party you deserve. You've got this great apartment to show off, so what's the harm?"

I looked at him in disbelief. "There's pornographic images on a twenty foot screen. You think that's appropriate when I've got children here?"

"It's Gil's standard backdrop. His video roll is artistic, not pornographic."

"It's not appropriate for kids, and you know it."

"I had no idea you were so conservative. You're worried about your son turning gay from seeing male bodies? You sound like Ralph Reed from the Christian Coalition."

I took a quick, deep pull on my cigarette. "It's not about being conservative or liberal."

"Isn't it? You wrote a bestselling novel that's a big fuck you to the literary establishment. What's the problem with celebrating gay liberation?"

"Rafe, don't lecture me and don't twist things around like I'm some kind of hypocrite. You turned this party into something you wanted with no respect for me."

He seemed to be taking that in for a moment, and then he shouted at me. "Everything was for you. I devoted myself to making you a success. I gave you fucking everything, and all you do is criticize and push me away."

The force of his words stunned me for a moment, but this conversation was a long time coming. I took one last draw from my cigarette, stubbed it out in a trash can and faced him.

"This isn't working out. Not personally or professionally. I want you and all your friends to get out of here."

He coughed out a laugh. "You're being irrational. The kids are going to bed, aren't they? It's time for the adults to play. Why can't you see that?"

I glared at him. "You can call it irrational if you want. What I'm saying is leave my apartment. I never want to see you again."

He turned from me and came back looking wild and fragile. "This is how you end it? In the middle of a party I put together for you? After all the favors I had to call in to make it happen? Putting my name on the line." He choked up for a moment and hid his face.

I never could stand seeing anyone cry, so that softened me up a little. "Rafe, for somebody else, it would've been perfect. But I'm trying to explain to you, we're not seeing eye to eye."

"You're an egotistical shit," he fired back. "I've been there for you through all your drama with Preston and your mental breakdowns. I waited for you when you told me you needed time with your son and niece. And now you want to discard me because I went out of my way to do something special for you?"

That got me past putting things gently. What he did was a blatant betrayal, and I didn't like the man he was.

"You're in my home, with my people. I don't know how I could've explained any better, this was supposed to be a party to thank the people I care about. You made it a promotional event. Behind my back."

"Yes I did. Because it's good for your career. I devoted two years of my life promoting you, and giving everything I've got."

"Rafe, I understand and appreciate that. I take responsibility for my part in blurring the lines in our relationship. I should've kept things professional from the start."

"You never gave a shit about me, did you? You were just stringing me along to get what you wanted."

I sighed. "That wasn't it. Rafe, you fought to take the lead on marketing. I never meant to take advantage of your feelings for me, and I tried to talk to you about these things a dozen times."

"And now that you've achieved success, you're done with me. Enjoy it. I'll let you in on a little secret. If you weren't Gaston Bondurant's son, you wouldn't have been able to sell your book to a third tier publisher. That's why Jullan signed you. Did you think it was because of your talent? You're such a narcissist."

He was making things easier and easier. "Okay. I guess we do see eye to eye after all. You don't want to work with me, and I don't want to work with you. The only thing left is for you to leave."

He stared at me with a wounded face. I met his gaze and nodded. Rafe peeled out of the room, and I stayed back to give him the dignity of leaving on his own terms.

THAT PARTY WAS one big disaster. I just wanted it over. I went to the bathroom to splash some water on my face, and then I headed over to the deejay. I told him I had an announcement to make, and he cut the music and gave me a microphone.

I thanked everybody for coming, and then I said I had to end things early to put my six-year-old son to bed. People groaned and booed, and some of the guys Rafe had invited called out that I should keep things going. I apologized and wished everyone a great night. I did feel bad. It wasn't even eleven o'clock, but after everything that happened, that night was over for me.

While everyone was milling around and figuring out where they were headed next, Jonathan found me. He must've picked up that something was off.

"You all right?" he asked.

"Yeah. I will be. Could you do me a favor? Wherever you all are off to, would you invite Duke and Preston along? They're only in town till tomorrow."

"Of course. But what about you? You've got Sophie to watch the kids, don't you? We're going to Boiler Room and then to Twilo. Junior Vasquez is spinning."

"I appreciate the invitation, darling, but I just don't have it in me tonight."

Jonathan studied me. "What happened? I saw Rafe leave in a hurry."

I squeezed his shoulder. "It's a long story, and I've got the deejay and the caterers to move on out of here. I don't want to hold you up. I'll have plenty to tell you tomorrow."

"I've got no problem hanging back if you want some company. This was supposed to be your big night. You sure you're okay?"

"I am. You know I'm always good for a raincheck to go bar hopping. I'm sorry we didn't have much time to hang out tonight."

"Don't worry about that. I just don't want to leave you if you're upset."

"Honey, I'm already feeling better. I just had to give my personal life a little detoxifying."

"Okay. I can't wait to hear about it. Call me tomorrow. And if you change your mind, you know where we'll be."

I gave him a big hug and stepped away to see what I needed to do to clean up. Most of the buffet had gone uneaten. I told one of the servers to take everything into the kitchen, and I'd figure out what I could keep and what they could take to a homeless shelter. While he went to get some help, I peeked over my shoulder. Jonathan was talking to Preston, Duke, and Sophie. It looked like the conversation was going well, and then Duke stumbled over to me.

"Arizona, Jonathan say he and his friends going to a club. He say we should all come along."

I nodded. "The night's young. You should see some New York nightlife."

"How come you not going?"

"I've got a lot of things to settle here."

"What you need? I help clean up, and we can go together to meet Jonathan."

He was a good little brother, but I needed some space to myself. "Duke, you came up all this way, and I want you to have a good time. I told Jonathan the same. I've got things under control here, and I just want to take things easy tonight. You can understand that, can't you?"

"Okay. If you say so." He hesitated, looking like he had something heavy on his mind. "Say, Arizona, you think it be okay if Sophie come too? She say she never been to a nightclub in New York 'fore."

I grinned to myself. "That'd be okay, Duke. I'll tell her she's got the night off."

He gave me a big, red-faced smile. I stepped over to Sophie to let her know I'd be watching the kids for the night. She looked real happy about that.

I SAID MY goodbyes to the remaining guests, including Janet and her family, and then I went to Dinah's bedroom to make sure she and Chase were tucked in. Later, I got held up in the kitchen, working out with the prickly chef what food he could leave and what he should take along with him. I understood that he was disappointed, but he was still getting paid the same. I helped one of his waiters pack my refrigerator and freezer with as much food as we could fit. His other staffers were just about through running their supplies out of the kitchen, and it sounded like people had cleared out of the apartment. I went out to the living room to see how things with the deejay were coming along.

Furniture had been pushed around, and the place was empty. When I turned to where Gil had set up, I spotted Preston helping him collapse the projector screen and zip it up in a big case. I stepped over.

"You didn't have to help pack up, but thank you," I told him.

"We almost finished."

He'd loosened his tie, undone the top button of his shirt, and his hair was damp. I felt bad he was spending his weekend doing manual labor.

"You gonna meet up with Jonathan and Duke?" I said.

"Nah. Them clubs never been for me. I tol' them I be fine stayin' in for the night."

I felt like a killjoy, but I won't say I minded him staying back. It looked like most of Gil's equipment was loaded up on a dolly. "What's left to do?" I asked.

Preston lifted the packed-up screen upright. "We just gotta take things down to his truck. The two of us be all right."

"Can I get you a beer when you come back up?"

"Sound good to me."

I helped him and Gil load things into the elevator and sent them down. Then I threw off my suit jacket and pushed furniture back in its place while the cater waiters carted their equipment out of the apartment.

I strolled over to the bar and poured myself four fingers of whiskey into a tumbler. I took a quick sip, and then I pulled out a bottle of Bud from the refrigerator compartment. The apartment was blissfully quiet. It suddenly felt luxurious having the place to myself.

Meanwhile, I was starving. It was nearly midnight, and I hadn't eaten anything since breakfast. I went to the kitchen and fixed two plates with potstickers, shrimps, roast beef, dinner rolls, tuna tartare, chicken skewers, and sesame noodles. I grabbed a pair of forks and napkins and brought it all into the living room.

I set the food down on a coffee table between my new Chesterfield sofas, and then I grabbed the drinks, sat down, and kicked off my loafers. I was tearing into the roast beef when I heard the door. Preston had returned. I straightened in my seat and made some space for him.

"He funny, that fella Gil," he said.

I scrunched up my brow.

"He must've thought I live up here." Preston grabbed the beer bottle and took a sip. "He want to know what bars was happening tonight and if I could show him around town."

I smirked. "That's called getting hit on."

Preston blinked, and then he waved me off.

"Come on. Has it been so long, you don't recognize when someone's taking an interest?"

"He's French-Canadian."

I chuckled. "What does *that* got to do with it?"

"He prolly just don't know his way around a foreign country."

I decided not to comment any further. One thing I always liked about Preston was his modesty. He could have ten guys hitting on him and not know the difference. I offered him some food, and he helped himself to a chicken skewer.

"Maybe I shouldn't tell you this, but I don't think he likes *you* too much," Preston said. "He say you hired him to work till four in the morning. I guess wrapping up early ain't good for his business or somethin' like that."

I chewed down a dumpling and took a swallow of liquor. Preston sat back and spread out his arms, getting comfy. "Guess it ain't the kind of night anyone expected." He let that hang in the air. I knew what he was getting at, and I filled him in on my fight with Rafe.

"So, I finally told him to beat it." I wiped the corner of my mouth. "I should've done it a long time ago."

Preston looked quietly amused. "I guess I can say it now. I never liked him. You know he never say a word to Duke or me or any of your friends all night?"

I wasn't surprised, though it chafed at me. "He never really wanted to get to know my family. Stuck up is what he is."

"I can't say I disagree. But the two of you were together for what? Over a year? You doin' okay?"

"I'm fine." I tossed back another gulp of whiskey and turned the tumbler in my hand. "I made a lot of mistakes. The party was supposed to be for all of you come up from out of town, and it turned into a big mess. I should've seen it coming from Rafe."

"I don't know, Arizona. You sure gave people something to talk about. Why, I can say I met Robin Leach from *Lifestyles of the Rich and Famous*."

I scowled at him. I still felt like a fool about the way things ended. Preston pointed his beer at me. "It's true. You had quite a crowd. Duke was having a good time."

"I think you're right about that. At least somebody had a good night." I glanced at him playfully. "How do you think things are going to work out with him and Sophie?"

He laughed. "I wouldn't have pictured it, but I dunno. At least he ain't runnin' into competition the places they going." He shrugged his eyebrows. "Duke might be smarter than you think."

I hadn't thought about that. I was willing to admit I might have underestimated my brother.

We dug into the food, and I got us refills of our drinks. "You didn't eat tonight either?" I asked him.

"I had a little here and there."

"How come?"

Preston took a draw on his second beer. "I don't know why, but I was kinda nervous for you."

"You were nervous for me?"

"I was. It was an important night for you. Now that you're a celebrity."

I blushed and told him not to make things out to be bigger than they were.

"You're on late night talk shows. Got your face in magazines. I don't know about these things, but I imagine that puts some pressure on you to live a certain way. I mean, you got this big apartment."

I frowned. "You sound like Rafe."

"Excuse you," he complained. "I was givin' you a compliment."

I tried to read his face. "You think I changed?"

"You feel different?" He eyed me as he tipped back his beer.

"No," I said. "But I'm asking you."

He kicked off his shoes and brought his legs up on the couch. "I tell you something. You got this luxury apartment. Living in New York City. With lots of people looking up to you. But I'll always see you as the boy who made friends with me in sixth grade. Not caring that people on your side of John's Island wasn't supposed to be friends with Cajun folk. And you always could get cocky sometimes, but you ain't let all the fame and money go to your head."

I was really glad to hear that. The truth was, I enjoyed spending time with Preston a whole lot more than being surrounded by all the New York luminaries Rafe had invited. He was getting me reminiscing and feeling a little cheeky. "We were more than friends back then," I reminded him.

"Mm-hmm."

"We were more than friends for a long time."

He minded his own thoughts. I gazed around the living room with its fancy paneled walls and high-end furniture, and the palatial view of the downtown skyline at night through the big southern-facing window. I was still getting used to the grandness of it all. I wondered if Preston thought it made me a show-off.

"You know the reason I got this apartment was for Dinah."

He smirked at me. "This what she earn for gettin' suspended

from school? What gonna be the upgrade next time she send a classmate to the ER?"

His teasing was getting me heated, but not in a bad way. "I mean, she helped me pick it out. She had a tough year. I'm going to need the space for when Chase and Sophie move in."

"You got space for moving in the first and second string of the New Orleans Saints."

I scowled.

"I jus' ridin' you, Arizona. You got the money to live in style, and I know Dinah like it up here. She seem happier than I seen her in a long time."

"She is. And we found her a school right here in the neighborhood. Just a regular public middle school. That's what she wanted."

Preston took another gulp of beer, looking pensive. "I glad for her. But last I heard, Chase was sayin' he want to stay in Louisiana."

I drew a deep breath. "I need to talk to him. Start getting him used to the idea. Worse come to worse, if he's dead set on doing another school year down there, I'll hold off on putting the house on the market. I talked to Sophie about that. She can bring him up for visits in the meantime."

"If I was you, I wouldn't give him the choice. He's six years old, and you his daddy."

I wasn't sure how to take that. He sounded like he was just giving me advice, but I felt bad taking Chase away from him. It was also sinking in I'd be living far from Press. The past few months, things had been warming up between us again, and he'd seen me through some dark times. I wasn't going to be able to hop in the car and drive forty-five minutes to see him whenever I wanted.

I waited for him to look at me. "You've got a place up here too now. What would it take to get you to spend some time in New York?"

"You got me for the weekend. Come Monday, I'm back to work at the shop."

I felt hollow inside. "Well, you've got an open invitation. If you find yourself with a weekend free."

He picked at the label on his beer bottle. "Next time Duke's on leave, if he wanna visit, I guess I could come along. Be nice to see Dinah when I can."

It felt like we were edging around something we'd both been feeling. At least, I hoped he was feeling it too. I leaned a little closer to him. "I miss you, Press. You been there for me when I needed you most."

He smiled a little. "When I do get up here again, I can buy my own ticket. I tol' you the shop's doin' well."

I loved seeing him take pride in himself. I rested my hand on his shoulder. "You and me, we made a family. It doesn't feel like it's whole anymore without you." I drew a big breath of courage. "You remember when you asked me if we were doing right? The day you moved out? You ever think the answer is no? 'Cause I've been thinking that."

He held his beer bottle on his knee and said nothing. I considered that wasn't such a good sign, but something about the awful party had put things in focus for me. I had to tell him how I felt. I raised my hand to the back of his scruffy neck.

"Press, you said you let me go, and you were letting God decide if I'd come back to you." I looked down and chewed my lip a little, working out what to say. "You know, I got the title of my book from that country song 'When the Fallen Angels Fly?' I'm not religious like you, but that's how the two of us feels to me. I've been a fallen angel. I strayed when I shouldn't have, and the only thing I want is to come back to you." His face softened, and I leaned close to kiss his lips. All my feelings for him welled up. I tried to find his gaze, and he swiped his face and finally spoke.

"You sure you're not saying that 'cause things didn't work out with Rafe?"

I looked him in the eye. "Things were never working out with Rafe. I needed somebody when you pulled away from me, but there wasn't one day I stopped having feelings for you. Hand to my heart."

Preston turned his head while he took that in. I was on pins and needles, wondering if he'd fallen out of love with me and what I said had come too late. Then he grasped my hand. "Like we always say, the feelings never been the problem. But how we supposed to fit together?"

Well, it might've been overeager of me, but I straddled his legs, getting real comfy with him. I pushed aside a lock of his hair that was falling on his face. "I don't have all the answers, but maybe we just try."

He held my sides, and we kissed, wet and deep. All of the sudden, that night took a big turn for the better.

21

SOME PEOPLE SAY everyone has one soulmate in the world or one love of their life. I don't know if that's true, but I never loved anyone like I loved Press, and I know he felt the same way about me. We'd gone our separate ways before, and we found each other once again that Saturday, August 12th, 1998 on my thirtieth birthday. We made love that night, and afterward, I was blissful in his arms. For the first time in a long time, I felt like I didn't have to fight for someone to understand me and just accept me for who I am. I felt a purpose to my life, and that was being with Press.

That's not to say we figured out exactly how we were going to be together right away. Preston had his business, his family, and his church in Louisiana, and I couldn't ask him to give that up. Nor could I live with moving back down there full-time. I needed the freedom that New York City had to offer, and Dinah needed to be in that environment, too. It felt like Preston and I were finally accepting these things about each other and realizing it didn't mean one of us had to change.

Like I said, we didn't have all the details worked out, but after that weekend, we went to bed together every night on the phone. I told him I talked to Chase, and while he was warming up to the idea of living in New York, it was too late to get him enrolled in a new school. He'd be going to second grade at St. Thomas's, at least for the fall, so while I had him for part of August, I planned a big weekend before he and Sophie had to fly back down to Louisiana.

I rented us a house in Fire Island, and Preston came up to join us. We bought kites and boogie boards, took the kids to the beach, and got them body-surfing in the big, cold waves of the Atlantic Ocean. We cooked out on a grill for dinner, made s'mores and played games, and after everyone went to bed, Preston and I cuddled up on a chaise lounge on the deck, just listening to the surf and taking in the stars and the ocean air. Later, we snuck into bed and fooled around, and stayed up talking until early in the morning.

Despite the distance between us, in some ways, our relationship was better than when we were living together. We'd known each other as teenagers and young adults, and now we were discovering each other all over again at thirty. I loved the man he'd become. He had an easygoing attitude that came from feeling more confident about managing his shop. He also had a lot more to say about how things should be for gay people. Maybe that came from the welcoming church he'd been going to. We could have conversations about politics and current events without it turning into a fight. He'd grown, and I'd done some growing too. I understood his family had their ups and downs about him being gay, and that wasn't their fault, really. They were products of their community and their church, but they were expanding their minds little by little since Preston had come out.

I flew down to Louisiana with Dinah the following weekend, and Preston stayed over at my place. The times we saw each other were extra special, and we didn't have the stress of sharing a home and arguing over petty things like whose turn it was to take out the trash. Preston told me he'd been a fool to let me go and that he wanted us to be together, no matter what it took. I didn't disagree with him.

I never spoke to Rafe again, though he tried reaching me. He left me messages saying he wanted to apologize and make things better, but I couldn't see any good coming from that. I certainly wasn't interested in rekindling our romance, and I was skeptical about being able to reset our relationship as working colleagues and friends. I'd come to the conclusion he didn't know himself very well. He'd just keep saying things he thought he meant, lying to himself I guess you could say. I'd been through that with Chase's mama. I wished I had recognized it sooner and saved myself some grief, but like I told Jonathan, I was a work in progress.

Anyway, to wind back a few clicks, the Monday after we broke up, I called Julian to say Rafe and I were having creative differences. I didn't have to spell it out. I'm pretty sure Julian knew what I was getting at. He assigned another marketing manager to work with me, and I made sure she understood I needed to be selective with media appearances. My book was still selling well, so I had that liberty. It gave me time to work on my next novel while taking care of Dinah and flying back and forth from New York to Louisiana.

I had another major loose end to tie up from my house-warming party, and that was my daddy. He'd stormed out, furious at me, but wouldn't you know, he called me a few weeks later like nothing had happened. I played along. I was feeling bad about the whole thing.

"Now that Chase is in second grade, I thought I'd do something special for him over Labor Day weekend," he said. "How 'bout you come down, too? We can take him to NOLA or have something at the house. Bring your friend Rafe along, if you want."

"Rafe's not my 'friend' anymore. As a matter of fact, Preston and I are seeing each other again."

"Is that right? I can't keep up with you. Well, then bring Preston along."

I chewed my lip. Jonathan was turning thirty that weekend,

and we were planning to celebrate our birthdays. We'd booked a big house in Rehoboth Beach with six of our friends. Preston was coming up, and I had Dinah tagging along. We figured she was old enough to entertain herself. I suppose I could've invited my daddy and Chase, but I couldn't see them having a good time while us gay boys were looking to party that weekend. I took a big swallow of courage.

"I've got plans up here, but I'll be down to Thibodaux in September. What do you say to planning a little something then?"

I braced myself while he was silent on the other end of the line.

"Well, if you don't want to come on my account, I understand. But you've barely seen your son this summer."

I winced. "Daddy, it's not on your account. I've got plans. And I had Chase up here with me for ten days right after the two of you came back from Europe."

"He tell you about the trip?"

"Yes, he did. And I appreciate it. Daddy, you understand, I'm juggling two kids now? I'd like Chase to be living with me up here, but I've got to find a school for him, and that takes time. I'll be down to Louisiana as soon as I can, and the three of us can spend the weekend together."

"You just give the dates to Eileen. Chase has been wanting to try sailing camp at the yacht club. That's on weekends in September, so there could be a conflict. But Eileen will sort things out."

Eileen was his executive secretary, and she kept his calendar. I wasn't crazy about him telling me to go through her, but I was itchier about something else he said.

"Chase wants to go to sailing camp? What's a six-year-old going to learn about sailing?"

"They've got a program for kids seven to nine, and I can pull some strings to get him enrolled. He's only a month short of seven."

I was pretty sure he was the only one interested in Chase

learning about sailing. I could've said this or that about being left out of the decision, but I let it go. It sounded harmless enough. I told him I'd follow up with Eileen, and we ended that conversation peaceably.

THE NEXT FEW weeks flew by. We had a great time in Rehoboth, celebrating our birthdays over Labor Day weekend, and then I had to get Dinah settled in her new school. Press and I kept in contact, and meanwhile, I had deadlines to meet for commissioned essays at *Esquire* and *Out* magazines. I enjoyed writing those articles where I reflected on what it meant to be gay in 1998. I'd recently found out one of my classmates from Columbia died of AIDS, and I decided to write about that and AIDS complacency and all the bills getting passed across the country prohibiting same-sex marriage. Those were things I'd always been passionate about, and I remembered Jonathan telling me to use my privilege as a published author for good. That's what I was going to do with my little platform—talk to readers about fairness and social justice. Meanwhile, when I could fit in the time, I got some work done on my next novel.

Dinah loved her middle school. She signed up for an after-school program where kids played music and wrote poetry, and after just one week, she brought two friends to the house. I was so proud of her. It was tough being the new kid in school, and Dinah had really come out of her shell and struck up friendships with her classmates.

One girl, Ayesha, lived with a foster family, and I supposed they could relate to each other, not having their birth mamas in their lives. Another girl, Brittany, was from Honduras and lived with her grandmother in the Lower East Side. The three of them couldn't have looked any different on the outside, and it made me happy that they didn't care, and they'd found a lot of things in common. One weekend, I took them all out to a Japanese restaurant and then over to the Nuyorican Poet's Café to see Jonathan and a line up of spoken word artists. While I took her friends home in a town car, they were talking a mile a minute about how cool the poets were.

With Dinah flourishing, I thought about spending some time with Chase. I called him every night, but some of those conversations were short. I couldn't tell what was going on with him exactly since he didn't have too much to say, but I was concerned.

Then, around the middle of September, Preston called me on a Friday night, saying he drove over to the house to pick up Chase for their scheduled weekend and Sophie told him Chase was staying with my daddy. I figured there had to have been a miscommunication. I told Press I'd sort it out with Sophie.

I rang her up right away and come to find out, Daddy had been taking Chase every weekend since Labor Day. Sophie said she thought I knew. I made it clear I sure didn't know about that arrangement, and any requests to take Chase had to go through me first. After the call, I felt a little bad about getting heated with her. She shouldn't have to be in the position of telling him no. But I was fit to be tied. He'd certainly overstepped his boundaries before, but he'd never done something so sneaky.

As I thought things through, I stopped short of calling him that night. It was too late for a driver to bring Chase over to Preston's, and I didn't want to upset him. I apologized to Preston and explained how I was feeling, and he agreed. I needed to have one of my talks with Daddy real soon, and I was thinking it was best done face-to-face.

Dinah had two days off from school for the Jewish holidays at the end of September, so I worked out a long weekend for us to go down to Louisiana. I called Sophie to let her know the dates, and she said Chase didn't have anything going on. Then I remembered something from my last conversation with my daddy.

I called his secretary Eileen, and she informed me Daddy had Chase on his calendar for that weekend, though she wasn't sure about the details. A short time later, Daddy called me himself to say he had Buck picking Chase up after school that Thursday. They were taking a quick trip to Lexington, Kentucky for the Breeders' Cup. He said I should bring Dinah and Preston over for dinner on Saturday.

I had to exert some self-control. I wasn't pleased about him taking such liberties, especially when I had planned a trip so Dinah and I could spend time with Chase. But like I said, I was feeling that a face-to-face conversation was the best way to straighten things out.

We flew to NOLA, and Preston picked us up at the airport. He'd arranged to take time off from the shop so he could spend the long weekend with us. Thursday night, we kept things low key, ordering in a fried chicken dinner while Dinah got Preston and Sophie caught up on her new life in New York. She was excited to tell them about her new school, her new friends, and all the places we'd been to around the city. That girl had changed in so many ways. She went on about how much she'd missed Sophie's cooking, and she dragged the poor woman up to her room to show Sophie some of her new clothes and jewelry and ask her advice.

When they ran off, Preston and I looked at each other and laughed. Dinah had never been interested in fashion before, but with her new friends, she liked going to vintage stores and spent a lot more time picking out outfits to wear. Miss Dinah had also moved on from treating Sophie like her archnemesis. We were both happy about that.

Preston stayed over and slept in our old bedroom where we had the personal reunion we'd both been looking forward to. I'd missed that boy like mad and told him so. We had to figure out a way to be together without going for long stretches not seeing each other. Preston agreed, and he told me he was "looking into things." I couldn't pull out of him what that meant so I left it alone for now.

On Friday, I sent Sophie off in a town car for the weekend. She said she was visiting a friend in Baton Rouge, and I was happy to give her some time to herself. Later, Preston, Dinah, and I went to a barbecue at Uncle Willy's house. All of Dinah's cousins on

Preston's side were there, and they played horseshoes and cornhole in the backyard while I got caught up with the Montclairs. As usual, they all gave me a friendly welcome. Actually, it was extra friendly. Preston said he'd told a few of his folks that we'd gotten back together, and with the Montclairs, you tell one, and the whole lot of them knows your business.

I didn't mind. I mean, I'd always felt a little strange about his family treating me like a celebrity, and that went back before my book came out, all the way to when I was a teenager, and they found out I was related to Gaston Bondurant. But the Montclairs were good people. I'd grown real fond of Preston's Aunt Eugenia, his cousin Francine, who he was closest to, and even his brother Earl.

Now after we made some small talk, Earl had words for me like he always did. He started off by asking if I moved to New York because I was too good for Louisiana now. Francine lit into him about showing me some respect, but I said I didn't mind. I told Earl, as a matter of fact, I owed a lot to Louisiana for making me the man I was, and I'd never be too good for anyone in bayou country.

Earl rolled his eyes. He looked like he'd tossed back a few beers. "That what you say, but now you got Duke on the bandwagon, talking 'bout moving to New York."

I broke out in an incredulous grin. "You say Duke?"

Something strange was going on. People around us got quiet all of the sudden, and Francine and Preston's père were looking at Earl like he better shut his mouth.

Earl sneered. "Why I gotta act like it's some big secret? Y'all know Duke is up in Baton Rouge with Sophie this weekend." He pointed his eyes at me. "That's what I'm talking 'bout. You the one who introduced the two of them, and now he gettin' ideas. When Sophie move up with you, he wanna live in New York too."

I was caught between disbelief, complicity, and not a little bit of humor. I turned my head and raised a hand to my face in case any of that was showing. Helpfully, half of the Montclairs swarmed on Earl to cool him down. Then Preston came over, and we took a stroll around the side of the house.

I looked at Preston. "Duke's spending the weekend with Sophie?"

Preston's guilty face had me feeling like I was the only one in the parish who didn't know. "He say he want to tell you himself. I tol' him, he should let you know 'fore the weekend. I dunno. Could be Sophie was worried 'bout you findin' out. I sorry, Arizona. Maybe I shoulda tol' you."

I didn't need apologies from anybody. I was just in shock from the unlikeliness of the two of them getting together. Then I felt bad that Duke and Sophie were scared of what I would say.

"Press, I'm not mad." I snorted a laugh. "They've been seeing each other since my housewarming party?"

He nodded. "I only heard last week. I went over to my cousin René's house for the ballgame last Sunday, and Duke was there. He been on leave from the oil rig, and René and Earl pull out of him what been going on. I don't think he wanted me to know about it neither."

I hadn't talked to Duke since he'd been up in New York. I'd meant to keep in touch with him, but so many other things had been going on.

"If he and Sophie are seeing each other, I'm happy for them. Why would they want to keep it from me?"

"Could be 'cause you paying Sophie to take care of Chase. Y'know, it would kinda be like if Earl started dating someone at my garage. People would wonder if that be disrespectful since I own the place."

That sort of thing didn't bother me. Then I thought of something funny. "You're saying if Earl was knocking boots with Lyle or Jackson from the repair shop, you'd be telling him he was out of line?"

He grinned. "I don't know. I might be. But that ain't happening. I just saying people get worried 'bout things getting messy where family and business be concerned."

I cocked a smile at him. "Duke and Sophie. Now that's not a match anybody would've put on their lottery card, but I'm happy for Duke. He hasn't had much luck with women, and Sophie, she's a real good catch. You think they might make a go of it for the long term?"

"I guess we have to see."

22

When we got home that night and sent Dinah to bed, I remembered I hadn't told Preston about my daddy's invitation to have us over for dinner on Saturday. That might've been my way of blocking out the drama in store for me. I didn't want Press to feel left out that weekend when I was in town, but I told him I was also worried about fitting in a tricky conversation with my daddy while he and Dinah were around.

Preston understood the dilemma and said he was fine skipping the dinner. His cousin Francine had been talking about taking her kids ATVing that weekend over at Bayou Teche, and he said Dinah was interested in coming along. She'd made up with Louie, Gracie, and Stella at the barbecue, which was good to hear. Preston suggested he take Dinah on that trip, and they'd stay over at Francine's for a Saturday sleepover.

We worked out the plans while we were curled up on the sofa in the living room, and Preston was nibbling at my neck with one hand unbuttoning my shirt and the other slipping inside the front of my jeans. He'd bring Dinah home Sunday after he went to church. I could sleep over at my daddy's and drive back with Chase in the early afternoon. We could all spend most of Sunday together. Preston had me half out of my clothes and revved up, but he stopped short to say he wanted to take me out to dinner, just the two of us, on Sunday night, which was my last night in town. Sophie would be coming home in the evening to watch Chase. I saw no problem with the plan. I got his arms wrapped around me again and found his mouth with mine.

We slept in on Saturday. That had never been a problem for me, but I was surprised Preston was conked out at my side when I opened my eyes at ten o'clock. He'd always been out of bed by seven, even on the weekends. Sometime since we broke up, he'd fallen into a more laid-back lifestyle, I guess. It used to be he was always wanting to check in on his garage, and he hadn't mentioned it in two full days.

I wasn't complaining. We lazily pulled ourselves out of bed to see if Dinah was up and about. That Saturday, Preston made us brunch with pain perdu, sausages, and fried potatoes. I washed the dishes afterward while he and Dinah got packed up to head over to Francine's.

My dinner with Daddy wasn't until eight. He and Chase had a late afternoon flight back from Kentucky. So I showered and killed some time on the phone with Jonathan. The big news was he and Russell were moving in together, and Jonathan had convinced him to look at apartments downtown. Jonathan had become one of those gays who never ventured above 14th Street. Anyway, I was happy for him and happy for me. They'd be living near my apartment, and we could get together real easy. He had a weekly gig at the Nuyorican Poet's Café, and he had a job now at the Latino AIDS Commission. I was looking forward to going to their fundraising events.

Later, I ironed a new plaid suit I'd bought at Bergdorf's. My daddy liked his formalities, and at least I'd be looking good for our dreaded conversation. I put on a shirt and tie, fixed my suit in the mirror, and I puttered around the house as long as I could take it. Then I got in my Beamer, drove to Darrow, and arrived at Whittington Manor a couple minutes before seven thirty.

Mr. Wainwright met me at the door with more pep in his

welcome than usual, and things got stranger from there. I asked where I could find Chase, and Mr. Wainwright led me upstairs to my old bedroom.

Chase was on my bed, lying on his belly in his pajamas, playing with his Game Boy. I snuck over to surprise him, raised him in my arms and spun him around, and then I set him down and took a seat beside him on the bed. I asked him about the horse race, and he said it was fine and not much else.

That boy was tired. His blond hair was sun-streaked, and his face and limbs were browned, which must've been from being out on the water for his sailing lessons the past few weeks. He leaned all his weight against my side like he was ready for bed. I asked if he was coming down for dinner, and he said he'd already eaten. Mrs. Gundy made him lobster, potatoes, and corn when he got back from Kentucky a few hours ago.

I didn't think I'd misunderstood my daddy. He'd said it was going to be him, me, Preston, Chase, and Dinah for dinner. I was disappointed, though I could see Chase was worn out from his trip. I asked why he was sleeping in my room. He had his own across the hall. Chase shrugged and said his granddaddy had been having him sleep there lately.

I glanced around nostalgically. My school pennants were up on the wall along with my old bulletin board with photos, grade reports, and tickets from the rock concerts I'd gone to in high school and college.

That wall had some recent additions, however. I saw a framed newspaper article from the society pages of the *Times-Picayune*. I stepped over to take a look at it. There I was, with Chase's mama, Fiona Linklater, the first time I made the papers at twenty-two-years old. That wall was like a gallery now. Framed shots from my graduations. My second-place ribbon from a high school equestrian meet, and my honor cords from Middleton Academy and Columbia. Somebody had also framed my articles from *Vanity Fair*, *Rolling Stone*, the *New York Times*, and even my photo shoot from the *Advocate*. I could only reason that my daddy had done all of that. I was curious, but I remembered I'd left Chase by his lonesome.

I turned back to him, and he was lying across the bed with his head on a pillow. I supposed I was staying in a guest bedroom that night, which was ridiculous, but I didn't want to go through the trouble of moving Chase. I helped him get under the covers, but before he went to sleep, I had some things I wanted to say to him.

"I missed you. Did you miss me?"

He joggled his head.

"You know I love you, even when you're down here and I'm in New York."

He yawned.

I tickled his sides to make him squirm and laugh. "I'm taking you to live with me up there. You know that, don't you? I'm not taking no for an answer anymore. I'm no good without you, you see? Dinah says she's too old for bedtime stories, and I don't have anyone to read to at night."

He wrapped his little arms around my neck, and I laid next to him on the bed for a spell.

I brushed his sun-whitened hair. "I love you so much, darling. It could be I haven't been the best daddy lately. But I want you to know, I'm going to make it up to you."

His eyes were shut, but I saw a trace of a smile on his face. I noticed his My Little Pony doll with a rainbow mane on his nightstand. That's what he'd wanted when I took him to FAO Schwartz in New York back in February. He had no interest in the toy cars or trucks or baseball sets.

"And Chase, you know you're perfect just the way you are? There's going to be people who tell you different, but you just let them jog ahead and be yourself."

He was lights out. I tucked the little angel in and kissed him on the head. I stepped out of the room and closed the door.

The second floor of the house felt still and desolate. It reminded me of when I'd lived there as a kid and felt lonely and out of place. I should've headed downstairs to see where Daddy had set us up for dinner, but my gaze wandered down the hall to the eastern wing. That was where my grandmother and my daddy had separate rooms. I couldn't help taking a stroll that way.

My chest tightened as I stepped down the hall. When I'd first moved into the big estate at fifteen years old, I'd been told to never disturb my grandmother, and it was like that prohibition was bearing down on me again. I pushed forward. The last time I'd seen Virginia Bondurant, she'd been doing well, albeit using a wheelchair. I couldn't help myself from looking in on her.

I came up to her room. The door was open, and some lights were on. I hesitated. If she was still awake, she'd likely curse me out for barging in on her. Things sounded quiet. I took a deep breath to settle my nerves, and I stepped up to the threshold of her room.

Her room was deep with lots of shadowy hollows. I recognized her perfume hanging in the air along with something more medicinal. I figured she had to be in the room, what with the lamps on here and there, but I took three steps inside and scanned around and couldn't find her. Her bed was made up, and her sitting area was empty.

I stepped inside a little farther, glanced around the bed and froze. Someone was sitting at her vanity, and the figure confused me at first. From the back, she looked real petite, swimming in a satin housecoat. She was in her wheelchair. The Virginia Bondurant I'd known was vibrant. She'd had her stroke three years back when she was sixty-three, and before that she could've passed for a fashionable lady in her forties. The woman at that vanity desk looked like she was catatonic, at least from behind.

I carefully approached her. "Virginia. It's Arizona."

She didn't move one iota. I called out to her again and stepped a little closer. I hadn't asked how she was doing, and I felt a little guilty about that. Now I didn't feel like I owed my grandmother much, seeing as she'd never wanted me in her life, but she was my grandmother. I couldn't be so cold as to ignore completely that her health was declining. Her vanity was filled with all her ornamental bottles of skin products, make up, and perfumes, and on one shelf, there were a half dozen brown bottles from the drug store. I caught a glimpse of her reflection in the mirror and nearly backed away.

Slowly, she pivoted her wheelchair, and we were face-to-face. Everything felt like it was happening in slow motion, and I was suddenly freezing cold. She was wearing a blond wig that had come loose from her forehead, revealing gray, thinned hair. Her face was made up grotesquely in an imitation of beauty. Giant arches of shimmering blue eye shadow. Thick foundation that was too dark for her skin tone and smeared sloppily, leaving a pale perimeter around her hairline and the wrinkled underside of her chin. Bright pink lipstick that a child might've applied. Her yellowed eyes stabbed at me warily.

"Who are you?"

That strained voice cut through me. It held a vestige of her imperiousness, but it was also fearful in a way I'd never heard her speak.

"It's Arizona. Your grandson." I drew up in front of her so I was in the light. I gazed at her gently.

She wheeled back and stared at me like a wild animal. "Who are you?" She glanced around. "What are you doing here?"

I tried to temper her reaction and repeated what I'd said. She gripped the chair tightly with bony, manicured hands. Her bottom half seemed motionless, but above, she was tensed, and her eyes searched around desperately.

She raised her voice. "Poly? Fabienne? Somebody help me." She stared at me again. "Get out. You don't belong here. I'll have you thrown out. You'll never hurt me and my daughter again."

I backed away to leave her in her peace. Her daughter, my mama, died over thirty years ago. Virginia Bondurant had lost her mind. I hurried out of her room and gathered my breath in the hallway.

I FOUND MY daddy downstairs in the gentleman's parlor. He was dressed to the nines in a white linen suit, a striped shirt, and a bowtie. He asked what had taken me so long to join him for dinner. I told him I'd gone up to see Chase and left things at that. Daddy gave me a hug and drew me over to a dining table that had a big gold-accented floral centerpiece, gold linens and candles, and a pile of gold-wrapped presents next to my table setting.

Daddy was working on a Johnnie Walker. I told the staffer in the room to bring me the same. I was feeling out of sorts and not sure what to do with all the presents.

"What's all this?" I asked him.

"We never had a chance to celebrate your birthday last month." Daddy raised his drink. "Happy birthday, son."

I raised mine, and we threw back gulps.

"Where's Preston and Dinah?" he asked.

"Preston's cousins invited Dinah over for the night. We thought it would be nice for her to spend some time with them since she's only in town for the weekend."

"Then it'll just be the two of us. Like old times." He gestured for me to sit down at the table while he took a seat at the head. "Thirty years old," he remarked. "By the time I turned thirty, I'd doubled my daddy's company. Most of that was due to striking a deal with Kraft Foods to be their main sugar supplier. Must've been 1973."

An attendant carted in our first course, which was a cold vichyssoise, and Daddy got him sorted out with clearing away the extra table settings. Daddy was looking a little drawn and tired. He'd always been a workaholic. I didn't know how he did it all, and anyway, I was thinking twice about mentioning that I would've liked to have known he was having Chase eat earlier that night.

Daddy sipped a spoonful of his soup and glanced at me. "I suppose you haven't done bad either. Not many people get invited to the *David Letterman Show*."

I muttered thank you to him.

"You keep steering in that direction, you're going to have a good career ahead of you," he went on. "It's not something I can give you advice about. There's a lot of things I know, but writing isn't one of them. Your grandmother Helena, now she loved writing and drawing. Your uncle Nicolas, too."

"What about my mama?"

Daddy hesitated, thinking back. "Your mama did well at school. But I don't recall her having an interest in writing like you. Philippa only ever talked about wanting to be a dancer."

"What about Virginia?"

He bulged his lip. "She was always more of a reader than a writer. She used to go to bed with one of her novels every night. Couldn't tear her away from it."

He'd gotten me curious about my family history. It hadn't occurred to me before that writing could be in my blood. But before I could ask him more about his mama Helena, Daddy changed the subject.

"Now Chase, he's going to be a little sportsman. He takes after his granddaddy."

I gave him a crooked glance. "He's six years old."

"That's not too young for a boy to show his nature. The report from the yacht club was he was head of the class. I've been thinking about getting a boat. Maybe a daysailer to start. It'd give Chase a pastime to pursue in the warm weather months."

I'm not sure why that ticked me off, but it did, and I started to misbehave. "I never once heard Chase say he was interested in sailing. I think that's what *you'd* like him to do."

"You wouldn't have heard him talking about it because you haven't seen him in what? Two months? I'm just stepping in to cultivate his development."

My stomach burned icy hot. I had things to straighten out with him concerning Chase, and I was already getting a preview of how he was going to hit back, criticizing my parenting. Meanwhile, he had a pile of presents for me, which made it hard to confront him. I let his little jibe pass and thanked him for doing so much for Chase over the summer.

"I'm happy to do it," he said. "I took him all over the Capitol and even showed him the Speaker's gavel in the Hall of the House." He smiled to himself. "Did he show you his Washington Nationals bat and ball? I got us tickets to one of their games. In a club room overlooking home base with James Carville, his wife Mary Matalin, and their three-year-old Matty."

Chase hadn't mentioned that baseball game. I was pretty sure he could care less about the sport. The only thing he'd been excited to tell me about the summer was his Paddington Bear he'd gotten in London.

"We saw everything from soup to nuts in Europe." He screwed up his brow. "I don't think the two of us ever went to the Blue Grotto in Capri. I took Chase there in one of them gondolier boats. The waves were a little choppy that day, but he loved it." He gave me a wink. "For a man pushing fifty-seven, I did well keeping up with him. We hiked to the top of the Acropolis in Athens and went swimming off a Catamaran in the Aegean Sea." He scratched his beard. "Anyway, I think it was good for him to have a male influence for a change."

"How do you mean?"

"I'm talking about Sophie. The boy spends ninety-nine percent of his time with her. Now, I know she takes good care of him, but a boy needs a male role model too."

I coughed out a not so humorous laugh. "Chase has me and Preston. Now tell me again, how do you mean he needs a male influence?"

"I'm saying in his day-to-day life. Now you can argue all you want, but the fact is, you made a choice to move up to New York without him."

My face compacted. I couldn't produce a word.

Daddy hiked up an easy smile. "I know it's not easy when you've got a career going full throttle. But it's something for you to think about. The years go by real quick when you have a child."

I ruminated for a moment. Probably should've waited a little longer for my feelings to settle before opening my mouth. "Daddy,

I'm trying to have a nice dinner with you and not start a fight. I don't need you lecturing me about my son. I'm seeing to him being taken care of, and he's coming up to live with me at the end of the school year. And as a matter of fact, not all boys are interested in sailing and baseball. Chase has got a long way to go figuring out who he is, and I don't like you presuming one way or the other."

We sat in silence while a staffer took our soup bowls away. I avoided eye contact with Daddy.

"What's that mean, figuring out who he is?" Daddy said. "He's a boy. Why, when I was his age, I started riding lessons, and I loved when my daddy took me to the ballpark."

"When I was his age, I was helping my mama around the kitchen and playing dollhouse with my sister. What's your point?"

"If this conversation is headed in the direction I think it is, I have to tell you, son, I'm worn out already. So, you didn't have the advantages Chase has. I didn't have your advantages. My daddy didn't have mine. That's what this country is all about. People have the opportunity to do better than their parents did."

I wasn't going to get him to understand what I was saying, so I just went straight for the bigger issue. "You can't take Chase whenever you please, and not tell me about it."

His face went blank, and then he cracked a grin. "What are you talking about?"

"I'm talking about you taking him every weekend this past month."

"I told you he was going to sailing lessons on Saturdays."

"Yes, you did. But he has a weekend a month with Preston. Preston drove all the way over to the house to pick him up last Friday, and you'd already stolen him away without talking to either of us."

"Well that's just faulty wires in communication. I told you to check with Eileen about Chase's schedule."

I glared at him. "I'm the boy's father. Eileen manages *your* schedule, not Chase's."

"I've been flying home on weekends so that boy gets some

attention. I'm doing you a favor so your son doesn't spend all his time with a nanny."

I was finding my way around his guilt-tripping real fast. "I didn't ask for that favor, and I shouldn't have to call your secretary to find out what's going on with my son. Now, I'm telling you, as plain as can be, if you've got plans for taking Chase for the weekend, you clear it with me first." I cocked a look at him. "You're a US senator and a CEO. Where are you finding the time all of the sudden to spend every weekend with your grandson?"

A gulf of silence ensued.

"The main course is coming along," Daddy said. "Why don't you take a look at your birthday presents in the meantime?"

I knew his tactics. Trying to deflect from the point I was making. "Daddy, I appreciate all this. But there's a conversation we need to have. What's going on with you spending all this time with Chase? And you've got him set up in my old room? It doesn't make sense to me."

"I've been reevaluating my priorities." He took a sip of his whiskey. "Somebody needs to mind Chase's safety while you're off being a big shot in New York."

"Daddy, you're being dramatic. Chase has someone taking care of him twenty-four seven. When it's not me or Preston, he's got Sophie."

"You may think that's sufficient, but I'm telling you it's not. There's all kinds of crazy people out there. Since you won't let me hire private security for Chase, I've been coming down to see to his security myself."

I laughed madly. "You're taking him to horse races on weekends."

"Is it a crime for a grandfather to want to spend time with his grandson?"

"I say, it's not a crime, but you need to respect I'm Chase's daddy."

He threw down his napkin. "I see. So you don't have time for me, and now you don't want me to have time with my grandson."

I rolled my eyes.

"I suppose you've got your new life in New York now, and you're going to forget all about me. Never mind I took care of you for the past fifteen years."

I sighed, but as I looked at him, something clicked in my head. Now he'd always been needy in his own way. I remembered, last year, he got drunk at his birthday party and he told me he wouldn't live if he lost me. I'd chalked that up to the alcohol making him emotional, but I realized that night, he wasn't just throwing his weight around to boss me. He was sulking. It was like we'd reversed roles, and he needed me to parent him.

"Daddy, I'm not going to forget about you. Where's all this coming from?"

At that moment, a staffer brought the main course out from the kitchen. Broiled lobster tails with Mrs. Gundy's potatoes and peas. We sat in silence while he made up our plates and stepped from the room.

"Arizona, when a man reaches a certain age, he has a tendency to take inventory of his life," Daddy said. "What he's accomplished. The things that matter. And the one thing I come back to all the time is you. You're the only thing I made that's important, and you're slipping away from me."

"Daddy, you made B&B. You're a US senator. You're the most accomplished man I know. Now I appreciate what you're saying, and maybe I haven't been the best son at times, but I'm always going to be in your life. I just need you to trust me and let go a little. I'm thirty years old."

He cut up some of his food and didn't say anything at first. "I want you to make good choices, son. And good choices for Chase."

"They're my choices to make is what I'm trying to tell you."

Daddy went back to cutting up his food and not talking to me.

"Daddy, I suppose I should apologize for what I said at my housewarming party last month. I may not be happy about what you're doing all the time, but it's not my place to scold you about your private decisions. So, if you're angry about that, I'm saying I'm sorry."

He glanced at me but still said nothing.

"You've got me wondering if you accept my apology."

Eventually, he waved me off. "It's ancient history. Takes a man to admit when he's wrong." He threw back the rest of his whiskey and got the attendant's attention to bring him a refill. I'd just about drained my drink, so I said I was also ready for another.

"I don't understand why you're so worried about me and Chase moving to New York. I'd think you'd see a silver lining. Now that you're living in DC a good part of the year, we'll be closer to you."

He ate a couple forkfuls of lobster before turning to me again. "I'm aware of that. They've got commuter flights on the hour from LaGuardia to National Airport. Get you into town in forty-five minutes."

"Then what's the problem? They've also got some of the best schools in the country in New York. My agent, Janet, she's got her daughter enrolled in a private school where Mia Farrow sends her kids. I've been looking into it for Chase."

"Is that right? Well, I don't doubt they've got top notch schools, but they've also got a gang problem in New York, and don't tell me I'm wrong. I hear about it from my colleagues in the Senate."

I smirked at him. "Daddy, I made it through four years of college in New York and never did join a gang, did I?"

"You know what I'm talking about."

"The neighborhood I'm living in is probably safer than down here. Besides, Chase ought to learn about being independent. No better place to do it than New York."

He was quiet for a spell. "Son, I just feel, well, I guess they call it an empty nest. I never had you to raise as a boy, and now you're talking about taking Chase away from me." He turned his head, and his face crumbled.

"Daddy. C'mon. You know I'm not taking Chase away from you."

He wiped his face with his napkin and scowled at himself. "You'll have to excuse me. Acting like a weepy old man."

"You're not a weepy old man, but you've got me worried. I'm not looking to start an argument, but as long as I've known you, you lived your life for yourself and never had a complaint about being lonely." My stomach was twisted up a bit about bringing the next part out. "You never had a problem finding companionship. What's going on with that girl Viv?"

His eyes flashed, and he looked down at the table. "Son, I'm not bragging when I say I can find companionship with a certain kind of woman real easily. To tell the truth, it gets less interesting by the year."

I couldn't help myself from smirking. "Maybe you'd enjoy it more if you took them one at a time instead of trying to keep three or four in circulation."

He looked up at me, not so pleased. "You're poking fun at me is what you're doing. You think I'm a ridiculous old geezer?"

"All I'm saying is I want you to be happy, Daddy. You're a strong man with one heck of a life to share with somebody."

"I can find a woman to share my life with. What I can't do is rewrite the past."

I had an idea what he meant by that. It made me squirmy, and I was relieved when he changed the subject.

"Well, so you're going to be a real New Yorker now. Tell me about your new life in the big city."

I told him about the magazine articles I'd written over the summer. I said I had a novel I was working on, and I mentioned some of the outings I'd taken with Dinah.

"You get yourself one of those limousine services for you and the kids. I don't want Chase taking the subway."

"I've been taking the subway since I was eighteen years old. And that was before Mayor Giuliani militarized the police to make things safe for white tourists. It's not that bad."

"Don't argue with me, Arizona. It'll keep me up at night worrying about you."

I was learning that a big part of managing him was lying. I promised him we'd use a limousine service. I don't know why he was so worried about something happening to Chase or something happening to me. When I was sixteen, he'd had no problem with me going back and forth to Boston on my own. I could only guess it had something to do with him getting older, which truth be told, I didn't like facing.

Anyway, he lightened up after that. He got back to his usual self, and we had a real nice time that night. We joked around about the latest scandal in Washington while we dug into our lobsters and potatoes and had champagne and birthday cake after that. I opened his presents. It was an assortment of gags and his usual extravagant gifts. A silly beret from Paris. One of them newfangled Blackberry mobiles. Pepper spray, which he told me I was going to need in New York. A first edition of William Faulkner's *The Sound and the Fury,* and the latest Power Mac desktop, which I didn't really need. We laughed together about the gag gifts, and I told him he spent too much money on me, though I never really minded being spoiled by him.

With Daddy loosening up, I ventured into a topic that had been on my mind.

"I wasn't sure if I should tell you this, but after I tucked Chase in, I went to say hello to Virginia."

He glanced at me.

"She doesn't look like she's doing too well," I went on. "I tried talking to her, but she didn't recognize me."

Daddy sat back and straightened the napkin on his lap. "I told you, she has her good and bad days. Her nurse, Fabienne, must've been taking her dinner break when you went to Virginia's room."

Virginia being on her lonesome so much struck me as sad. I mean, I'd wished her all kinds of suffering for her treatment of me, but it's different when you witness the suffering. I wasn't sure how to feel. On one hand, my daddy's relationship with Virginia had been going south since the day I was born. She'd had her own affairs and was barely civil to him, so I couldn't fault my daddy for living his own life. On the other hand, Virginia was basically rotting away in her bedroom.

"I do wish there'd been time for the two of you to come to peace," Daddy said.

I sighed. "I can't hate her anymore. You know, she mentioned my mama? Like she was still alive."

Daddy brought out his cigarette case from his jacket pocket. A staffer came over and lit his Camel.

"She's been talking about your mama from time to time. It might sound bonkers, but I think it's nice. She's come around to loving her daughter in her own way." He peeked at me. "She loves you, too."

"You don't need to make it all pretty. She never wanted me in your life, or hers. I'm just saying it makes it a little easier for me to forgive her now that she's, well, not herself."

Daddy glanced away from me. I felt bad about bringing down the mood, but it was something we both needed to acknowledge.

"You going to forgive *me* before I'm old and lose my faculties, too?" he said.

I looked at him. I knew what he was talking about. We'd had some world class spars about him making me pretend I was his grandson in public and not taking me in for fifteen years because he couldn't find the balls to do it. Usually I got tight in the chest when the conversation came up, but in that moment, I realized I wasn't angry about any of that anymore.

"Daddy, I love you, and I forgive you. I know you've been trying to make it up to me since I was fifteen. I'm thirty, and it's time for me to accept the past is the past."

He glanced at me blearily.

"I mean it," I told him. "I know you did the best you could, and I'm not angry any more. I'll always love you, Daddy. I just need you to let me be my own man. That doesn't mean I don't want you in my life."

The staffer brought over our fourth or fifth round of Johnnie

Walker. We were quiet for a while. The booze was slowing my brain.

"Say. Since you and Chase are staying over, how 'bout we go out on the trails tomorrow?"

I balked. "In this humidity? It was ninety degrees today."

"The morning's not so bad, Mr. New Yorker. We can get an early start."

"Daddy, you got me drunk. I'm going to need to sleep in."

"You sound like an old man. But if you're not in the mood for an early ride, we can have a late breakfast and head over to the country club. Chase loves their swimming pool."

"I wish I could, but I promised Preston I'd bring Chase home so we can all spend some time together. Then Press is taking me out on the town for my last night."

"Where all you going?"

"I told him I wanted to try that new Italian place, Irene's. We'll probably head over to a jazz club after."

I think Daddy was fishing for an invitation. I felt bad about that. But Press and I wanted a romantic night for just the two of us.

Daddy stood up from the table on wobbly legs. I had no idea what he was doing, but he didn't make it too far before stumbling and looking like he was losing his balance. I got up and helped him straighten out.

"Where you going?" I asked.

"To fetch us some refills. I don't know where that attendant went."

It was after two o'clock in the morning. The attendant was probably in the kitchen, waiting to hear he could clear out for the night. "Daddy, I'm calling it a night. I'm just about three sheets to the wind, and I think you are too."

He held my face, a little forcefully. His eyes were glazed and sightless. It was definitely time to get him to bed.

"What you doing?" he asked as I tried to shoulder him along.

"I'm seeing you to bed is what I'm doing. We'll have breakfast in the morning before I take Chase home."

His hands fumbled on my shoulders and my neck. It was mildly painful, but I tolerated it because there was something going on with him.

"You've gotta be safe, son. I have these terrible nightmares something's going to happen. I don't want to lose you."

"Okay, Daddy." I got a grip around his side. He was sounding kind of disturbed, but I chalked it up to drinking too much.

"It's like a premonition," he slurred. "You might not believe in that, but I'm telling you, I seen it in my dreams." His voice croaked. "And I can't be losing you when I don't have nothing else in the world. You've gotta be careful, son. Someone put on a gris-gris, I think, and I'm worried about you."

I shuffled him along, not taking his babbling too seriously. "We're going to get you upstairs and comfy in your bedroom. You gave me a great birthday dinner. Thank you, Daddy."

23

I PACKED CHASE up and drove him home the next day, and we had a beautiful family reunion. Preston cooked chicken and shrimps on the barbecue, and when it started raining cats and dogs, we cleared out space in the living room, threw down a blanket, and had a picnic inside. Just Preston, Chase, Dinah, and me. The four of us hadn't all been together at home since New Year's 1998. Everybody was in a great mood, and I think I was smiling the hardest.

Dinah got Chase talking about sailing camp. He said it was okay, but he'd rather have been home with Sophie, working on the garden they'd planted in the backyard. I knew my daddy was full of BS. That boy took after me, not him. He liked helping around the house, reading books, and playing with his stuffed animals. However he turned out, gay or not, he was not going to be a sportsman.

We set up Cornhole in the dining room and played teams: Dinah and me versus Preston and Chase. It wasn't a fair match-up since Preston was so good at the game. After that, Press put together a bowling alley in the hall with plastic pins and a beach ball. We murdered the floors that day, but we passed a real good time. I had popsicles for the kids, and Dinah showed Chase how to build a house from popsicle sticks.

Sophie came home around six. It took every ounce of my better behavior not to tease her about her weekend and get her to admit she'd spent it with Duke. I could see they'd had a good time. Sophie had a big smile on her face and some sashay in her step. I didn't want to embarrass her. I figured she and Duke would tell me they were dating when they were ready.

Sophie took over watching the kids, and Preston and I jumped in the shower and got dressed real slick. I think it had been over two years since we'd had a night out together, and Preston gave me grief for not remembering. He knew, to the day: February 14th, 1996. Francine had taken Chase for the night, and we went on a river dinner cruise and stuck out like sore thumbs as the only gay couple on the entire boat. It came back to me then. The wait staff thought we were cute and kept our flutes filled with the complimentary champagne. We both got tipsy and checked into a club room at the Ritz-Carlton and had a lot of fun on the king bed. We'd stayed up all night watching movies and ordering room service because the fancy food on the cruise hadn't been enough to fill our bellies. Those memories warmed my heart. It used to be that Preston was the only thing I needed in the world to be happy, and I was feeling that again.

Anyway, I put on a new pinstripe shirt, a tie, slacks, and my new pair of bucks. Preston had brought along a nice outfit too. I trimmed his beard and got his wavy hair brushed the right way with a little gel. Then Press drove us to NOLA for a nine o'clock reservation at Irene's.

The place was classy. The dining room was dimly lit, and they had exposed brick walls and candles and flowers on the tables. It was perfect for a date night. Preston ordered us an expensive bottle of Italian wine, and we took a look at our menus. When I saw the prices, I gulped.

"We can go half and half on this," I told him.

"No, sir. I never took you out for your birthday. You think I'm some kinda cheapskate?"

"No. I just don't need you spending all your hard-earned money on dinner."

Preston frowned impartially. "The garage is doing well. Since people moved in to that new housing development on the other side of Route 90, we booked solid. I had to hire a second mechanic."

"I didn't know. Well, good on you." I reached my foot under the table and tapped it against his shoe playfully. Got a quiet smile on his face.

We put in our orders with the waiter, and I told Preston about my eventful dinner with my daddy, along with seeing Virginia. Out of all that, he chose to comment on something I hadn't expected.

"I agree with your daddy about one thing. You should be spending mo' time with Chase."

My nose twitched. "That's just what I need. The two of you ganging up on me."

"Kids grow up real fast." His face was somber, and he turned his wine glass in his hand. "You ain't traveling for your book no mo', are you?"

I sipped my wine. "I've just got that trip to Los Angeles next month to meet with the folks from Paramount." An idea occurred to me. "What do you think about bringing Dinah and Chase to Hollywood? We could make a week of it. I think it falls over Columbus Day."

"That's kinda soon. And the kids only get one day off from school that week. Chase already been missing a lot of Fridays and Mondays. Y'know, on account of your daddy."

I knew he'd been taking Chase to sailing lessons on Saturdays, but the old sneak hadn't mentioned pulling him out of school for long weekends. "I straightened my daddy out. He's not going to do that anymore. But I see your point. Well, I'll be back in just over a week for Chase's birthday." That was going to have to be a quick trip, flying down Monday and leaving Wednesday so I could get Dinah back for two days of school and meet up with Janet for our flight to LA on Friday.

"When I get back from LA, I can do a longer visit later in the month." Then I remembered my first parent-teacher conference at Dinah's school was happening in October, and I was also speaking at an event at Columbia around that time. "Or maybe November would be better. I could come down here or the two of you could come up to me."

Preston didn't answer. Something was on his mind. I waited it out, feeling a little antsy.

"You've got a lot on your plate. But this is sorta what I'm talking 'bout in terms of keepin' up with Chase. You his primary guardian."

"I'm slowing down. It's just, with Dinah, I can't be in two places at once right now."

"You wouldn't have to worry 'bout the back and forth if he was living up there with you," he said.

"That's the plan. After he finishes the school year." I fiddled with my appetizer fork. "I think I know now what you mean about him turning out like the two of us. He's young, but I see what you said about him being sensitive and more interested in girl-things."

"He got time to figure things out. But it's not going to be long till he's gonna have to deal with kids at school having opinions about him."

"You saying I should move him up sooner? It would make it harder for you to see him."

"Suppose I moved up too?"

Our eyes met, and then he glanced away with some color showing on his face. I watched him while my heart hovered in my throat.

"Press, I say, I'd like that a lot." I cracked a grin. "We really talking about this? How are you going to move up when you've got your garage?"

He knit his hands together on the table. "Firestone been after me to buy the shop. I didn't like the idea at first. My uncle Merle bought that lot in 1970 and built his garage from the foundation to the roof. But it's had a good run, and they say they'll keep my mechanics and pump boys. They offering half a million."

I couldn't hide the startled look on my face. I never expected to hear those words out of Preston's mouth. "You're really thinking about selling your shop?"

"I been waiting for the right time to talk to you about it. Y'know, face-to-face. It'd gimme some savings till I figure out what to do for work in New York. A fellow from church used to live up there. He say if I get my inspector's license and take a course in diesel mechanics, they got a lot of bus and truck companies that's always hiring."

I studied him. "You'd be okay moving away from your family?"

He looked down at his wine glass. "It wouldn't be easy, but I'm thirty years old. I gotta leave the nest sometime. Make a family of my own, the right way."

My heart was bursting, and it took me a minute to compose myself.

"Press, if that's what you want to do, well, I've been ready for you to move up to New York with me for ten years and counting. You'll have plenty of time to work on your licenses and training. We've got an apartment already paid for, and I'm bringing in a comfortable income for the four of us."

Preston glanced up at me. "I want to pay my own way. If we gonna do this, that's my one condition. It's important to me, Arizona. I know you done well for yourself, and you got your family's money. But working always been good for me. It's who I am. So, if we gonna give this a second try, you gotta let me be a man and contribute."

I had no problem with that. I knew it was important to Preston to pull his weight. It meant a lot to his pride. I was thinking it was also time to set up a meeting with Lawrence Barbet and review our options for getting Preston some parental rights what comes to Chase. It had been two years since we last looked into it. Back then, I'd just gotten full custody of Chase after his mama's grandfather had passed away. When a social worker from family court did a visit, I'd been upfront about my relationship with Preston, but we'd stopped short of filing for Preston to adopt Chase as his co-parent since that had never gone over well in Louisiana. I thought to myself, now that Louisiana courts were out of my hair, we might be able to work things out quietly with some legal paperwork, if not an outright adoption. Even better, once we established residency in New York, we might be eligible for a domestic partnership, which could make his parent status easier.

I was about to tell Press about that, but just then, a thirty-something woman in an expensive cocktail dress came over to the table with a big smile. She apologized for intruding, but she said she just had to tell me she loved my book. I saw a group of people from her table watching from across the room.

I thanked her kindly, and she asked if I wouldn't mind giving her an autograph. I nodded, and she brought out a postcard and a pen from her clutch purse. I got her name and wrote her a little note with my signature.

Afterwards, Preston and I were quiet for a while.

"You famous now," Press said. "I guess I wonder sometimes if you really want to settle down with someone like me."

"Press, you're all I've ever wanted. What's happening with my book didn't change that." I stretched my hand across the table to take his in mine. I could see that made him a little uncomfortable, being out in public. "Now, I could take this hand away if you want me to, but you can bet that table over there already knows I'm queer." I glanced around. Other diners were peeking at me, trying to place who I was. I turned back to Preston and spoke quietly. "Everyone in this here room could be recognizing me in the next few minutes. You're guilty by association, so I think the more important thing for us to be talking about is how you feel about that?"

He gave me a small, stiff grin. "You don't have to take your hand away. Feels funny, but, well, it's time I get used to it."

I kept gazing at him. I wanted to make sure he was being honest with himself. Press had never been comfortable with us holding hands in public or telling people about our relationship. I hadn't made the papers for a while, but after the whole thing with Dolly going to the tabloids, it was possible another gossip magazine would be interested in telling the world about my personal life. Preston's family had come around to accepting our relationship, but I didn't think they'd be happy seeing it in a grocery store magazine rack or on TV.

"I'm ready to be open about us," he said. "I spoke to my pastor 'bout it, and she think I ready too." He wiped his mouth with his free hand. "My family knows about me, Arizona. Everyone from my père to my cousin René who you like so much."

I sat back. "How'd René take the news?"

Preston snorted. "He be saying fag this and fag that when we at the gun range with my brother Harry a few weeks back. I walked up to him and say, 'You got a problem with gay men, you got a problem with me.'" His face turned rosy. "That got him 'pologizing, and now he asks 'bout you every time we see each other."

I chuckled.

"Anyway, it's not a problem for me, and I be lyin' if I said I ain't been thinking it'd be better for us to raise Chase in New York. He gonna be a strong kid, but he shouldn't have to go through what we been through growing up here. You right about that." He sat back a little in his seat. "I'll miss Louisiana, but I'll miss you mo' if we livin' a thousand miles apart."

I squeezed his hand, and then I set mine back on my lap so the waiter could serve us our appetizers. While that was going on, I thought of something. "You won't have a problem finding a church. They've got a lot of churches that welcome people like us."

"I know. My pastor tol' me they got a congregation on 71st Street. I can take the A or C train up there from your stop at West Fourth."

I raised my eyebrows. I was touched that he'd put so much thought into the move. We had some details to hash out, and we talked through them over our baked oysters oreganata and crawfish fettuccine. Press needed a few months to seal the deal with Firestone and turn his garage over to them, and he had to put his house on the market. Meanwhile, I could work on applications to get Chase enrolled in that private school Janet told me about. Next spring, I'd need to start looking for a buyer for my house, bring Chase and Sophie up to New York, and figure out what I had to ship up from the old house and sell the rest of it. That all seemed doable, and it started sinking in that things were really happening. In less than a year, Preston and I would have a home at my Fifth Avenue apartment with Chase and Dinah.

Then Preston brought a velvet jewelry box out of his pocket. I was pretty sure I knew what was inside. It had been a long time ago, but I remembered that blue box he'd given me at my seventeenth birthday party. I scowled at him and opened it up. Inside, there was the silver ring he'd bought for me when he asked me to get engaged.

Preston watched me, carefully and a little nervously. I was overwhelmed and not helping him much. I steadied myself and looked him in the eye. "You held on to it all this time?"

"I looked into hocking it, but I couldn't even get the eighty dollars I spent." The bastard grinned real big.

I fit the little band on my finger. "Well, you can't take it back now. If it means what I think it means."

"You mine now, Arizona. You can't wander away no mo'."

"Who's wandering?"

Press gave me a wise look, and then he took my hand in his again, admiring the engagement ring. "I get you an upgrade soon as the deal with Firestone go through."

"No sir. This one's perfect," I told him.

After dinner, we took a stroll down Chartres Street. The French Quarter was hopping with rowdy bands of young people and drunken tourists. Nobody blinked an eye about the two of us holding hands. Not that such things didn't happen sometimes, but generally, people were used to gay couples in the French Quarter, and we could be ourselves. It had been a long day for both of us, so I told Press we could skip the jazz club and just check out the musicians at Jackson Square for a while. I was buzzing from the wine, which I'd mostly drank myself since Press was driving. It was a real happy buzz. In fact, the last time I remembered being so happy in New Orleans was when I first took Press out on the town. We were seventeen years old, sneaking into gay bars. I remembered the wonder on his face and how proud I'd been to show him around. Now we were walking down the middle of the street holding hands, and it felt like we were King and King of NOLA.

That bottle of wine had gone to my bladder. I should've used the restroom before we left Irene's. I told Press I'd just relieve myself in an alley. People did it all the time, including me back in my bar-hopping days. I spotted an alley off the street and snuck into it to do my business.

Just past a dumpster, there was a shadowy space that looked perfect for the deed. I popped open my belt and trousers, pulled down my briefs, and groaned from the relief of letting the water go. I even laughed out loud about the circumstances. I was tipsy. Then someone came up behind me and jabbed me in the back.

"Gimme your money."

I thought it was a joke, so I turned around without even pulling up my pants. "We playing stick-em-up now?"

That alley was dark, but I could tell it wasn't Preston. The fellow I saw was shorter, leaner, and antsy. He wore a hooded sweatshirt that covered the sides of his face. He wasn't amused by my pecker hanging out.

"Gimme your fuckin' money."

He was holding something inside the pouch of his sweatshirt. I'd never been in such a predicament before. I was having a hard time believing I was in a predicament even then so I got brassy.

"I ain't got no money on me, so why don't you fuck off?"

I bent down to pull up my pants, and then he thrust out a pistol and shouted at me with his voice tremoring.

"Gimme your wallet. Right now."

I held up my hands. "Okay. Take it easy," I told him. The guy was practically bouncing on his feet. A junkie, I imagined. I tried to hold his gaze while I lowered my right hand and dug out my wallet from my pocket. He nudged his head toward the pavement. I threw my wallet down.

"Arizona? Everything okay?"

The stranger and I both looked in the direction of that voice. Cold terror flooded me. Preston was coming to see what was going on, and the junkie was glancing back and forth in a panic. Then he pointed his pistol at Preston with a quivering hand.

I didn't think twice about what to do. I rushed at the junkie while his pistol was turned. He was as tight as a coil and pretty scrawny. I took him by surprise and backed him against a building with a grip on his arm which was holding the gun. Then he shirked his arm free, and a blast deafened my ears and ate up my vision with white hot fireworks.

For a couple of seconds, I thought that strange explosion had knocked my legs out from under me and I just needed a breather to get my limbs working again. My ears were ringing so bad, it was like lightning had struck a foot away from where I'd been standing. The world rocked. I hadn't even felt my body hit the asphalt, but I was definitely laid out on my back.

Then I realized I couldn't breathe. A stupefying pain shot through my chest as though I'd been impaled by a rusty battering ram. I gagged and tasted blood. Every atom of strength in my body had been sapped away with the exception of my reflexes. My throat wrenched to expel the internal fluids that were drowning me.

For the briefest of moments, I was aware of Preston propping me up and screaming for help. I knew it was too late. I'd been shot in the chest at practically point blank range. It sure wasn't how I'd pictured my death the few times I'd thought about it. That was supposed to be a long time away, fifty, sixty years off, I'd hoped. But that bullet had sawed right through my heart and lungs, and facts were facts. A cold curtain fell over me. I didn't even have time to panic.

I wanted to tell Preston I was sorry for getting myself into such a mess. I just needed him to keep holding me for as long as I had left. He was fading away. Everything was fading away. The world peeled back, and I was somewhere else without the pain and just a tumble of thoughts and images in my head.

I was flying like an angel, higher and higher, drifting to an infinitely quiet place. It was strange at first. All my life, I'd been ready to fight, and there was nothing to fight anymore. A gentle current just carried me into the night sky. I didn't even have to flap my arms. I guess that left me with an inner peace I'd been looking for all along. Truth was, I'd been loved by so many people. I had so much gratitude in my heart, I couldn't be sore that I'd only gotten thirty years. I just wished real strong that people would forgive me. My babies Chase and Dinah. My love Preston. Daddy. Duke. Jonathan. *I'll be looking over all of you from heaven.*

Then, there was nothing left but motes of light disappearing one by one.

ABOUT THE AUTHOR

Romeo Preminger has been called the master of the romantic thriller. He's the author of over a dozen books including the Southern Gothic ARIZONA series, the branded romantic thriller series GUILTY PLEASURES EDITIONS, erotic romance stand-alones, and some naughty shorts called STORYBOOK EDITIONS.

Romeo lives on the East Coast with his husband. Beyond writing, some of his favorite jobs on his resume are a brief stint as a zookeeper, an even briefer stint as a hot dog vendor, and a more substantial career as a counselor and advocate for LGBTQ+ youth. For more about Romeo, visit: https://romeopreminger.com or connect with him on Twitter at https://twitter.com/Preminger Romeo.

Sign up for his mailing list and get news on sales and upcoming releases:

https://mailchi.mp/78bc1368af1e/team-romeo

THE STORY CONTINUES WITH THE
CHASE SERIES

WHEN I WAS six years old, my daddy was murdered in an alley in New Orleans, and I stopped talking for four years. All I remember is I didn't want to be in the world anymore, and I guess the only way I could do that at the time was by drawing into myself where nobody could find me. My daddy and my père tucked me into bed one night, and my nanny Sophie woke me up in the morning to say my daddy was never coming back. From that point on, I didn't like going to sleep at night. I was afraid that if I did, the next time I opened my eyes, somebody else would have left me.

Sophie and I moved into my granddaddy's estate, Whittington Manor, and the last time I saw my père and my older sister Dinah was when they came to the house after the funeral. My granddaddy didn't want me going to my daddy's funeral, and after that day, I guess he didn't want me seeing my pére or Dinah either. Technically, Dinah and I were stepcousins, but she'd always been like a big sis to me. My daddy adopted her because his stepsister couldn't take care of her, and we grew up in the same house. My père had raised me with my daddy since my mama died when I was two months old. I was too young to ever know my mama. She just existed in my imagination, based on a few photos I'd seen of her.

I came to understand my family took a lot of explaining for most people, but as best as I can remember, I was happy living with a daddy and a père and a sister who wasn't related to me by blood. It never seemed unusual to me. Then, in just a span of days, they were gone. I didn't know what I'd done to lose them, but the way my granddaddy treated me, it had to have been something terrible. I thought maybe I was a cursed child, just come into the world unworthy of people sticking around on my account.